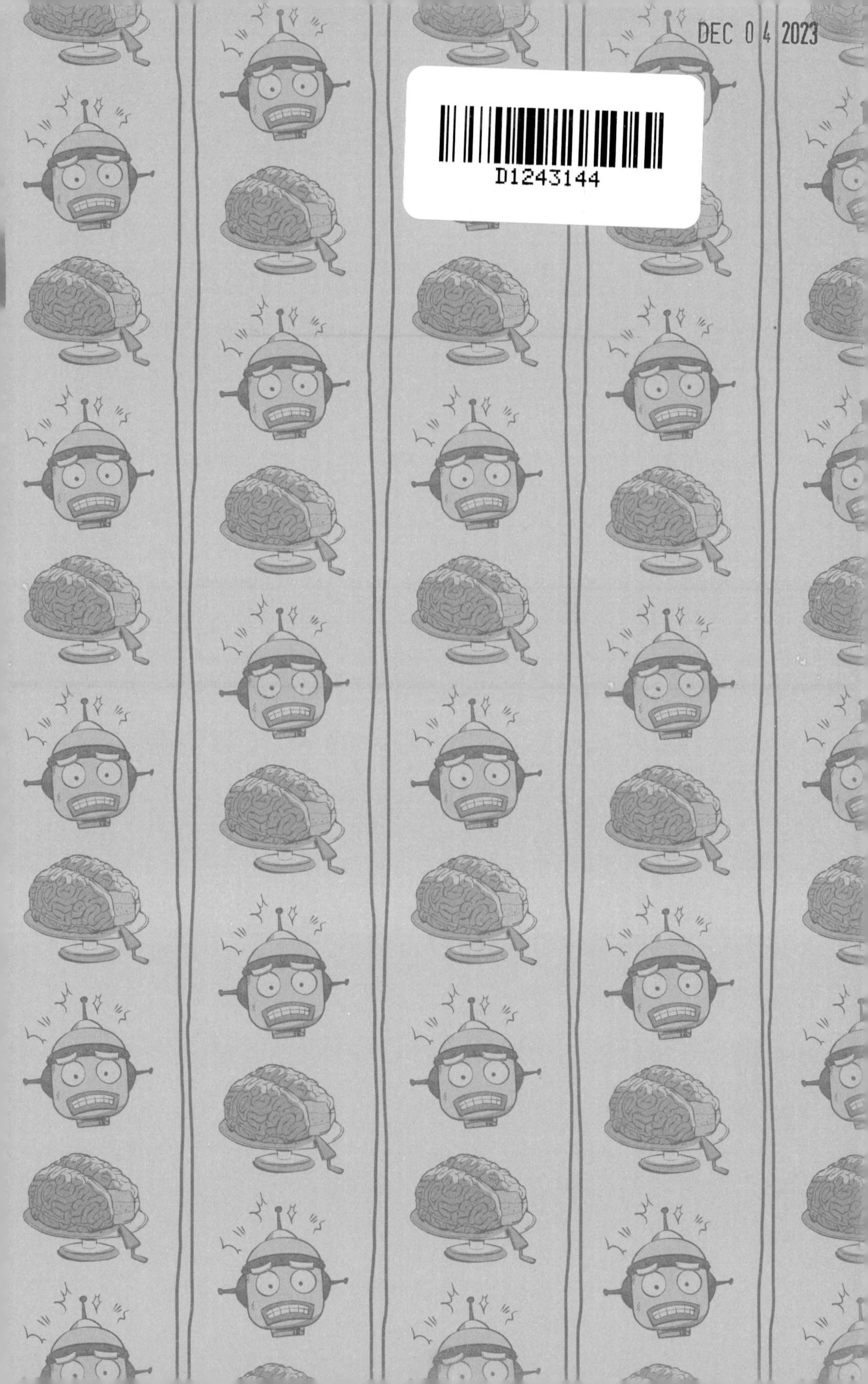

PLANTS VS. ZOMBIES™

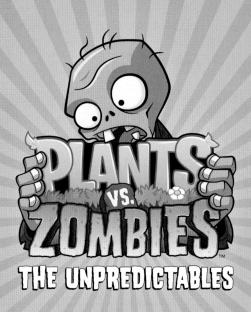

THE UNPREDICTABLES

Written by PAUL TOBIN

Art for this volume by JESSE HAMM (pencils, pages 1 to 24, and inks, pages 1 to 12), LUISA RUSSO (pencils and inks, pages 25 to 72), LES McCLAINE (inks, pages 13, 14, 15), and PHILIP MURPHY (inks, pages 16 to 24)

Colors by HEATHER BRECKEL

Letters by STEVE DUTRO

Cover by JESSE HAMM

DARK HORSE BOOKS

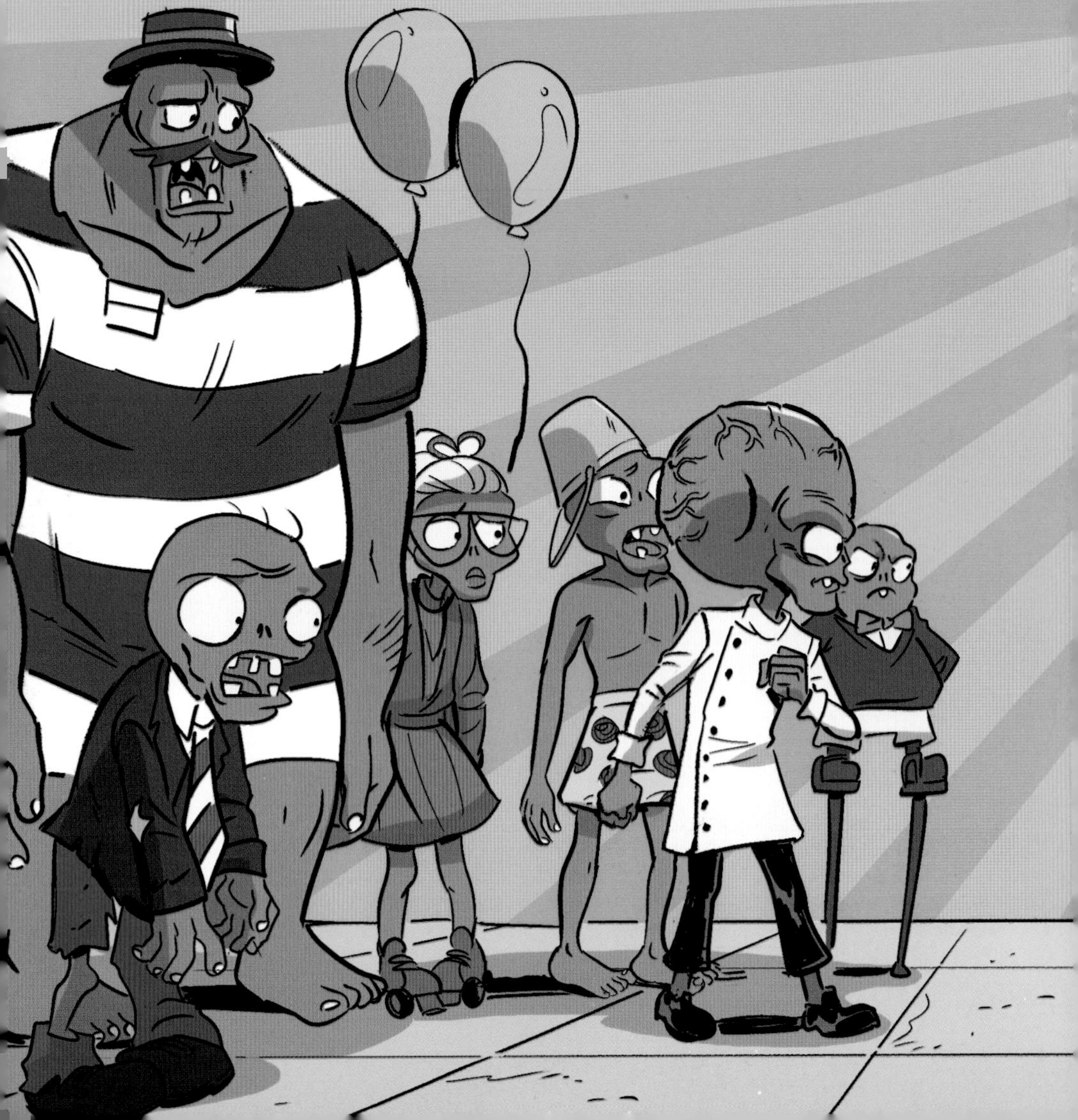

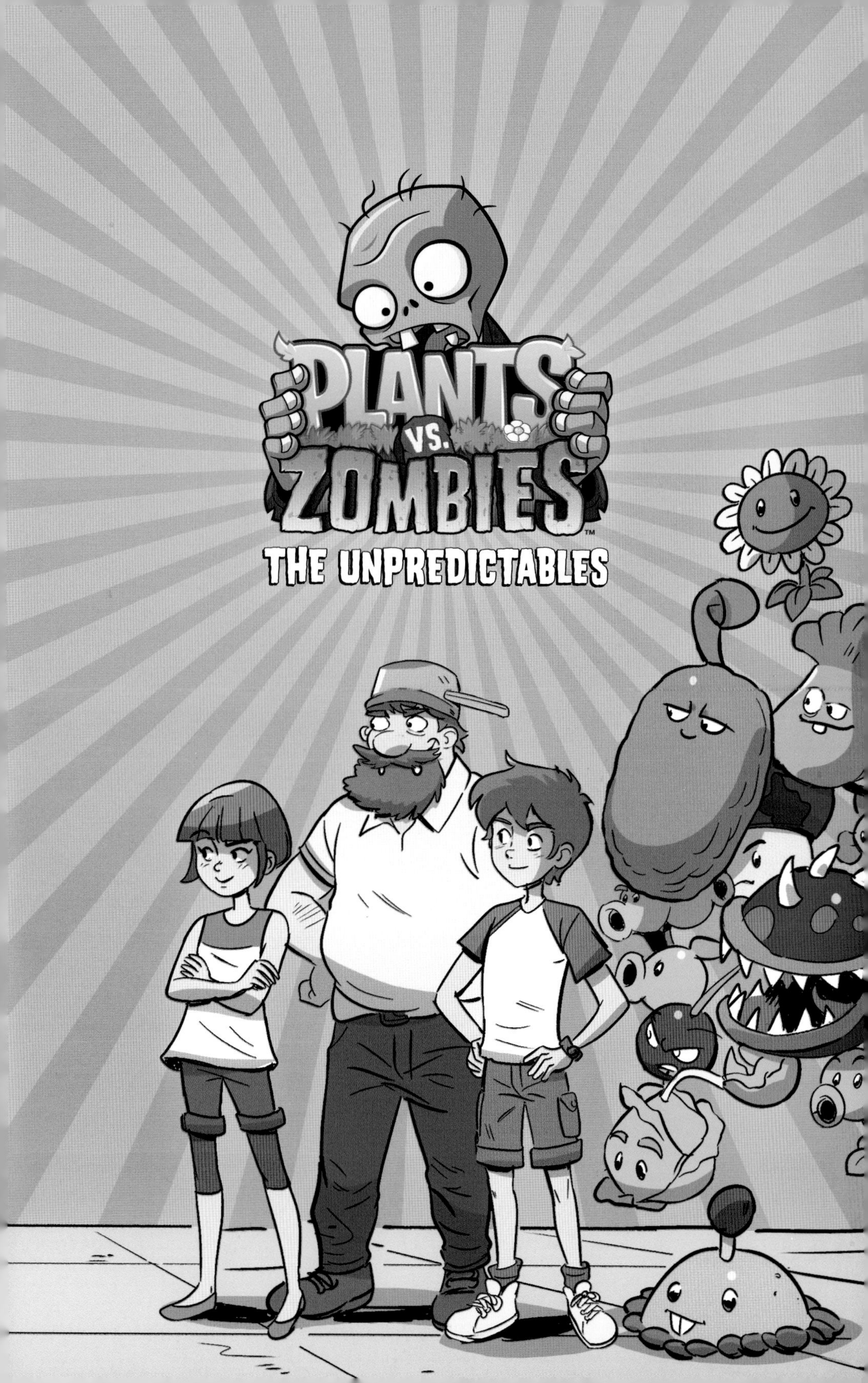
PLANTS VS. ZOMBIES™
THE UNPREDICTABLES

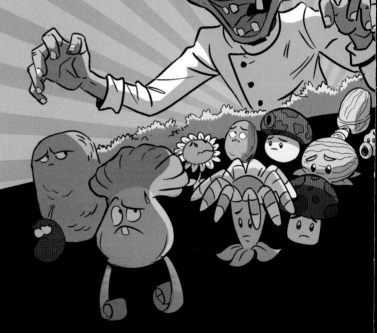

President and Publisher MIKE RICHARDSON
Senior Editor PHILIP R. SIMON
Editor JUDY KHUU
Associate Editor ROSE WEITZ
Designer KATHLEEN BARNETT
Digital Art Technician ALLYSON HALLER

In loving memory of Jesse Hamm.

Special thanks to Joshua Franks, Ryan Jones, Jessica Leung, Christopher Olsen, Kristen Star, Matt Townsend, and everyone at PopCap Games and EA Games.

First Edition: October 2023
Ebook ISBN 978-1-50672-096-8
Hardcover ISBN 978-1-50672-093-7

10 9 8 7 6 5 4 3 2 1
Printed in China

MIX
Paper from responsible sources
FSC® C109093

DarkHorse.com
PopCap.com

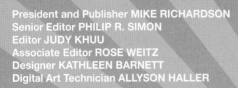

No plants were harmed in the making of this graphic novel. However, the zombie named Big Trouble was injured during some costume changes, and Zomboss is infuriated with stairs.

PLANTS vs. ZOMBIES: THE UNPREDICTABLES | Published by Dark Horse Books, a division of Dark Horse Comics LLC. 10956 SE Main Street, Milwaukie, OR 97222 | To find a comics shop in your area, visit comicshoplocator.com |

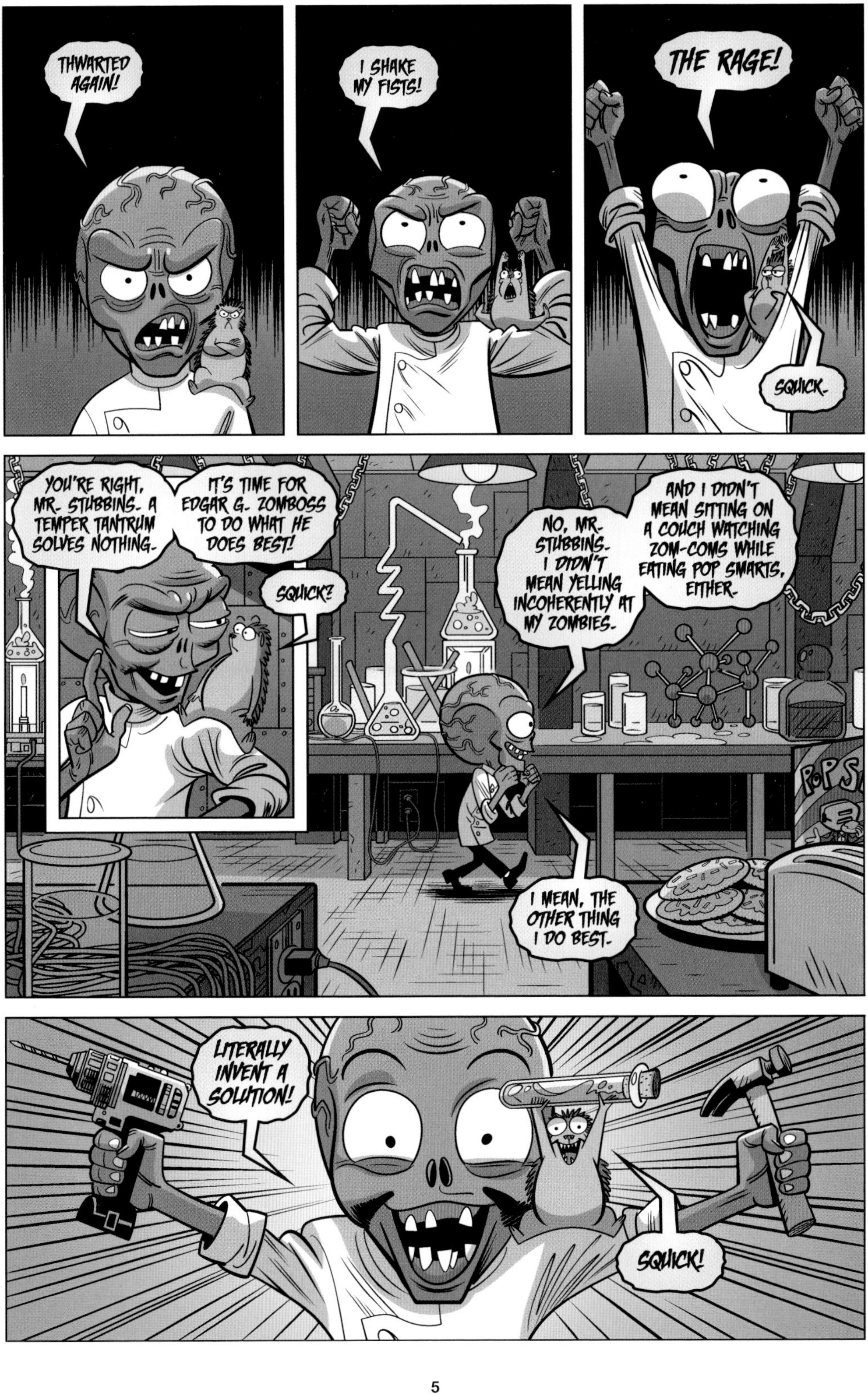
THWARTED AGAIN!
I SHAKE MY FISTS!
THE RAGE!
SQUICK.
YOU'RE RIGHT, MR. STUBBINS. A TEMPER TANTRUM SOLVES NOTHING.
IT'S TIME FOR EDGAR G. ZOMBOSS TO DO WHAT HE DOES BEST!
SQUICK?
NO, MR. STUBBINS. I DIDN'T MEAN YELLING INCOHERENTLY AT MY ZOMBIES.
AND I DIDN'T MEAN SITTING ON A COUCH WATCHING ZOM-COMS WHILE EATING POP SMARTS, EITHER.
I MEAN, THE OTHER THING I DO BEST.
LITERALLY INVENT A SOLUTION!
SQUICK!

MINUTES LATER...

PUTT PUTT PUTTER

BANG!

PLAPP!

SQUOINT!

FLOBBER! BANK!

SUCCESS! EUREKA! JACKPOT!

I'VE CREATED... ANTI-THWART CREAM!

FOOP FOOP

YES, JUST APPLY A LITTLE TO YOUR SKULL, AND IT GETS RID OF ALL UNSIGHTLY THWARTS!

OKAY, GONNA NEED A LITTLE MORE HERE.

SPLORTCH! SPLORTCH!

ECONOMY SIZE FOR BIG HEADS

SQUICK?

GOOD QUESTION, MR. STUBBINS. HOW DOES ANTI-THWART CREAM WORK?

IT'S SIMPLE, ACTUALLY...

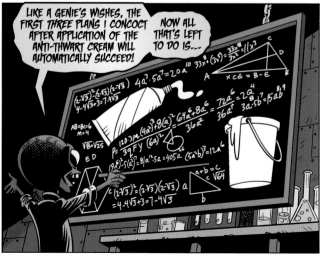

LIKE A GENIE'S WISHES, THE FIRST THREE PLANS I CONCOCT AFTER APPLICATION OF THE ANTI-THWART CREAM WILL AUTOMATICALLY SUCCEED!

NOW ALL THAT'S LEFT TO DO IS...

6

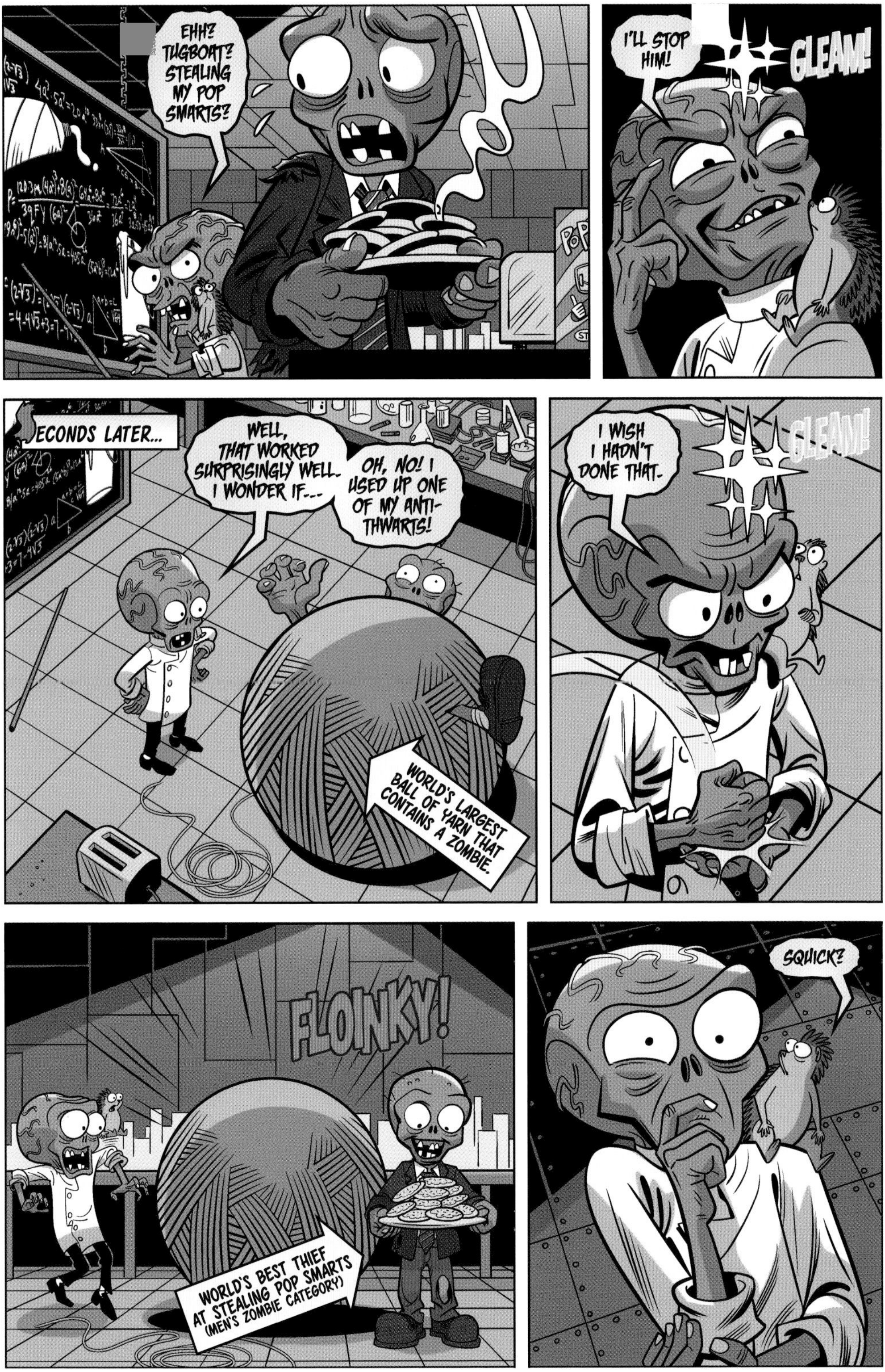
EHH? TUGBOAT? STEALING MY POP SMARTS?
I'LL STOP HIM!
GLEAM!
ECONDS LATER...
WELL, THAT WORKED SURPRISINGLY WELL. I WONDER IF...
OH, NO! I USED UP ONE OF MY ANTI-THWARTS!
WORLD'S LARGEST BALL OF YARN THAT CONTAINS A ZOMBIE.
I WISH I HADN'T DONE THAT.
GLEAM!
FLOINKY!
WORLD'S BEST THIEF AT STEALING POP SMARTS (MEN'S ZOMBIE CATEGORY)
SQUICK?

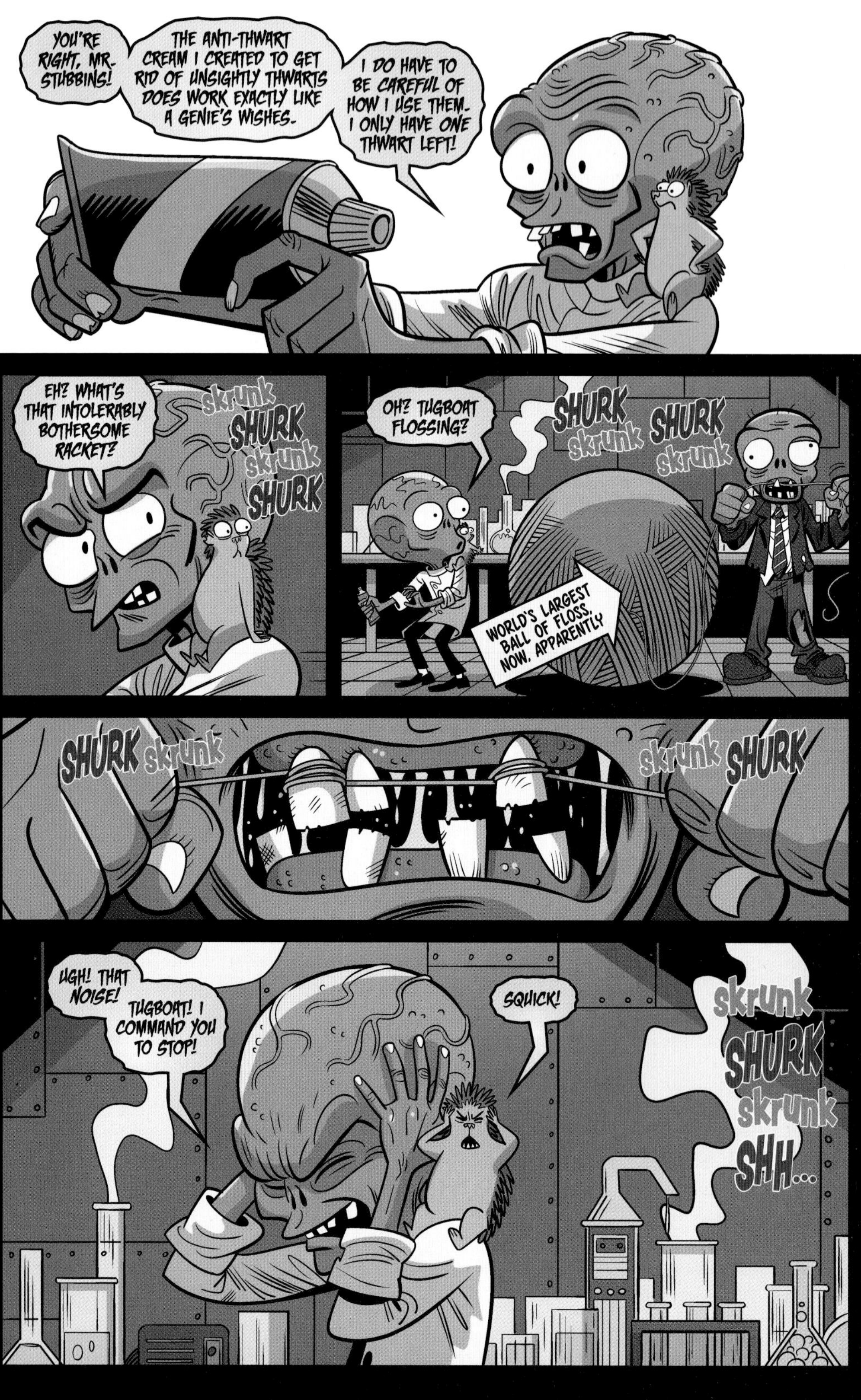
YOU'RE RIGHT, MR. STUBBINS!
THE ANTI-THWART CREAM I CREATED TO GET RID OF UNSIGHTLY THWARTS DOES WORK EXACTLY LIKE A GENIE'S WISHES.
I DO HAVE TO BE CAREFUL OF HOW I USE THEM. I ONLY HAVE ONE THWART LEFT!
EH? WHAT'S THAT INTOLERABLY BOTHERSOME RACKET?
skrunk SHURK skrunk SHURK
OH? TUGBOAT FLOSSING?
SHURK skrunk SHURK skrunk
WORLD'S LARGEST BALL OF FLOSS, NOW, APPARENTLY
SHURK skrunk
skrunk SHURK
UGH! THAT NOISE!
TUGBOAT! I COMMAND YOU TO STOP!
SQUICK!
skrunk SHURK skrunk SHH...

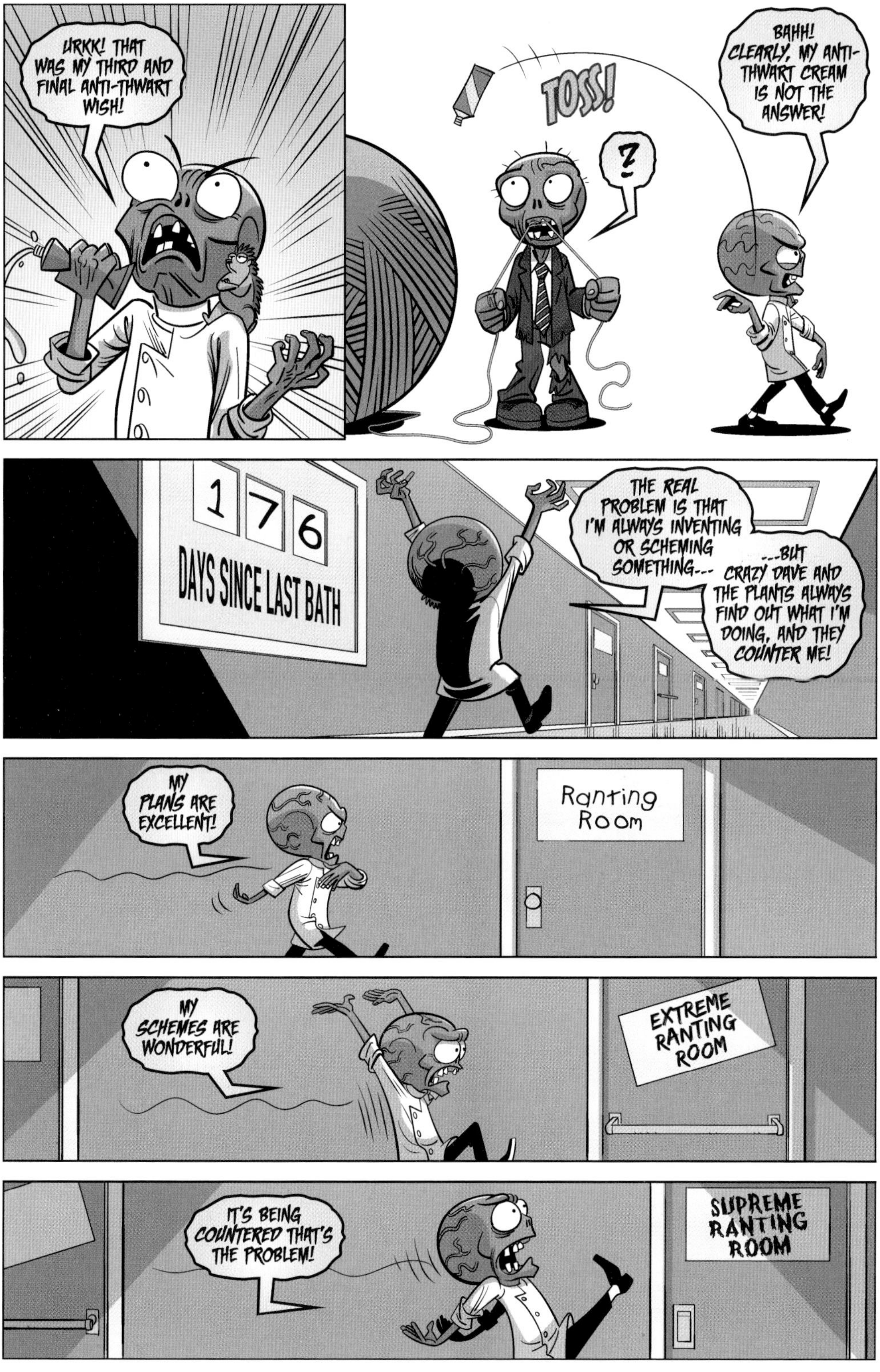
URKK! THAT WAS MY THIRD AND FINAL ANTI-THWART WISH!
TOSS!
?
BAHH! CLEARLY, MY ANTI-THWART CREAM IS NOT THE ANSWER!
176
DAYS SINCE LAST BATH
THE REAL PROBLEM IS THAT I'M ALWAYS INVENTING OR SCHEMING SOMETHING...
...BUT CRAZY DAVE AND THE PLANTS ALWAYS FIND OUT WHAT I'M DOING, AND THEY COUNTER ME!
MY PLANS ARE EXCELLENT!
Ranting Room
MY SCHEMES ARE WONDERFUL!
EXTREME RANTING ROOM
IT'S BEING COUNTERED THAT'S THE PROBLEM!
SUPREME RANTING ROOM

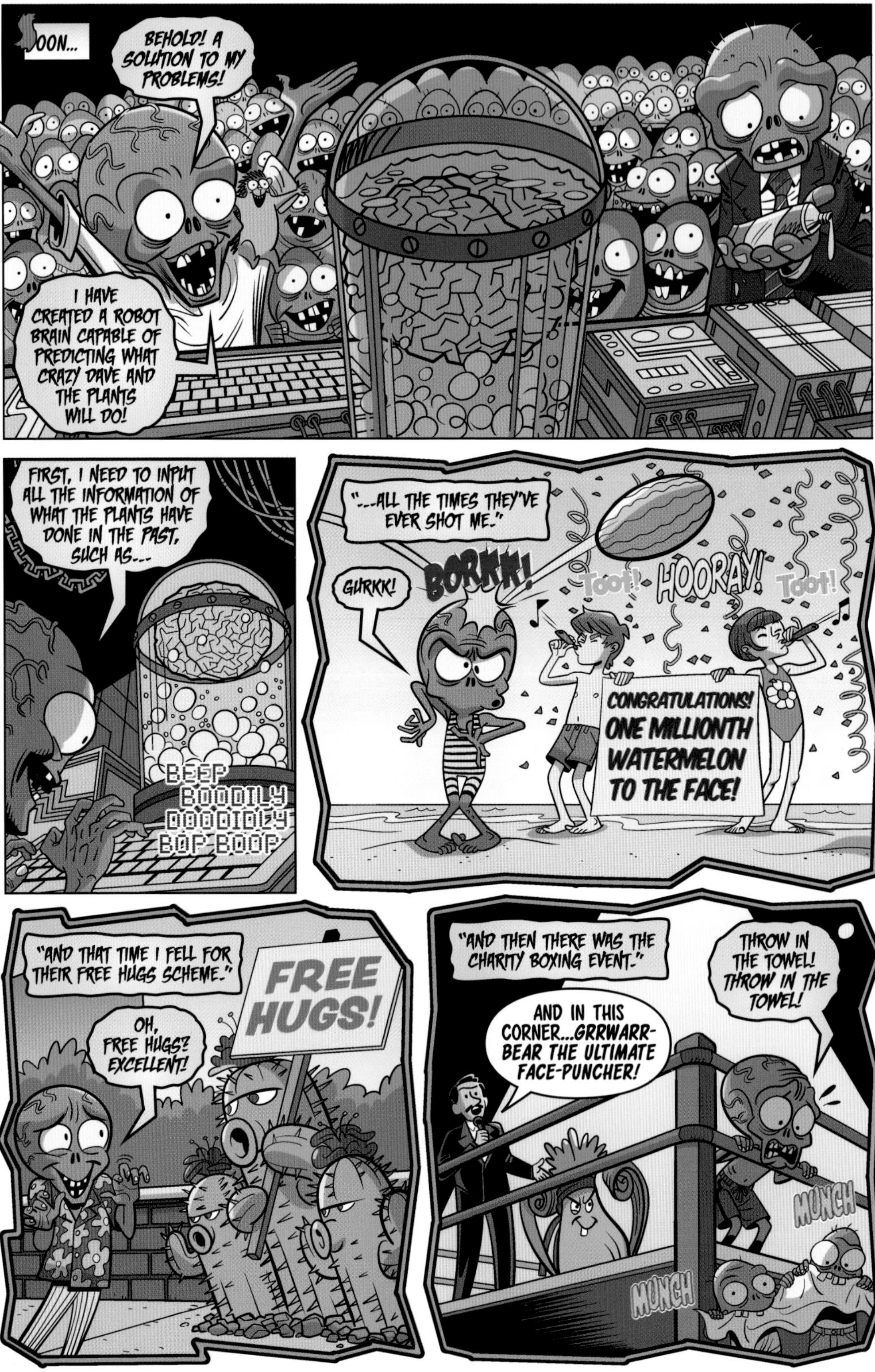
SOON...
BEHOLD! A SOLUTION TO MY PROBLEMS!
I HAVE CREATED A ROBOT BRAIN CAPABLE OF PREDICTING WHAT CRAZY DAVE AND THE PLANTS WILL DO!
FIRST, I NEED TO INPUT ALL THE INFORMATION OF WHAT THE PLANTS HAVE DONE IN THE PAST, SUCH AS...
BEEP BOODILY DOODIDLY BOP BOOP
"...ALL THE TIMES THEY'VE EVER SHOT ME."
GURKK!
BORKK!
TOOT!
HOORAY!
TOOT!
CONGRATULATIONS! ONE MILLIONTH WATERMELON TO THE FACE!
"AND THAT TIME I FELL FOR THEIR FREE HUGS SCHEME."
FREE HUGS!
OH, FREE HUGS? EXCELLENT!
"AND THEN THERE WAS THE CHARITY BOXING EVENT."
THROW IN THE TOWEL! THROW IN THE TOWEL!
AND IN THIS CORNER...GRRWARR-BEAR THE ULTIMATE FACE-PUNCHER!
MUNCH
MUNCH

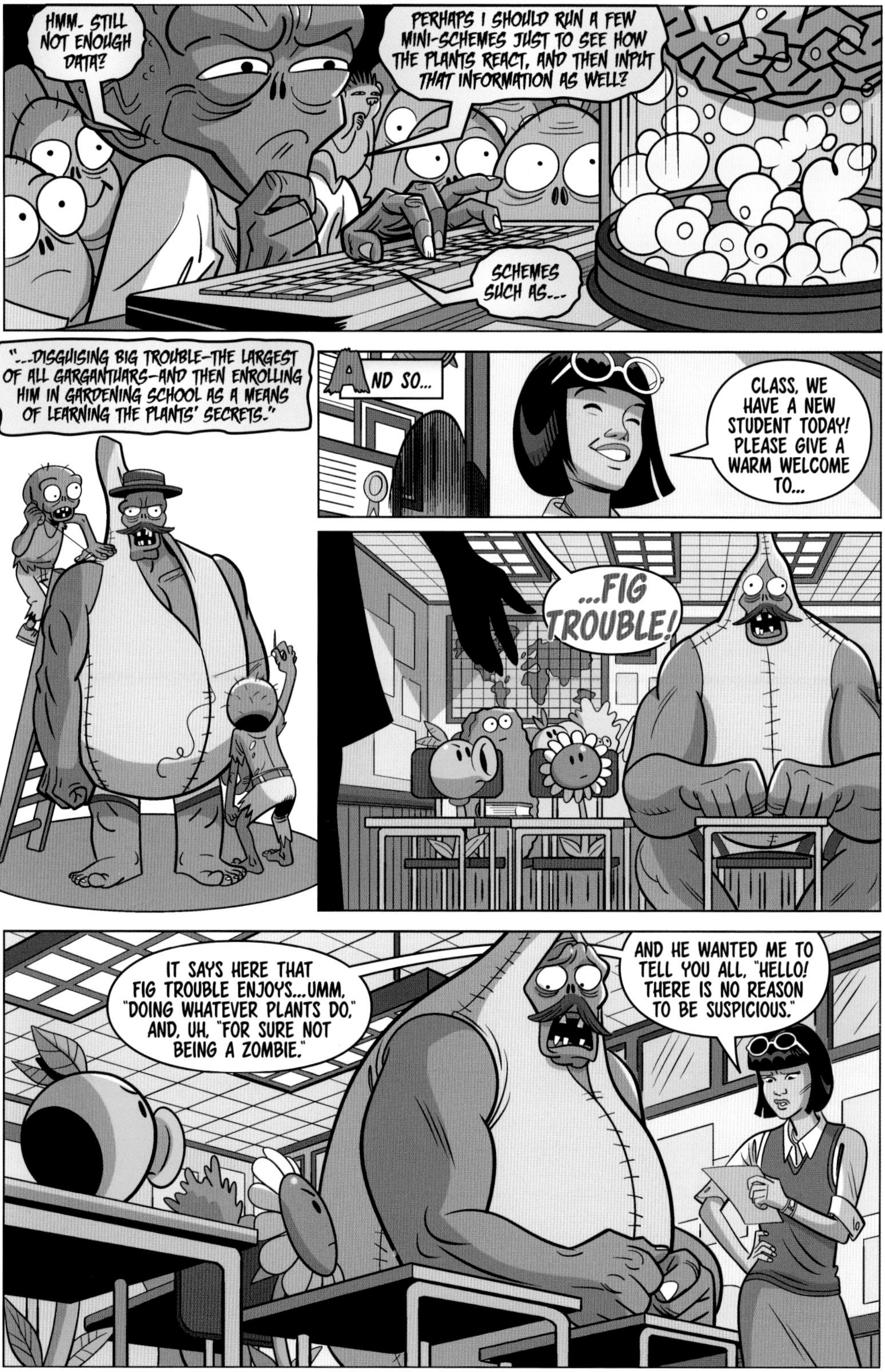
HMM. STILL NOT ENOUGH DATA?
PERHAPS I SHOULD RUN A FEW MINI-SCHEMES JUST TO SEE HOW THE PLANTS REACT, AND THEN INPUT THAT INFORMATION AS WELL?
SCHEMES SUCH AS...
"...DISGUISING BIG TROUBLE—THE LARGEST OF ALL GARGANTUARS—AND THEN ENROLLING HIM IN GARDENING SCHOOL AS A MEANS OF LEARNING THE PLANTS' SECRETS."
AND SO...
CLASS, WE HAVE A NEW STUDENT TODAY! PLEASE GIVE A WARM WELCOME TO...
...FIG TROUBLE!
IT SAYS HERE THAT FIG TROUBLE ENJOYS...UMM, "DOING WHATEVER PLANTS DO," AND, UH, "FOR SURE NOT BEING A ZOMBIE."
AND HE WANTED ME TO TELL YOU ALL, "HELLO! THERE IS NO REASON TO BE SUSPICIOUS."

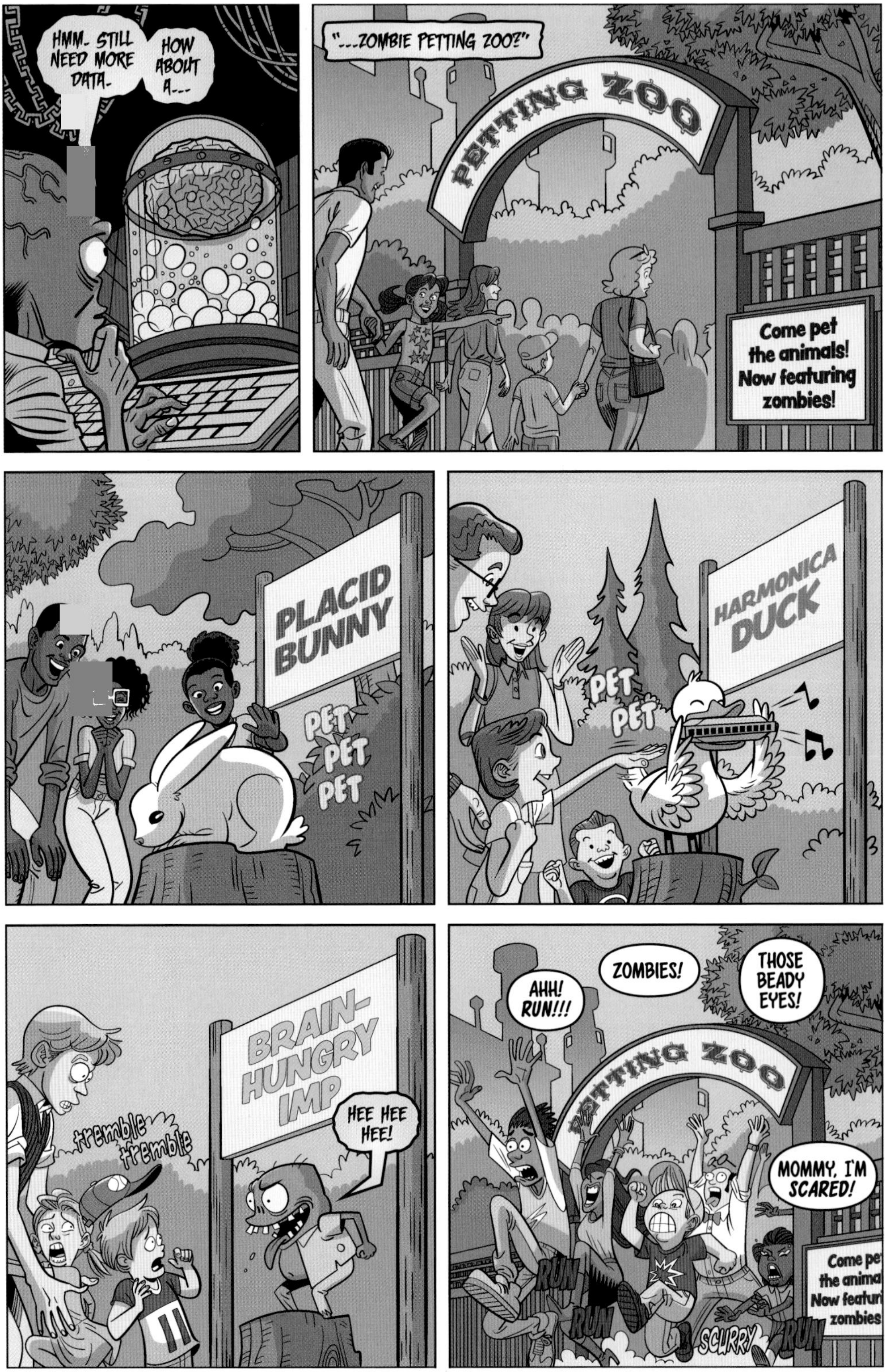
HMM. STILL NEED MORE DATA.
HOW ABOUT A...
"...ZOMBIE PETTING ZOO?"
PETTING ZOO
Come pet the animals! Now featuring zombies!
PLACID BUNNY
PET PET PET
HARMONICA DUCK
PET PET
BRAIN-HUNGRY IMP
tremble tremble
HEE HEE HEE!
AHH! RUN!!!
ZOMBIES!
THOSE BEADY EYES!
MOMMY, I'M SCARED!
RUN
RUN
SCURRY
RUN

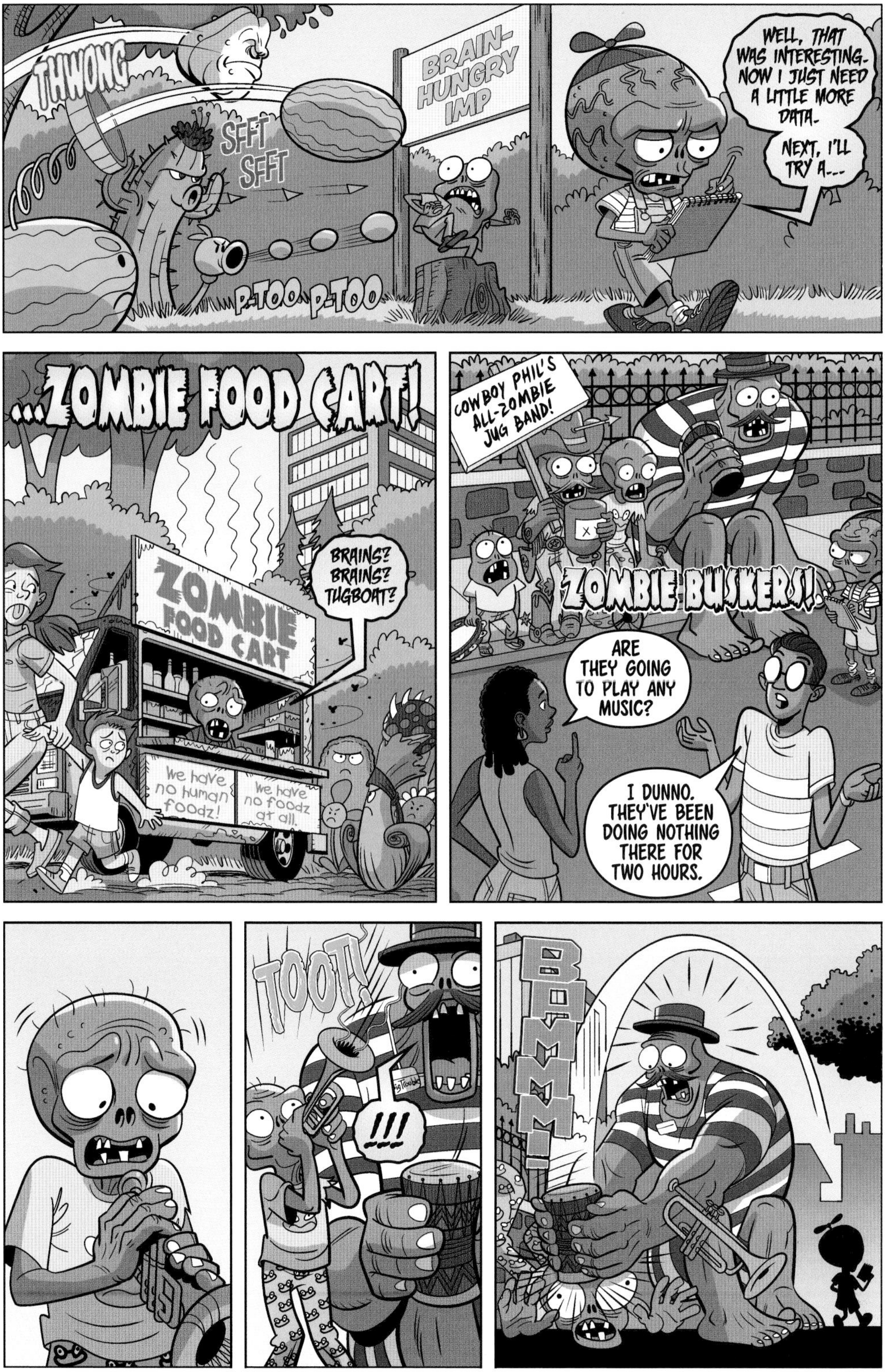
THWONG
SFFT SFFT
BRAIN-HUNGRY IMP
P-TOO P-TOO
WELL, THAT WAS INTERESTING. NOW I JUST NEED A LITTLE MORE DATA.
NEXT, I'LL TRY A...
...ZOMBIE FOOD CART!
ZOMBIE FOOD CART
BRAINS? BRAINS? TUGBOAT?
We have no human foodz!
We have no foodz at all.
COWBOY PHIL'S ALL-ZOMBIE JUG BAND!
ZOMBIE BUSKERS!
ARE THEY GOING TO PLAY ANY MUSIC?
I DUNNO. THEY'VE BEEN DOING NOTHING THERE FOR TWO HOURS.
TOOT!
!!!
BAMMM!

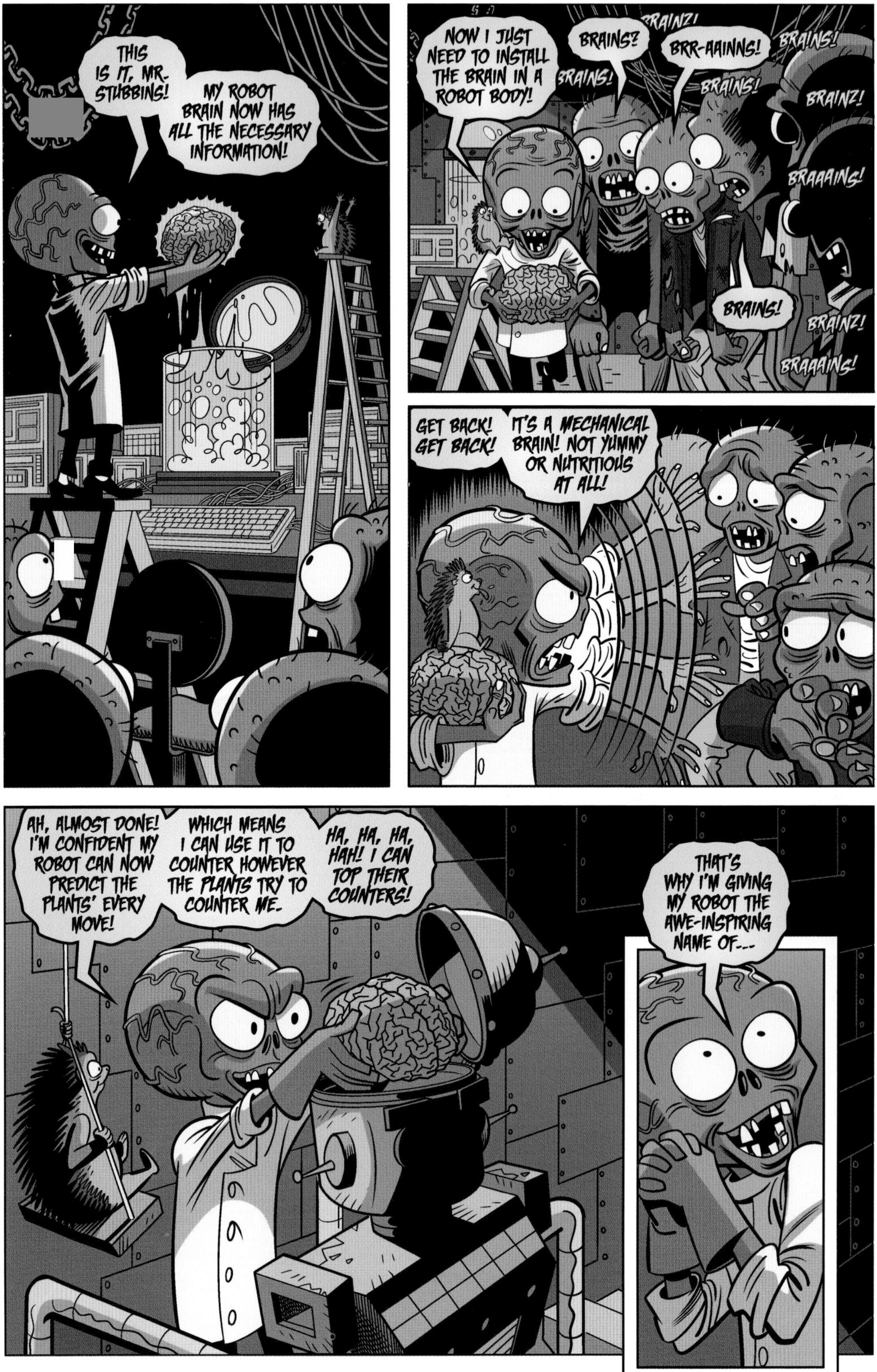
THIS IS IT, MR. STUBBINS!
MY ROBOT BRAIN NOW HAS ALL THE NECESSARY INFORMATION!
NOW I JUST NEED TO INSTALL THE BRAIN IN A ROBOT BODY!
BRAINS?
BRR-AAINNS!
BRAINZ!
BRAINS!
BRAINS!
BRAINS!
BRAINZ!
BRAAAINS!
BRAINS!
BRAINZ!
BRAAAINS!
GET BACK! GET BACK!
IT'S A MECHANICAL BRAIN! NOT YUMMY OR NUTRITIOUS AT ALL!
AH, ALMOST DONE! I'M CONFIDENT MY ROBOT CAN NOW PREDICT THE PLANTS' EVERY MOVE!
WHICH MEANS I CAN USE IT TO COUNTER HOWEVER THE PLANTS TRY TO COUNTER ME.
HA, HA, HA, HAH! I CAN TOP THEIR COUNTERS!
THAT'S WHY I'M GIVING MY ROBOT THE AWE-INSPIRING NAME OF...

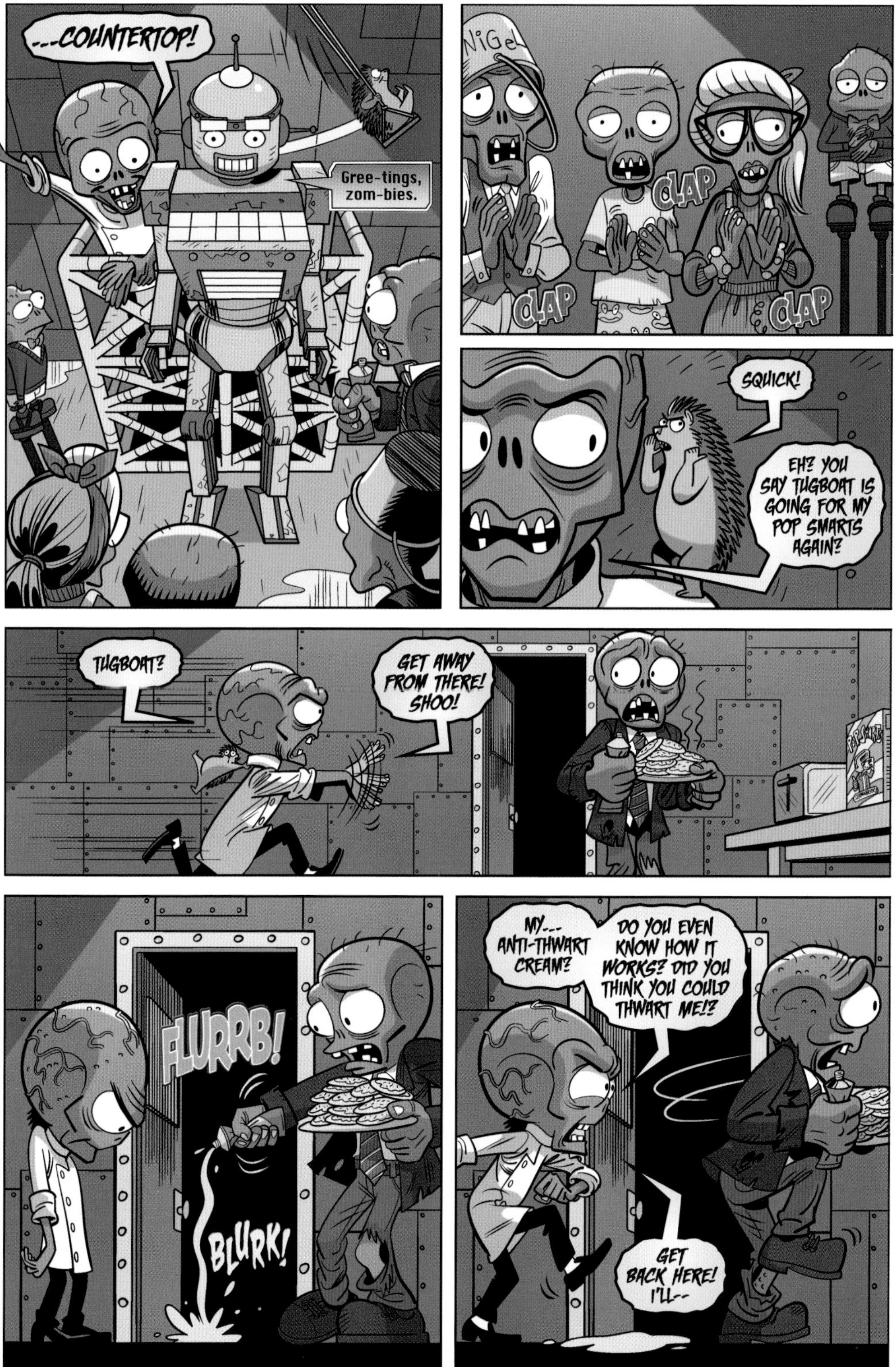

...COUNTERTOP!
Gree-tings, zom-bies.
NiGel
CLAP
CLAP
CLAP
SQUICK!
EH? YOU SAY TUGBOAT IS GOING FOR MY POP SMARTS AGAIN?
TUGBOAT?
GET AWAY FROM THERE! SHOO!
FLURRB!
BLURK!
MY... ANTI-THWART CREAM?
DO YOU EVEN KNOW HOW IT WORKS? DID YOU THINK YOU COULD THWART ME!?
GET BACK HERE! I'LL--

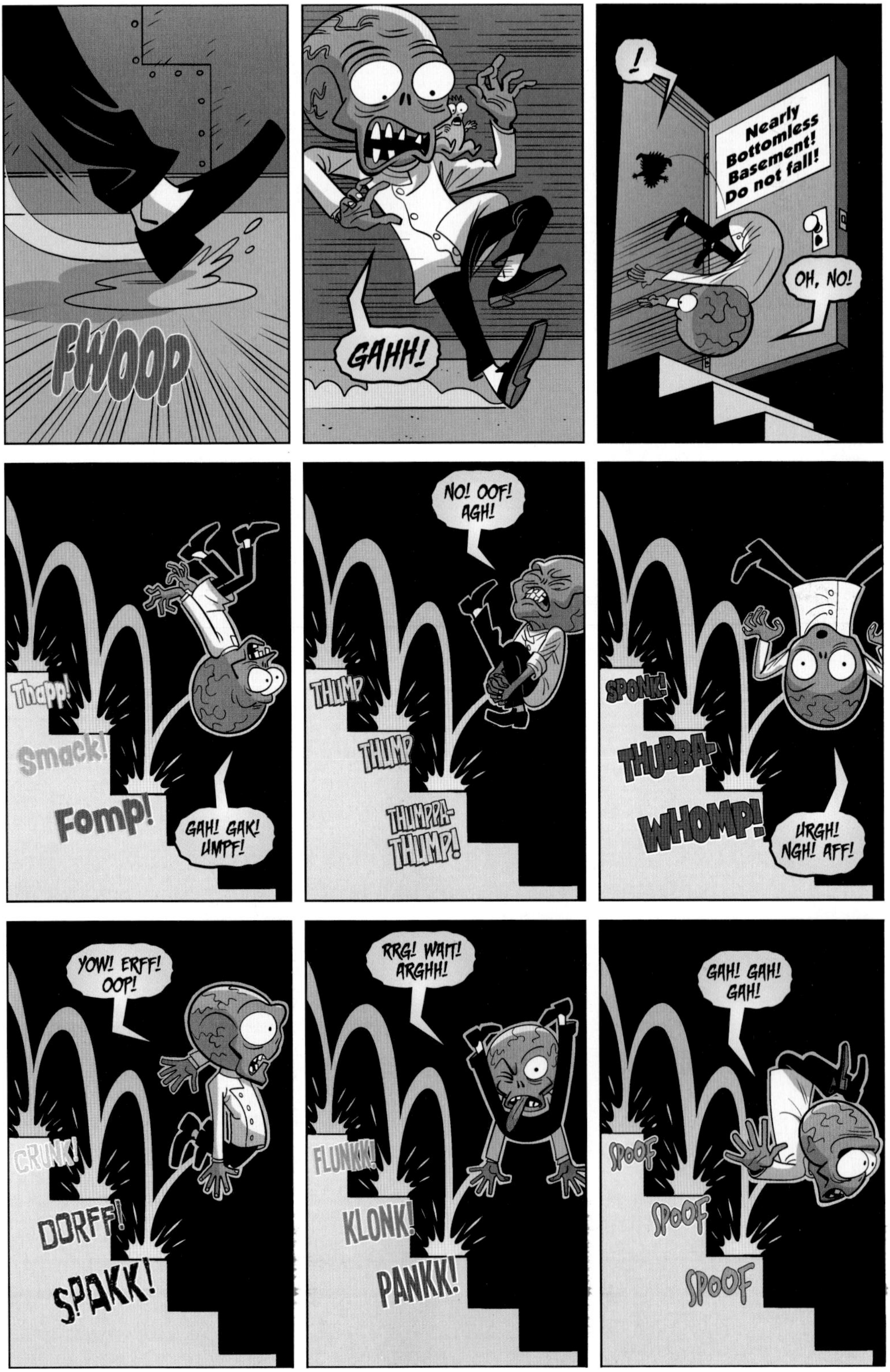
FWOOP
GAHH!
!
Nearly Bottomless Basement! Do not fall!
OH, NO!
Thapp!
Smack!
Fomp!
GAH! GAK! UMPF!
NO! OOF! AGH!
THUMP
THUMP
THUMPPA-THUMP!
SPONK!
THUBBA-
WHOMP!
URGH! NGH! AFF!
YOW! ERFF! OOP!
CRUNK!
DORFF!
SPAKK!
RRG! WAIT! ARGHH!
FLUNKK!
KLONK!
PANKK!
GAH! GAH! GAH!
SPOOF
SPOOF
SPOOF

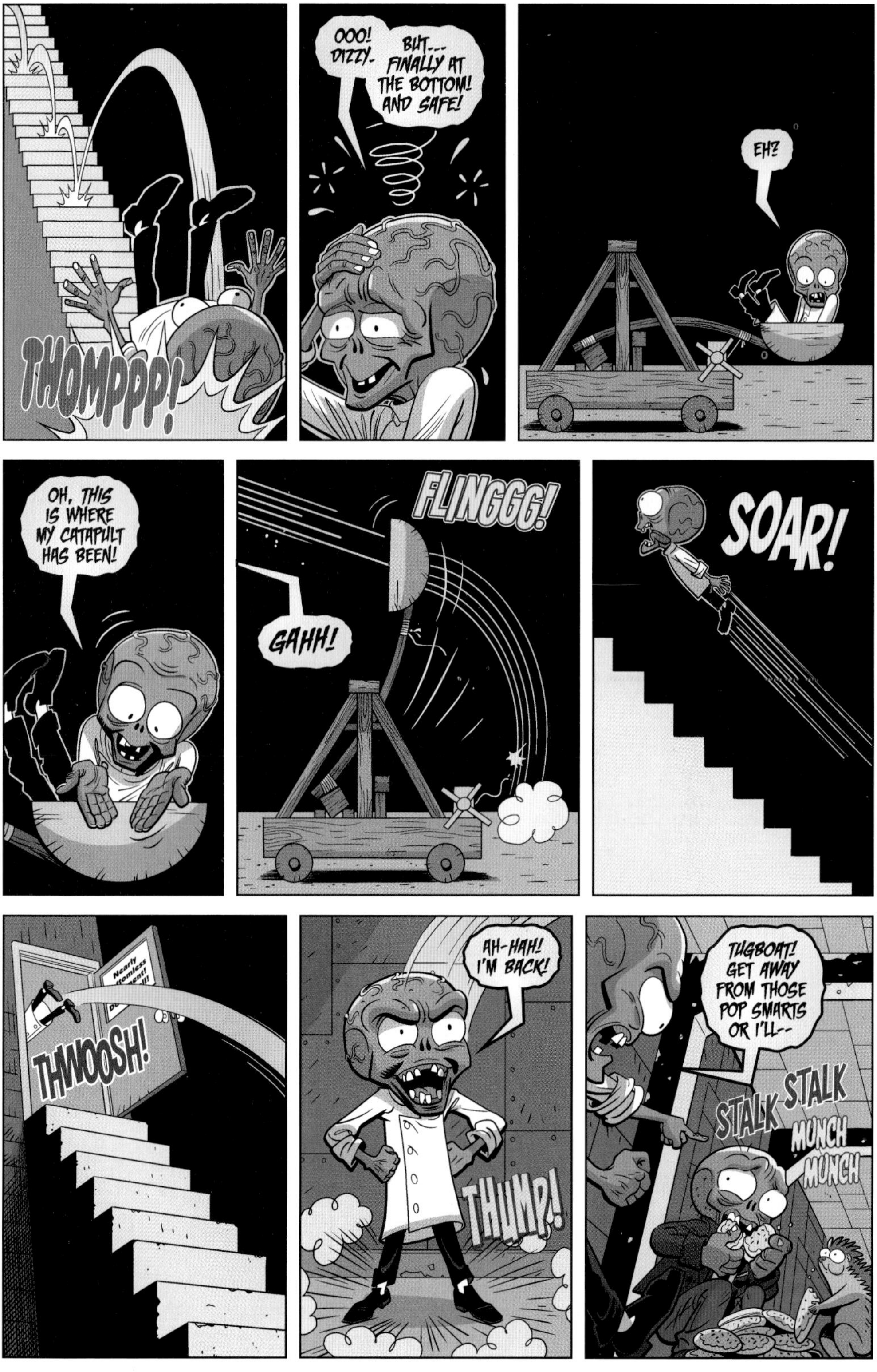
THOMPPP!
OOO! DIZZY.
BUT... FINALLY AT THE BOTTOM! AND SAFE!
EH?
OH, THIS IS WHERE MY CATAPULT HAS BEEN!
FLINGGG!
GAHH!
SOAR!
THWOOSH!
AH-HAH! I'M BACK!
THUMP!
TUGBOAT! GET AWAY FROM THOSE POP SMARTS OR I'LL--
STALK STALK
MUNCH
MUNCH

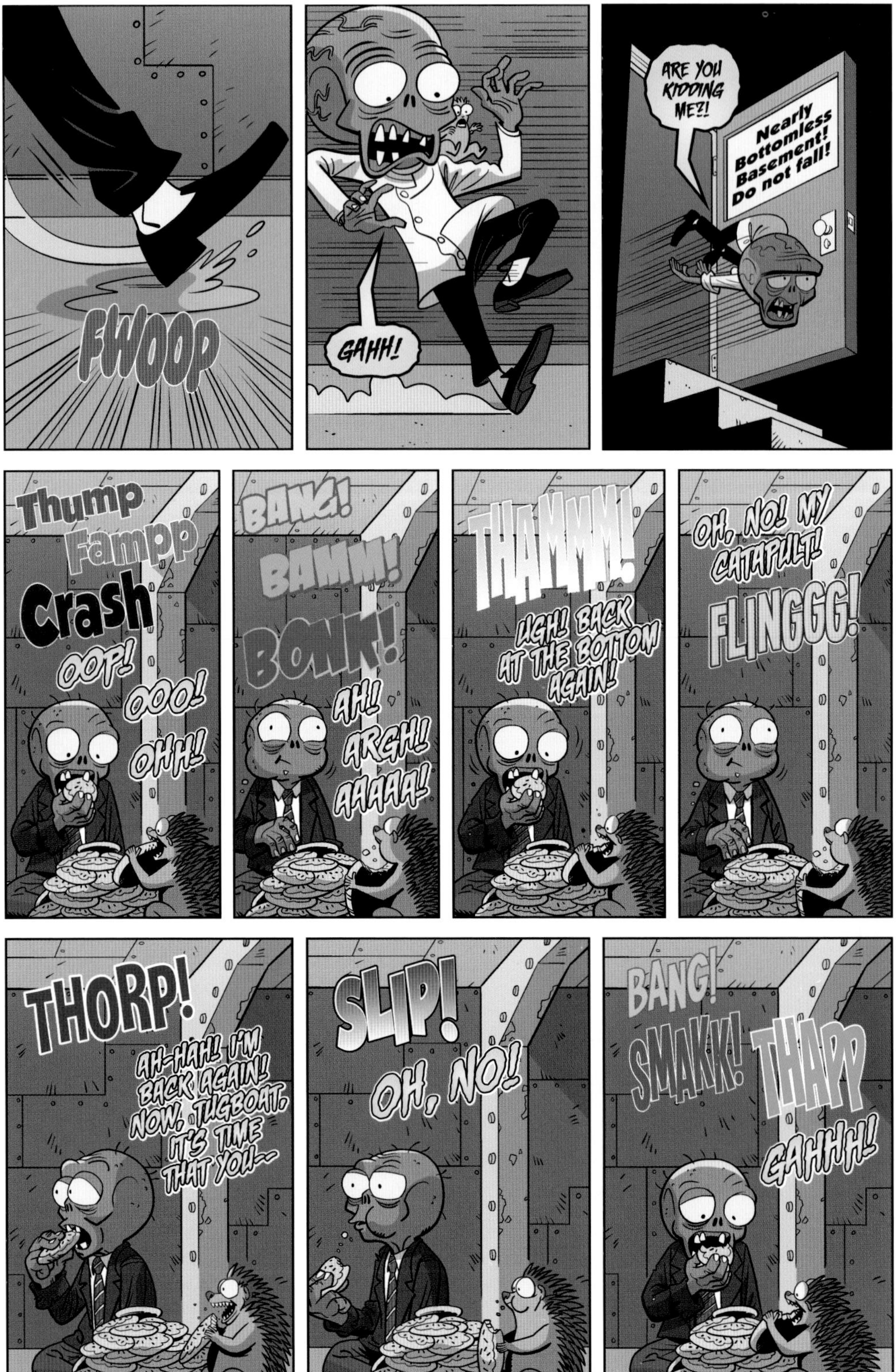
FWOOP
GAHH!
ARE YOU KIDDING ME?!
Nearly Bottomless Basement! Do not fall!
Thump
Fampp
Crash
OOP!
OOO!
OHH!
BANG!
BAMM!
BONK!
AH!
ARGH!
AAAAA!
THAMMM!
UGH! BACK AT THE BOTTOM AGAIN!
OH, NO! MY CATAPULT!
FLINGGG!
THORP!
AH-HAH! I'M BACK AGAIN! NOW, TUGBOAT, IT'S TIME THAT YOU--
SLIP!
OH, NO!
BANG!
SMAKK!
THAPP
GAHHH!

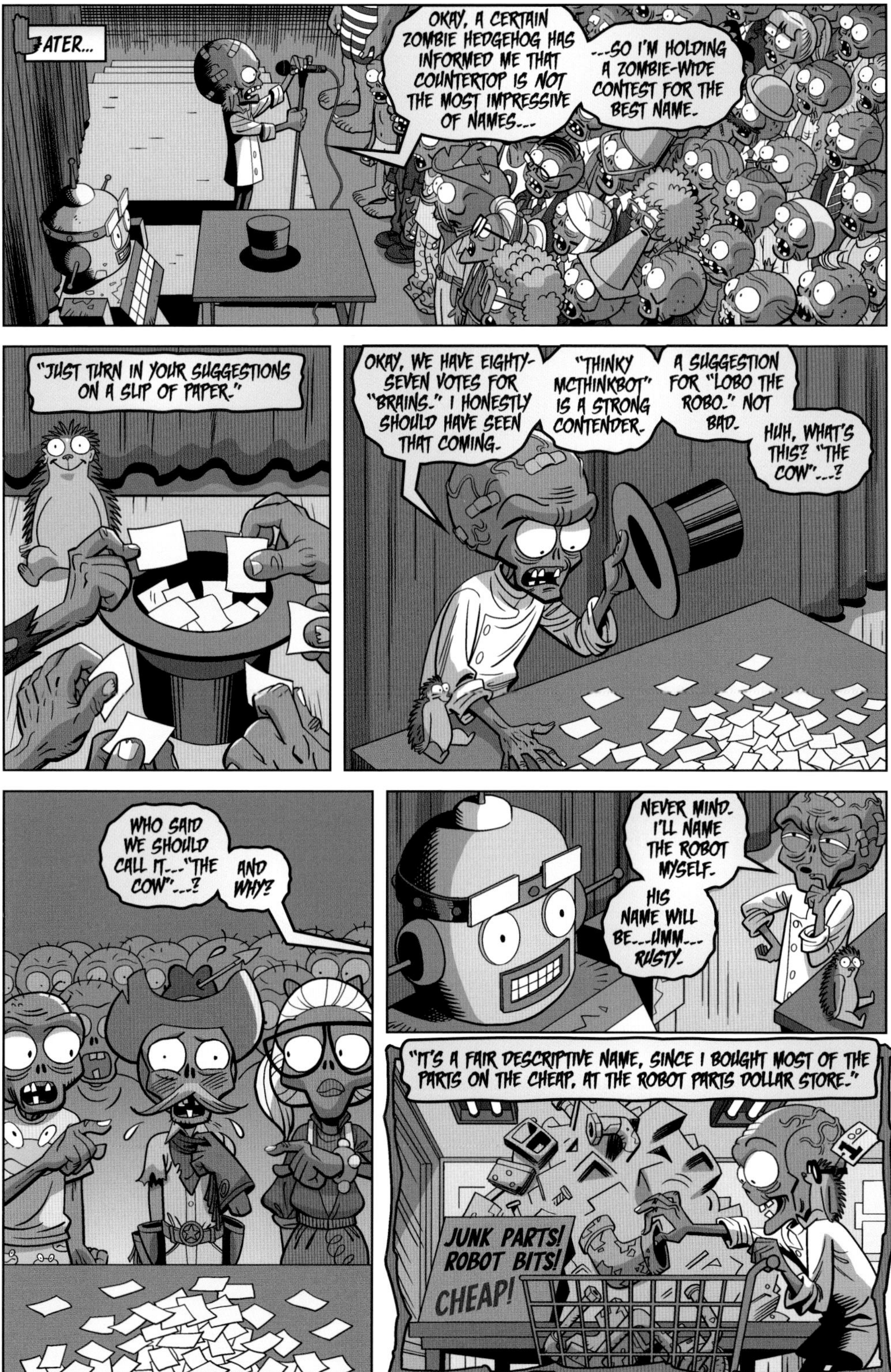
LATER...
OKAY, A CERTAIN ZOMBIE HEDGEHOG HAS INFORMED ME THAT COUNTERTOP IS NOT THE MOST IMPRESSIVE OF NAMES...
...SO I'M HOLDING A ZOMBIE-WIDE CONTEST FOR THE BEST NAME.
"JUST TURN IN YOUR SUGGESTIONS ON A SLIP OF PAPER."
OKAY, WE HAVE EIGHTY-SEVEN VOTES FOR "BRAINS." I HONESTLY SHOULD HAVE SEEN THAT COMING.
"THINKY MCTHINKBOT" IS A STRONG CONTENDER.
A SUGGESTION FOR "LOBO THE ROBO." NOT BAD.
HUH, WHAT'S THIS? "THE COW"...?
WHO SAID WE SHOULD CALL IT..."THE COW"...?
AND WHY?
NEVER MIND. I'LL NAME THE ROBOT MYSELF.
HIS NAME WILL BE...UMM... RUSTY.
"IT'S A FAIR DESCRIPTIVE NAME, SINCE I BOUGHT MOST OF THE PARTS ON THE CHEAP, AT THE ROBOT PARTS DOLLAR STORE."
JUNK PARTS! ROBOT BITS! CHEAP!

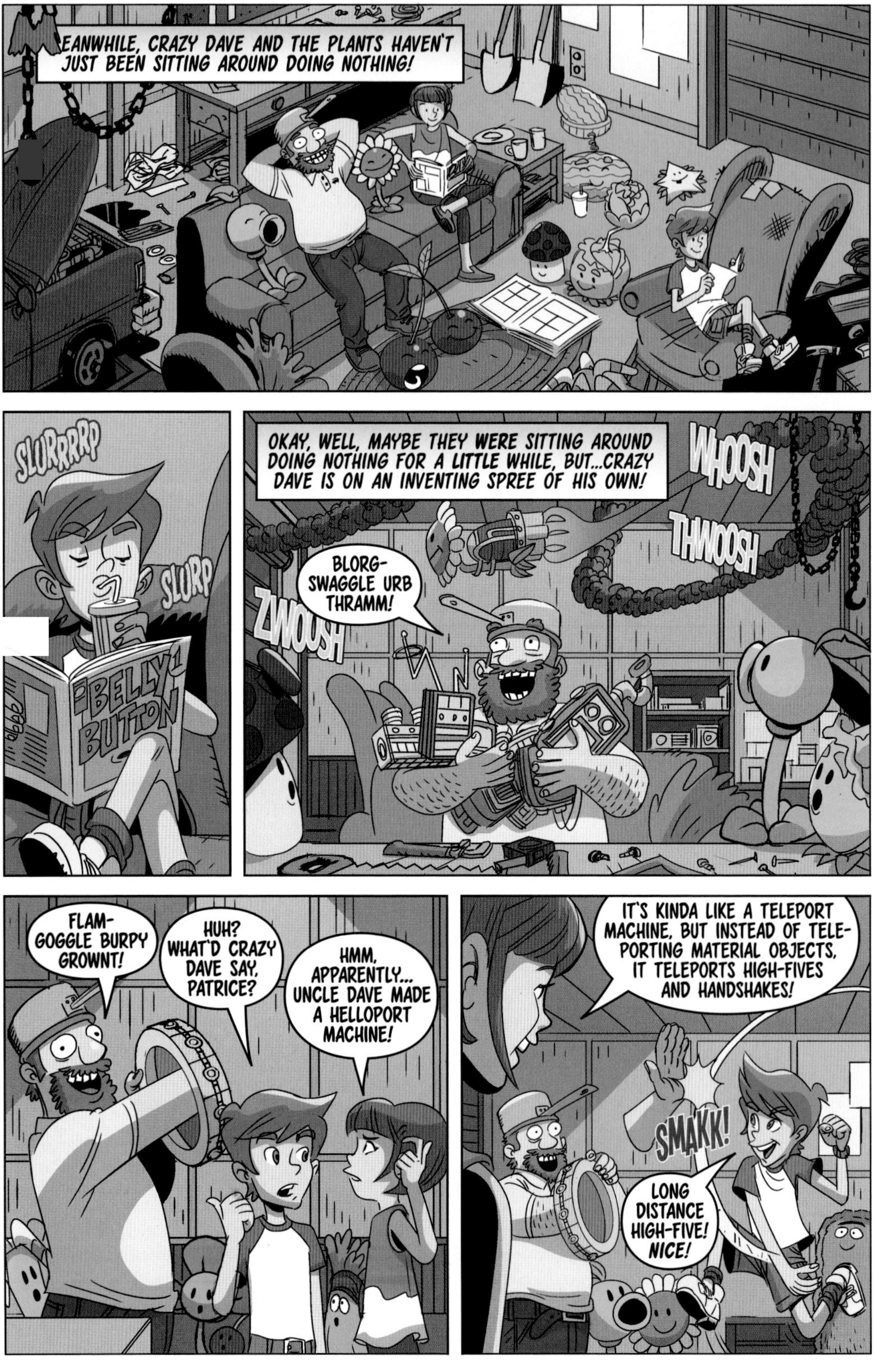

MEANWHILE, CRAZY DAVE AND THE PLANTS HAVEN'T JUST BEEN SITTING AROUND DOING NOTHING!
SLURRRRP
SLURP
BELLY BUTTON
OKAY, WELL, MAYBE THEY WERE SITTING AROUND DOING NOTHING FOR A LITTLE WHILE, BUT...CRAZY DAVE IS ON AN INVENTING SPREE OF HIS OWN!
WHOOSH
THWOOSH
ZWOOSH
BLORG-SWAGGLE URB THRAMM!
FLAM-GOGGLE BURPY GROWNT!
HUH? WHAT'D CRAZY DAVE SAY, PATRICE?
HMM, APPARENTLY... UNCLE DAVE MADE A HELLOPORT MACHINE!
IT'S KINDA LIKE A TELEPORT MACHINE, BUT INSTEAD OF TELE-PORTING MATERIAL OBJECTS, IT TELEPORTS HIGH-FIVES AND HANDSHAKES!
SMAKK!
LONG DISTANCE HIGH-FIVE! NICE!

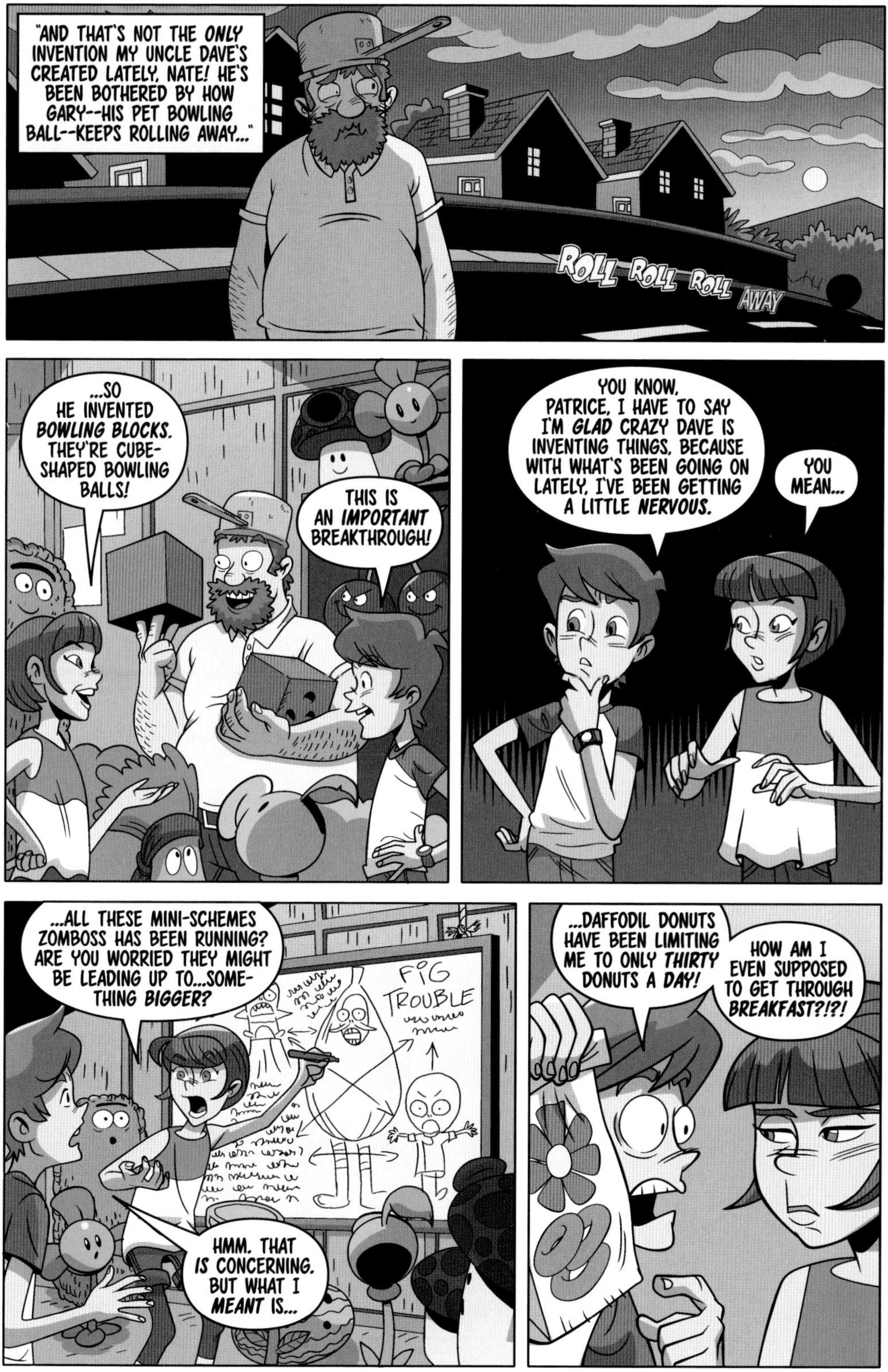
"AND THAT'S NOT THE ONLY INVENTION MY UNCLE DAVE'S CREATED LATELY, NATE! HE'S BEEN BOTHERED BY HOW GARY--HIS PET BOWLING BALL--KEEPS ROLLING AWAY..."
ROLL ROLL ROLL AWAY
...SO HE INVENTED BOWLING BLOCKS. THEY'RE CUBE-SHAPED BOWLING BALLS!
THIS IS AN IMPORTANT BREAKTHROUGH!
YOU KNOW, PATRICE, I HAVE TO SAY I'M GLAD CRAZY DAVE IS INVENTING THINGS, BECAUSE WITH WHAT'S BEEN GOING ON LATELY, I'VE BEEN GETTING A LITTLE NERVOUS.
YOU MEAN...
...ALL THESE MINI-SCHEMES ZOMBOSS HAS BEEN RUNNING? ARE YOU WORRIED THEY MIGHT BE LEADING UP TO...SOMETHING BIGGER?
FIG TROUBLE
HMM. THAT IS CONCERNING. BUT WHAT I MEANT IS...
...DAFFODIL DONUTS HAVE BEEN LIMITING ME TO ONLY THIRTY DONUTS A DAY!
HOW AM I EVEN SUPPOSED TO GET THROUGH BREAKFAST?!?!

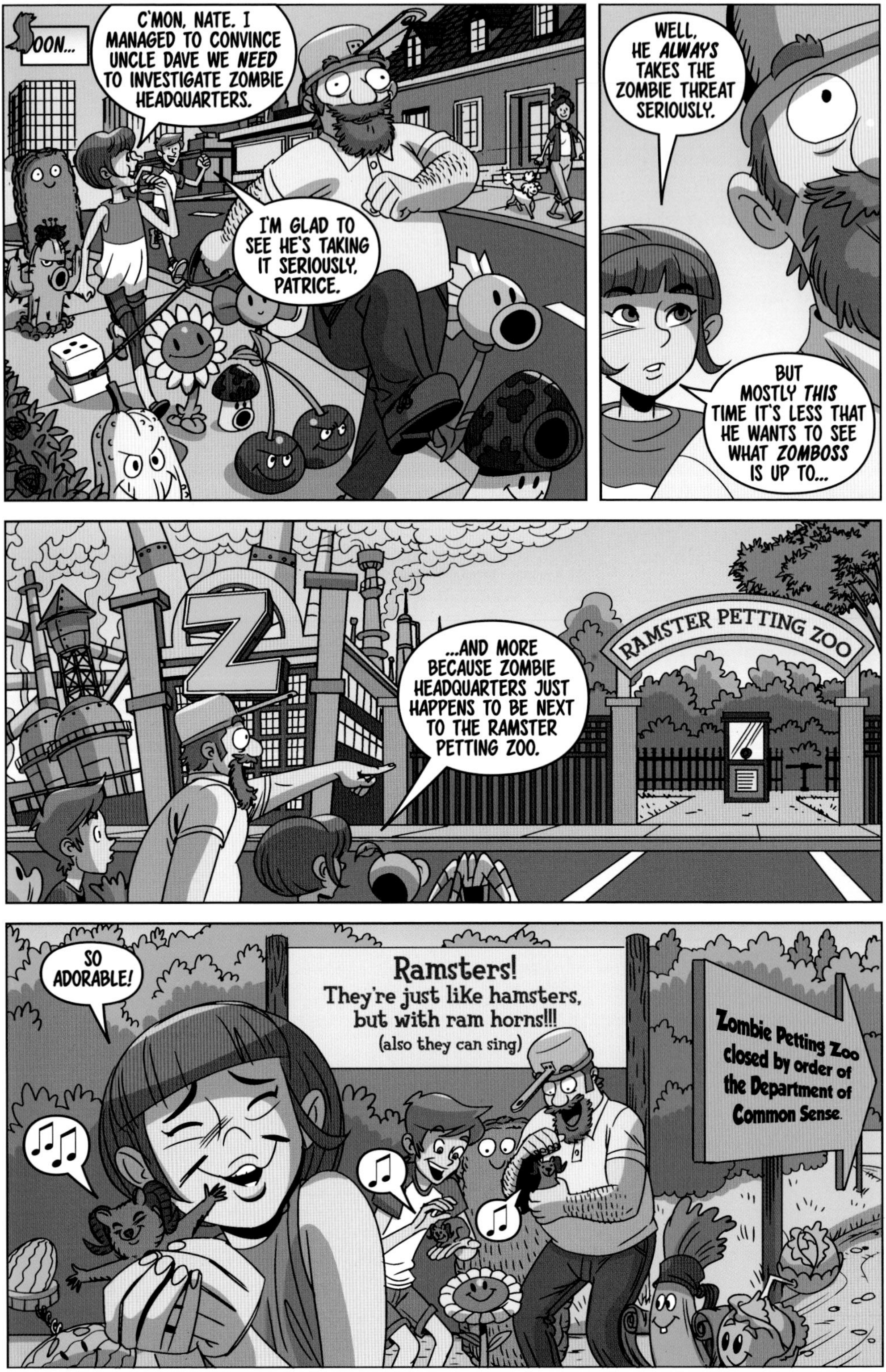
SOON...
C'MON, NATE. I MANAGED TO CONVINCE UNCLE DAVE WE *NEED* TO INVESTIGATE ZOMBIE HEADQUARTERS.
I'M GLAD TO SEE HE'S TAKING IT SERIOUSLY, PATRICE.
WELL, HE *ALWAYS* TAKES THE ZOMBIE THREAT SERIOUSLY.
BUT MOSTLY *THIS* TIME IT'S LESS THAT HE WANTS TO SEE WHAT *ZOMBOSS* IS UP TO...
Z
RAMSTER PETTING ZOO
...AND MORE BECAUSE ZOMBIE HEADQUARTERS JUST HAPPENS TO BE NEXT TO THE RAMSTER PETTING ZOO.
SO ADORABLE!
Ramsters!
They're just like hamsters, but with ram horns!!!
(also they can sing)
Zombie Petting Zoo closed by order of the Department of Common Sense.

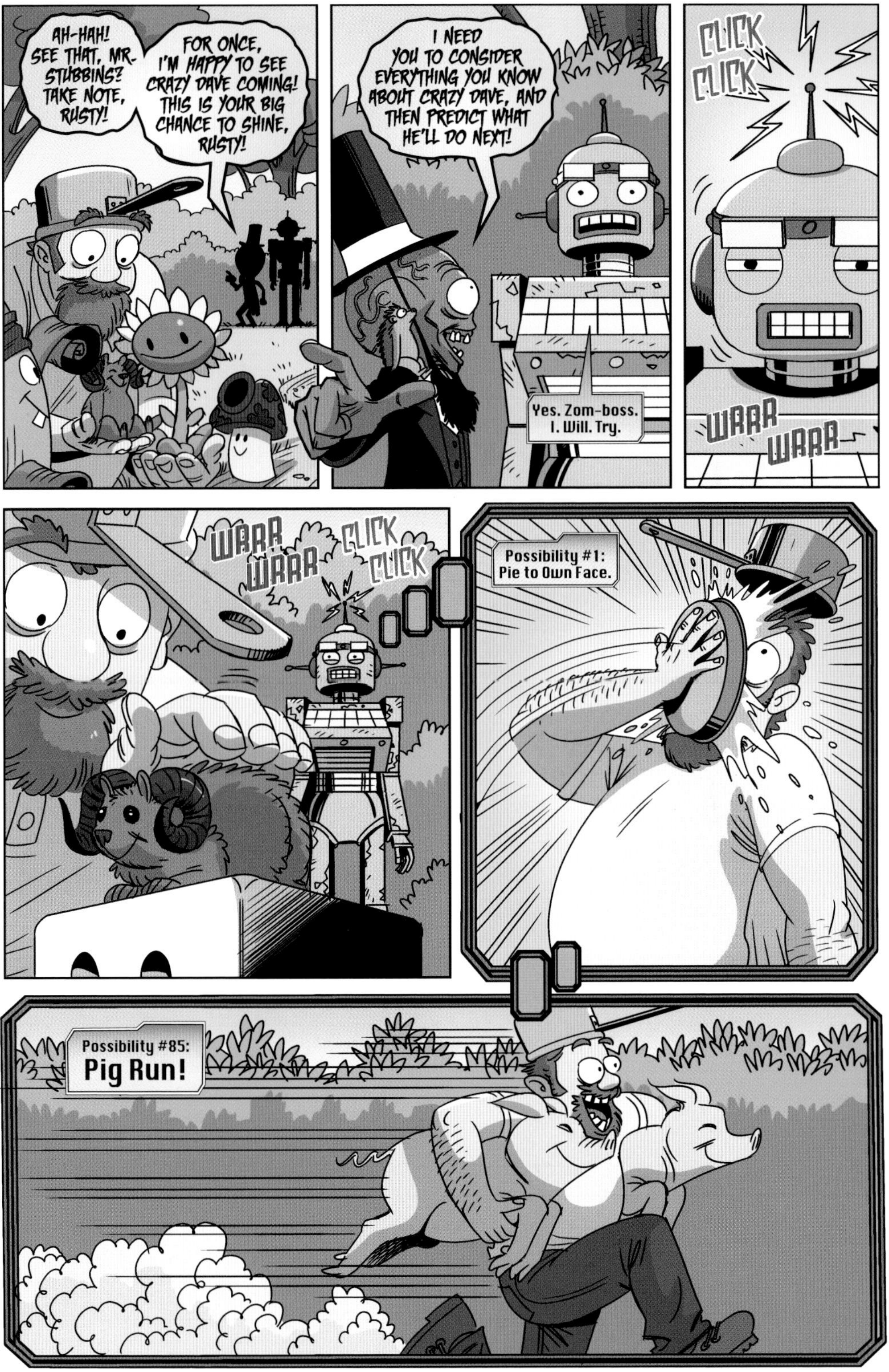
AH-HAH! SEE THAT, MR. STUBBINS? TAKE NOTE, RUSTY!
FOR ONCE, I'M HAPPY TO SEE CRAZY DAVE COMING! THIS IS YOUR BIG CHANCE TO SHINE, RUSTY!
I NEED YOU TO CONSIDER EVERYTHING YOU KNOW ABOUT CRAZY DAVE, AND THEN PREDICT WHAT HE'LL DO NEXT!
Yes. Zom-boss. I. Will. Try.
CLICK CLICK
WRRR WRRR
WRRR WRRR
CLICK CLICK
Possibility #1: Pie to Own Face.
Possibility #85: Pig Run!

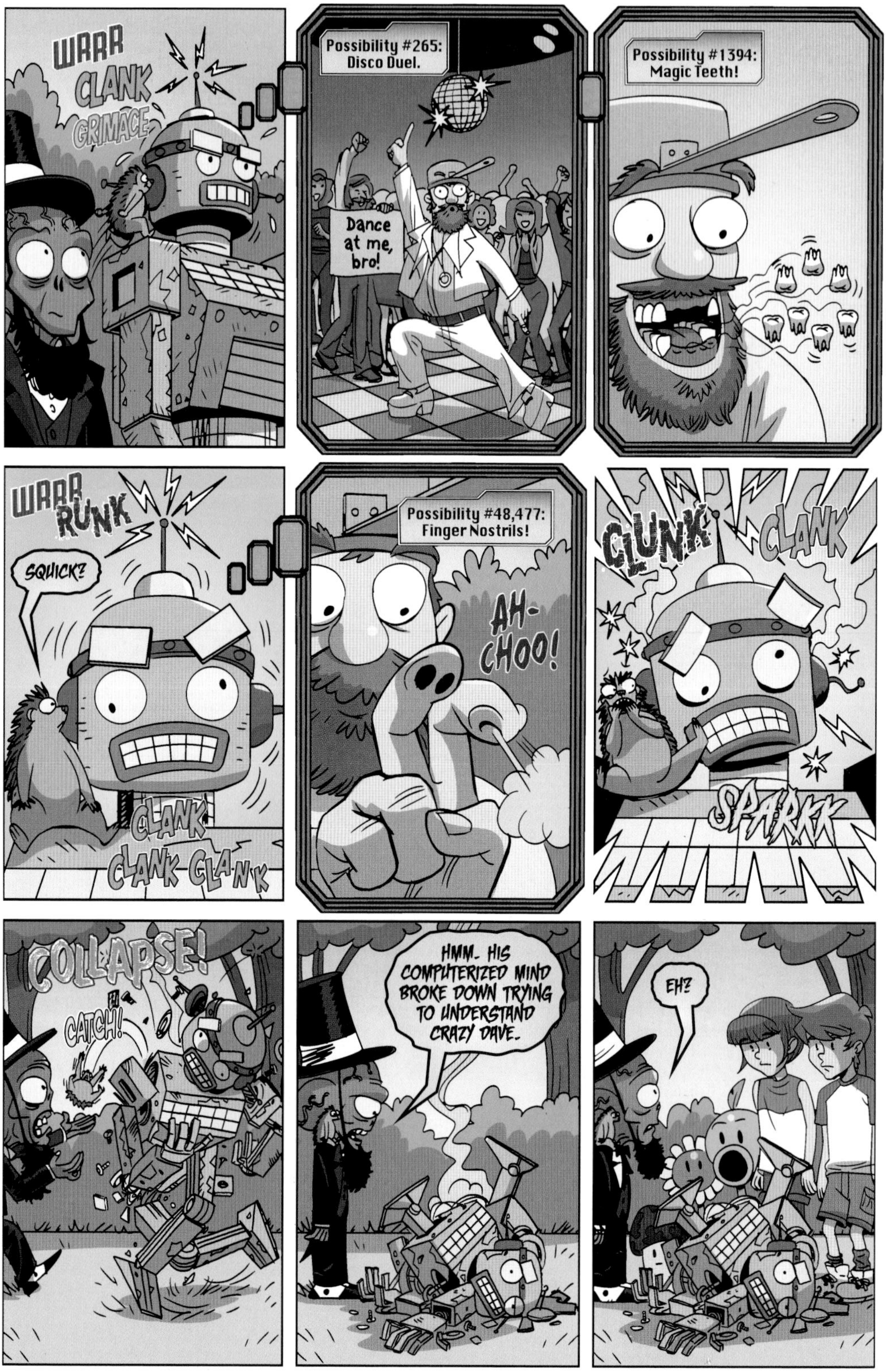
WRRR
CLANK
GRIMACE
Possibility #265: Disco Duel.
Dance at me, bro!
Possibility #1394: Magic Teeth!
WRRR
RUNK
SQUICK?
CLANK
CLANK CLANK
Possibility #48,477: Finger Nostrils!
AH-CHOO!
CLUNK
CLANK
SPARKK
COLLAPSE!
CATCH!
HMM. HIS COMPUTERIZED MIND BROKE DOWN TRYING TO UNDERSTAND CRAZY DAVE.
EH?

C'MON, EVERYONE. I GUESS ZOMBOSS IS NO THREAT AFTER ALL.

IT'S RAMSTER FEEDING TIME! LET'S BUY THEM ICE CREAM!

DID YOU...? DID I HEAR...? DID YOU SAY...?

I'M NO THREAT?

ZOMBOSS ISN'T A THREAT?

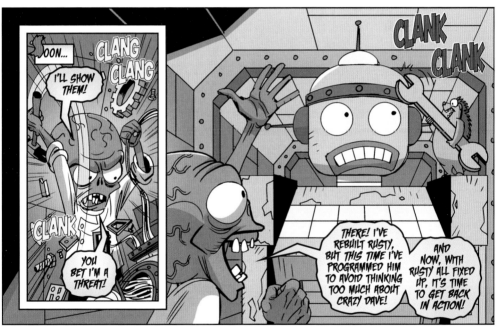

...OON...

I'LL SHOW THEM!

CLANG CLANG

CLANK

YOU BET I'M A THREAT!

CLANK CLANK

THERE! I'VE REBUILT RUSTY, BUT THIS TIME I'VE PROGRAMMED HIM TO AVOID THINKING TOO MUCH ABOUT CRAZY DAVE!

AND NOW, WITH RUSTY ALL FIXED UP, IT'S TIME TO GET BACK IN ACTION!

ALTHOUGH MAYBE IT'S TIME TO GET INTO DISGUISE AND GO TO THE PETTING ZOO?

BECAUSE, SERIOUSLY, THOSE RAMSTERS REALLY ARE ADORABLE.

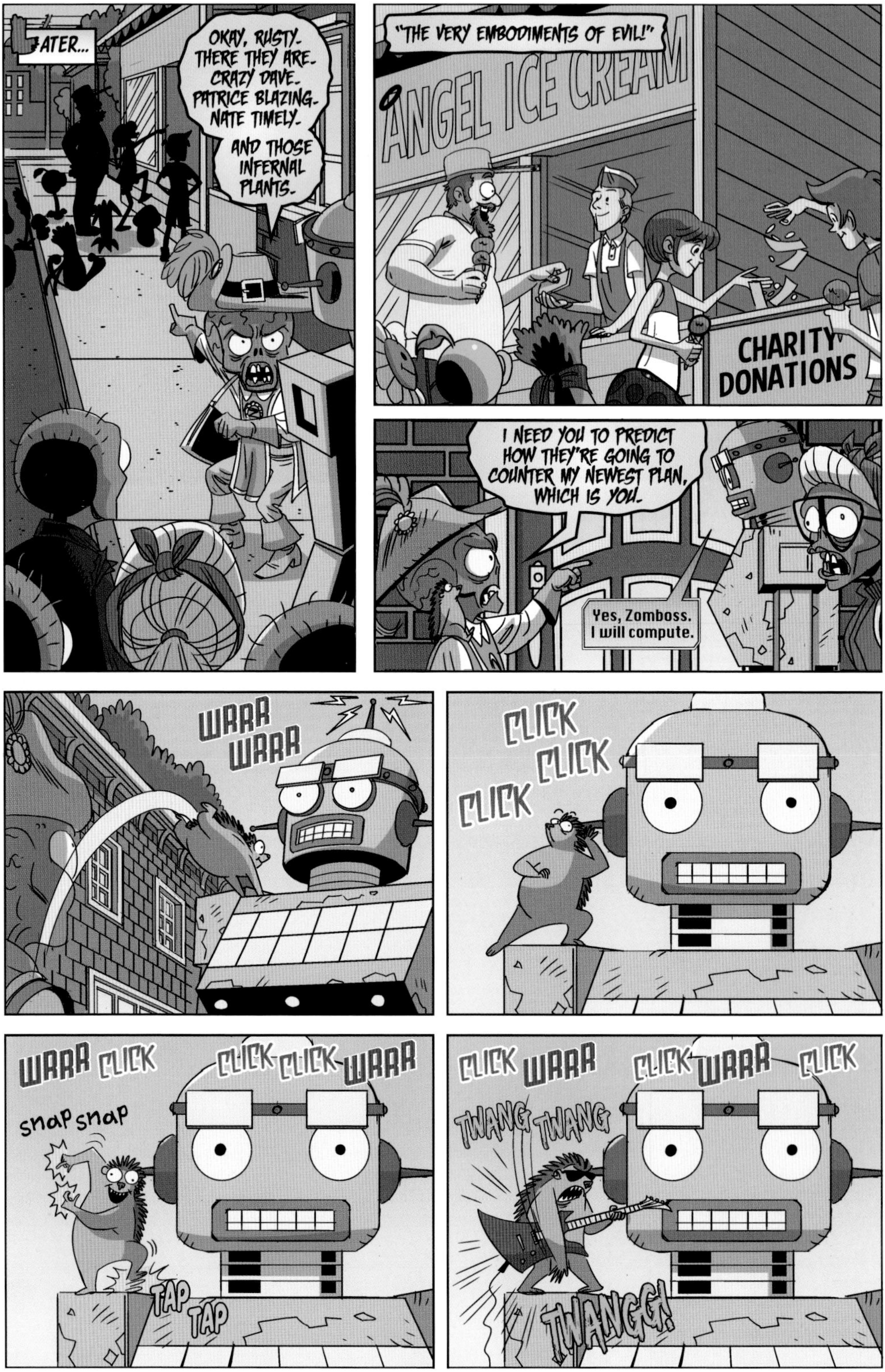
LATER...
OKAY, RUSTY. THERE THEY ARE. CRAZY DAVE. PATRICE BLAZING. NATE TIMELY.
AND THOSE INFERNAL PLANTS.
"THE VERY EMBODIMENTS OF EVIL!"
ANGEL ICE CREAM
CHARITY DONATIONS
I NEED YOU TO PREDICT HOW THEY'RE GOING TO COUNTER MY NEWEST PLAN, WHICH IS YOU.
Yes, Zomboss. I will compute.
WRRR WRRR
CLICK CLICK CLICK
WRRR CLICK CLICK CLICK WRRR
snap snap
TAP TAP
CLICK WRRR CLICK WRRR CLICK
TWANG TWANG
TWANGG!

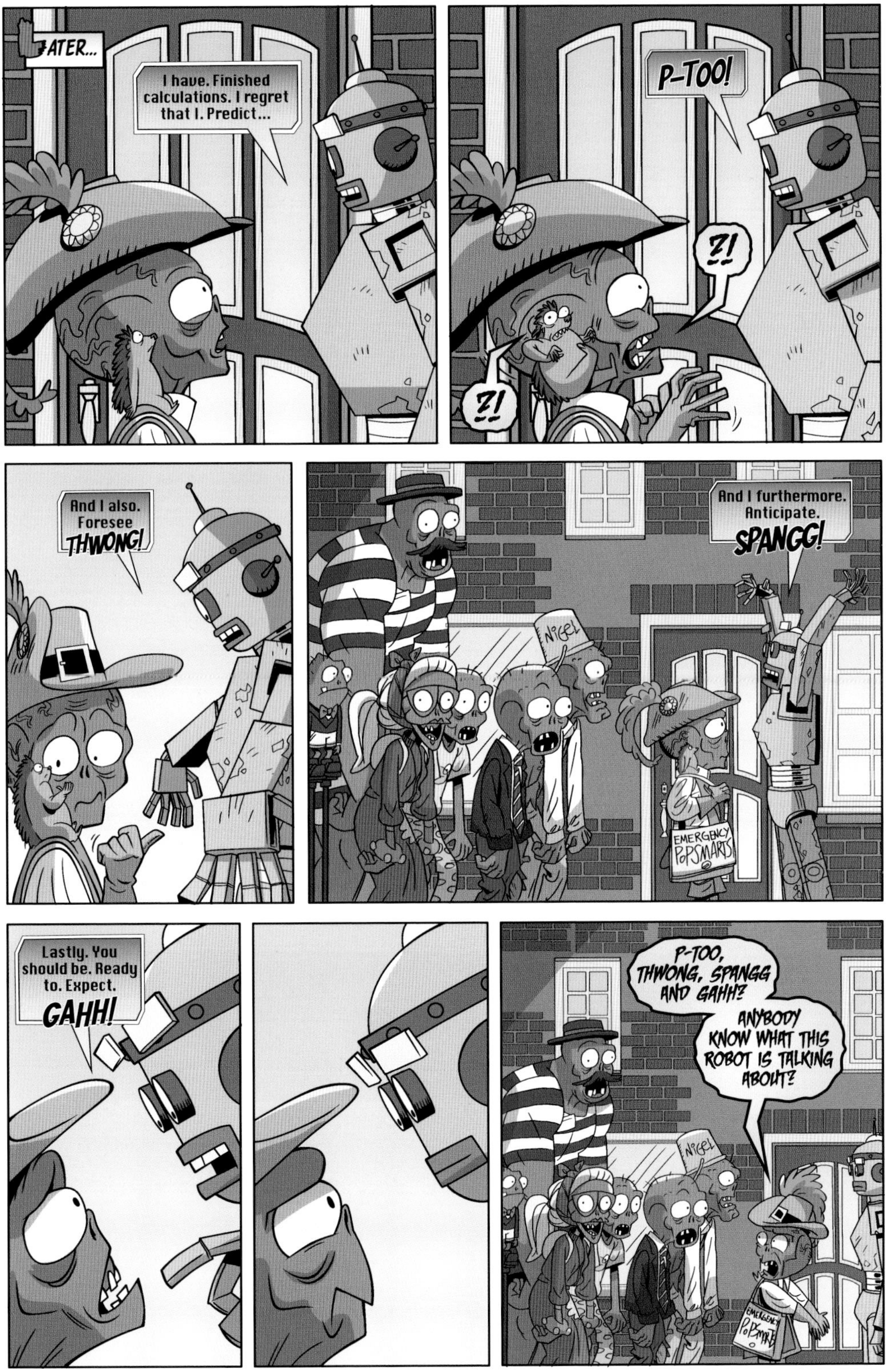
LATER...
I have. Finished calculations. I regret that I. Predict...
P-TOO!
?!
?!
And I also. Foresee THWONG!
And I furthermore. Anticipate. SPANGG!
NIGEL
EMERGENCY POPSMARTS
Lastly. You should be. Ready to. Expect. GAHH!
P-TOO, THWONG, SPANGG AND GAHH?
ANYBODY KNOW WHAT THIS ROBOT IS TALKING ABOUT?
NIGEL
EMERGENCY POPSMARTS

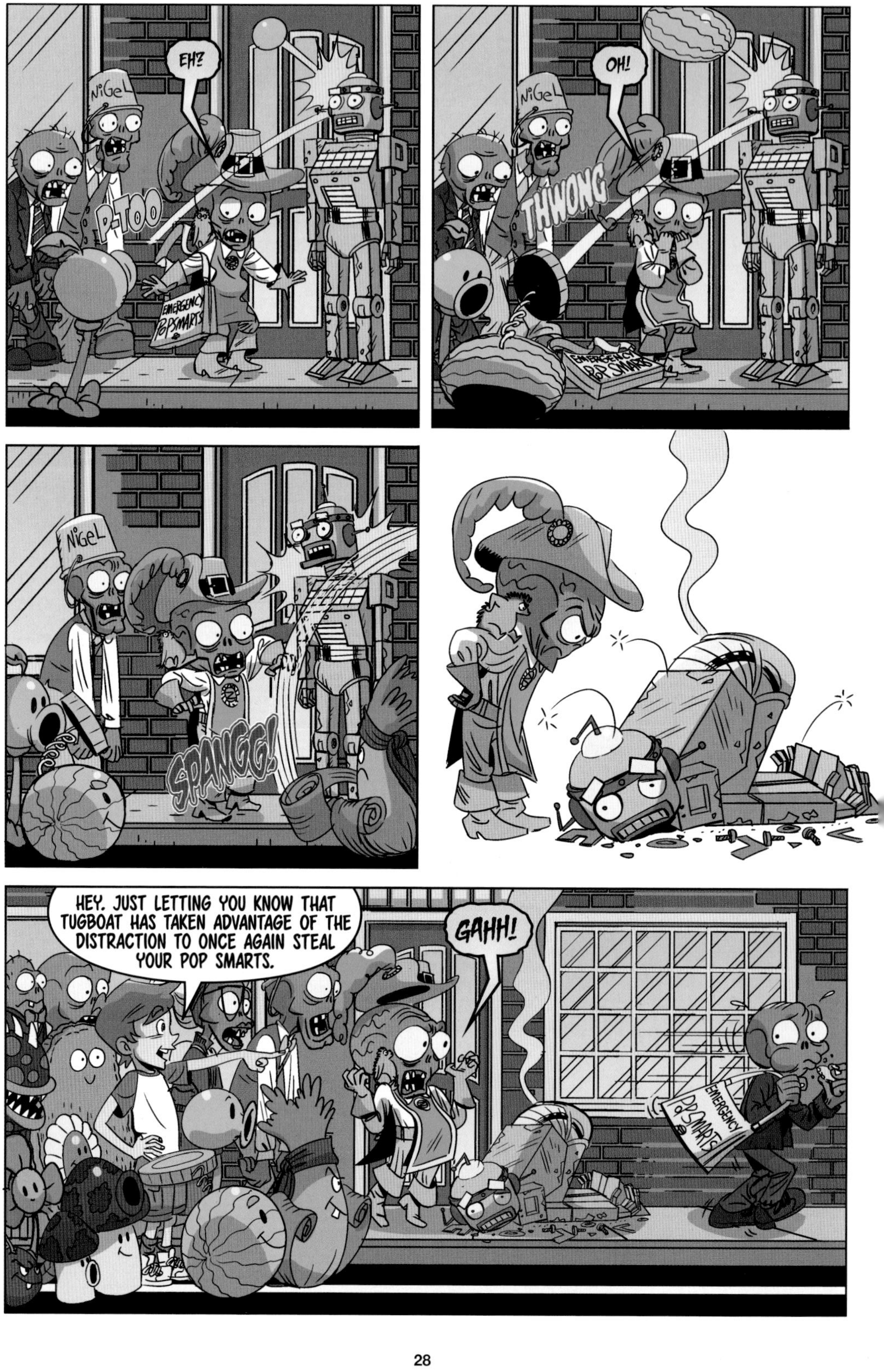
EH?
NiGeL
P-TOO
EMERGENCY POPSMARTS
OH!
NiGeL
THWONG
EMERGENCY POPSMARTS
NiGeL
SPANGG!
HEY. JUST LETTING YOU KNOW THAT TUGBOAT HAS TAKEN ADVANTAGE OF THE DISTRACTION TO ONCE AGAIN STEAL YOUR POP SMARTS.
GAHH!
EMERGENCY POPSMARTS

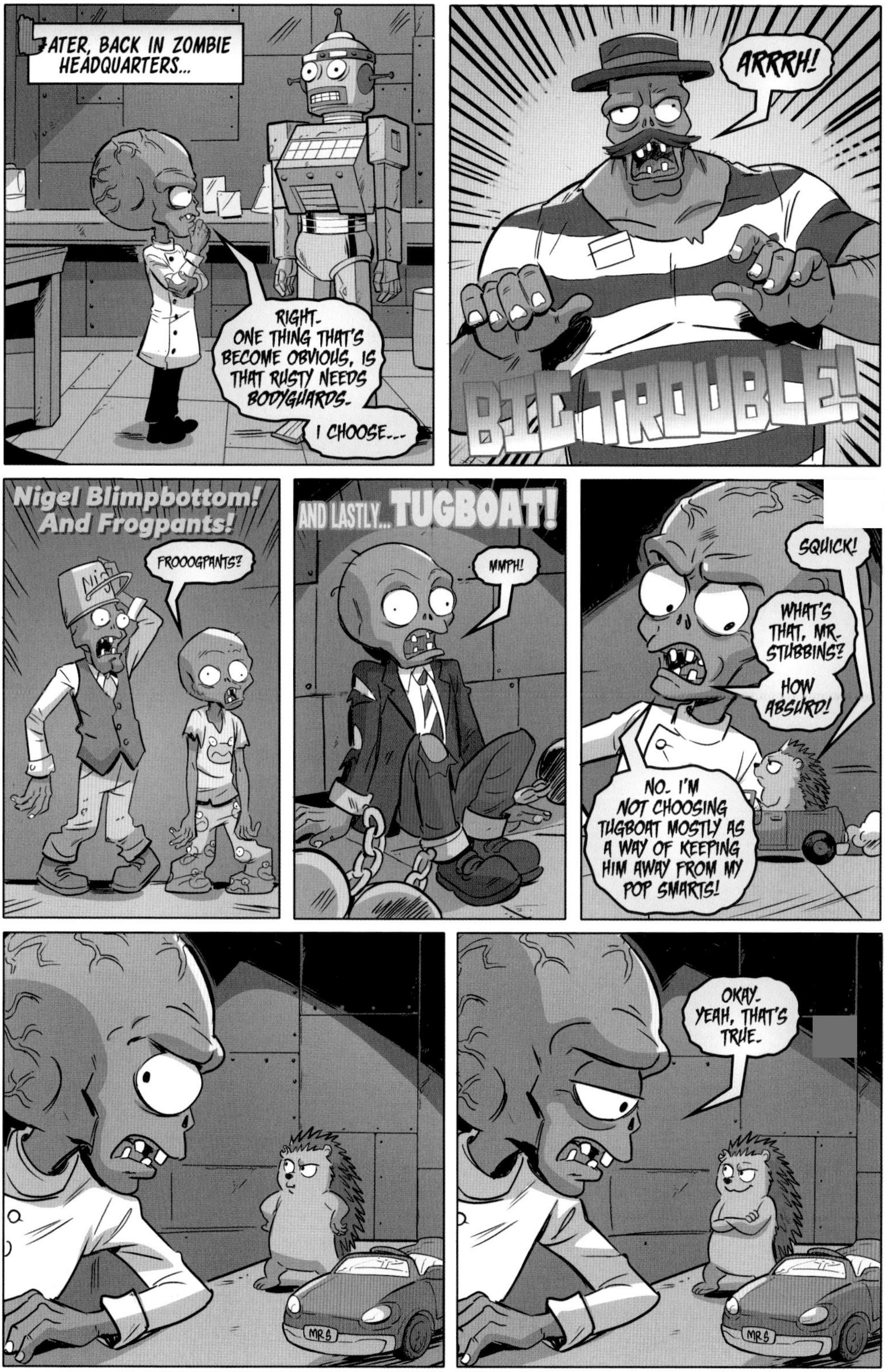
LATER, BACK IN ZOMBIE HEADQUARTERS...
RIGHT. ONE THING THAT'S BECOME OBVIOUS, IS THAT RUSTY NEEDS BODYGUARDS.
I CHOOSE...
ARRRH!
BIG TROUBLE!
Nigel Blimpbottom! And Frogpants!
FROOOGPANTS?
AND LASTLY... TUGBOAT!
MMPH!
SQUICK!
WHAT'S THAT, MR. STUBBINS?
HOW ABSURD!
NO. I'M NOT CHOOSING TUGBOAT MOSTLY AS A WAY OF KEEPING HIM AWAY FROM MY POP SMARTS!
OKAY. YEAH, THAT'S TRUE.

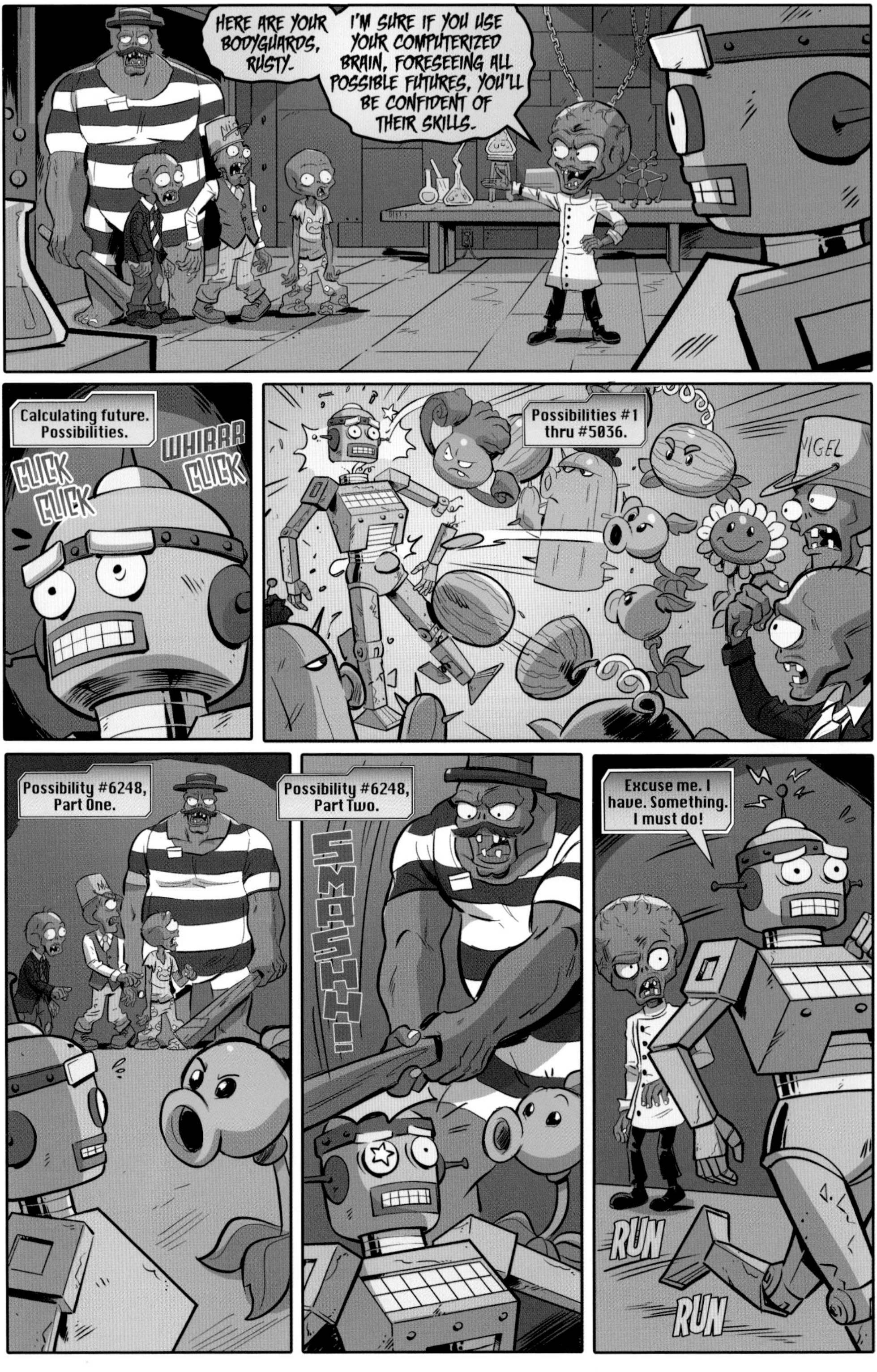
HERE ARE YOUR BODYGUARDS, RUSTY.
I'M SURE IF YOU USE YOUR COMPUTERIZED BRAIN, FORESEEING ALL POSSIBLE FUTURES, YOU'LL BE CONFIDENT OF THEIR SKILLS.
Calculating future. Possibilities.
CLICK CLICK
WHIRRR CLICK
Possibilities #1 thru #5036.
NIGEL
Possibility #6248, Part One.
Possibility #6248, Part Two.
SMASHHH!
Excuse me. I have. Something. I must do!
RUN
RUN

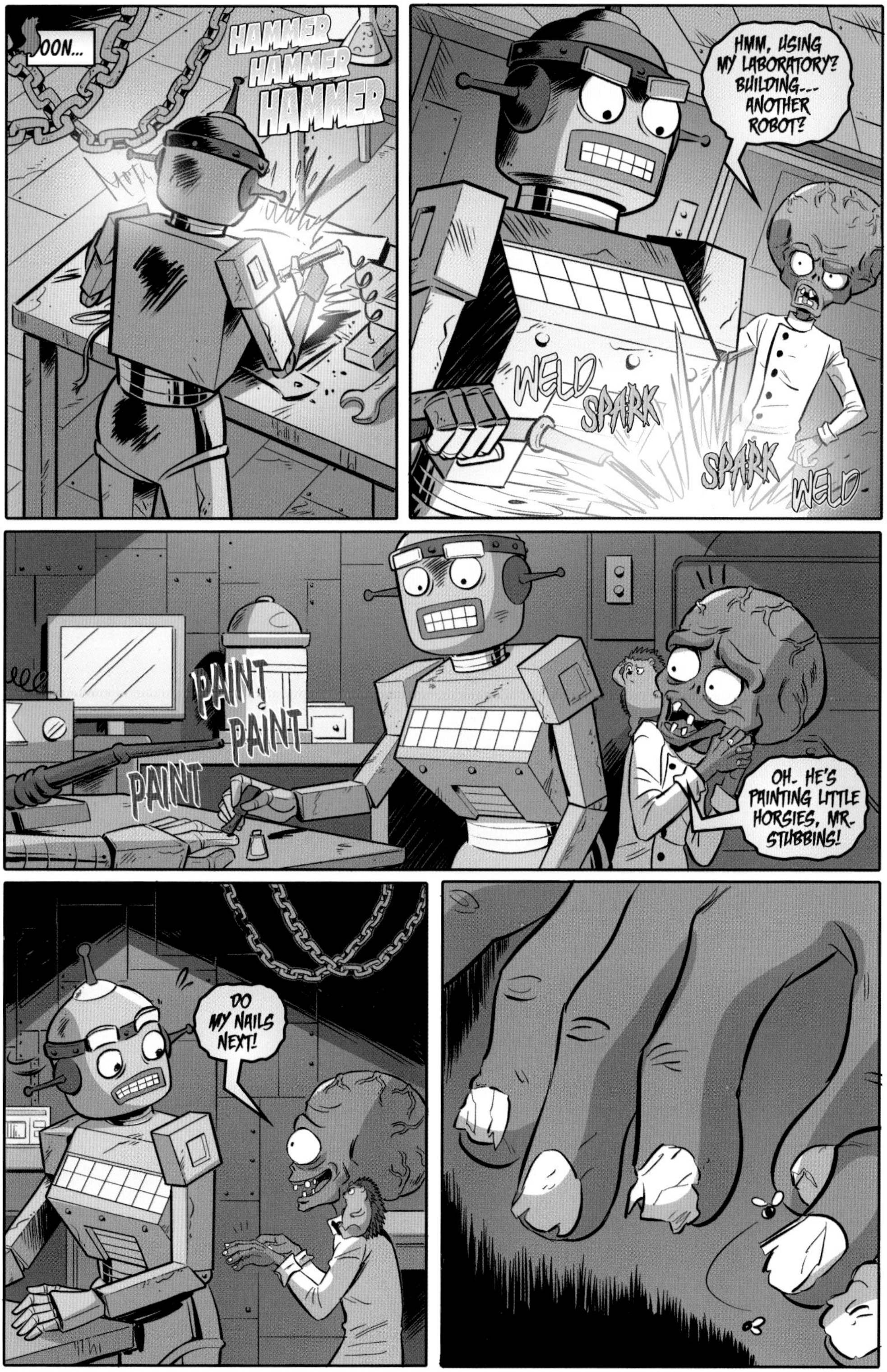

...OON...
HAMMER HAMMER HAMMER
HMM, USING MY LABORATORY? BUILDING... ANOTHER ROBOT?
WELD
SPARK
SPARK
WELD
PAINT
PAINT
PAINT
OH. HE'S PAINTING LITTLE HORSIES, MR. STUBBINS!
DO MY NAILS NEXT!

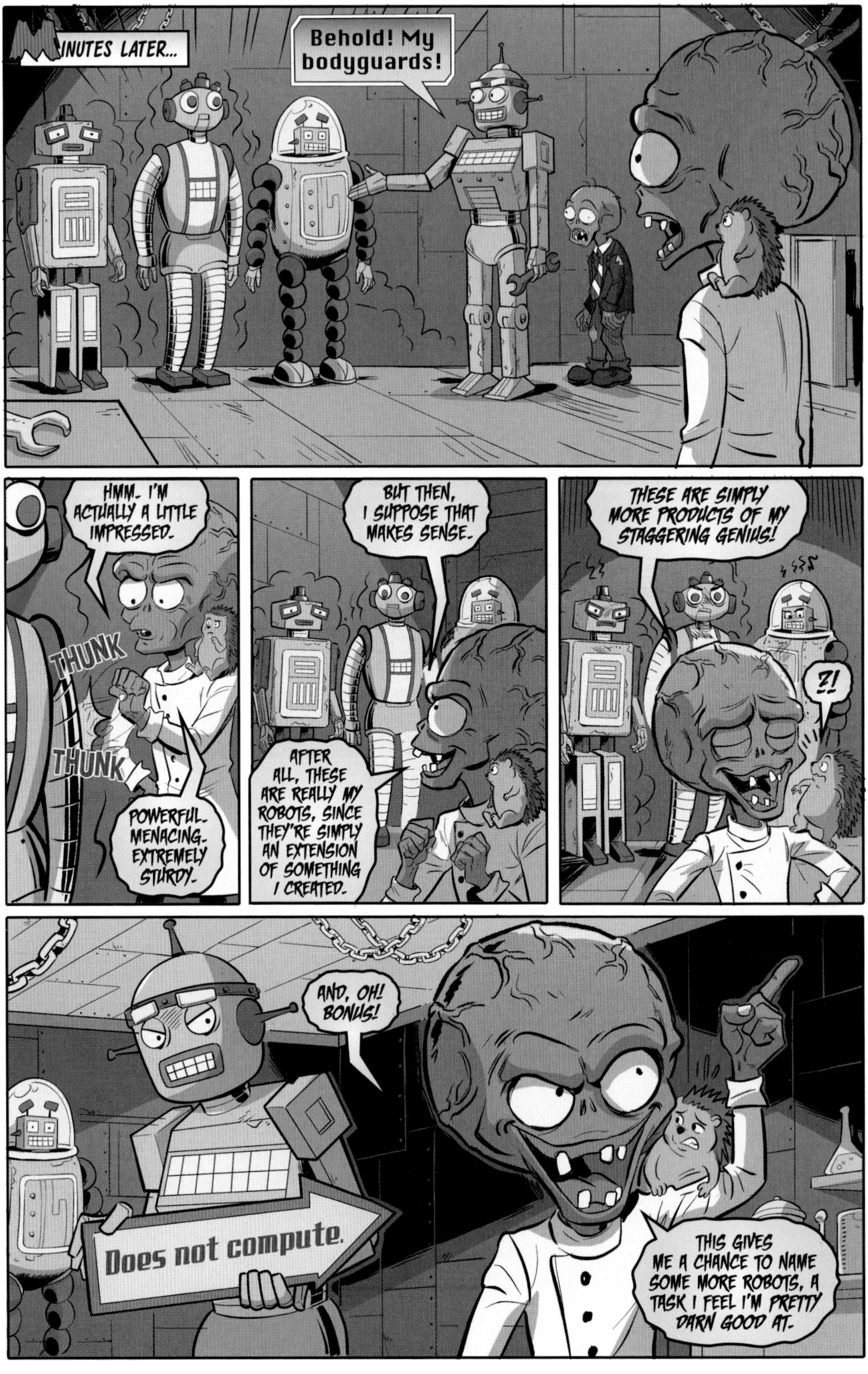
MINUTES LATER...
Behold! My bodyguards!
HMM. I'M ACTUALLY A LITTLE IMPRESSED.
THUNK
THUNK
POWERFUL. MENACING. EXTREMELY STURDY.
BUT THEN, I SUPPOSE THAT MAKES SENSE.
AFTER ALL, THESE ARE REALLY MY ROBOTS, SINCE THEY'RE SIMPLY AN EXTENSION OF SOMETHING I CREATED.
THESE ARE SIMPLY MORE PRODUCTS OF MY STAGGERING GENIUS!
?!
AND, OH! BONUS!
Does not compute.
THIS GIVES ME A CHANCE TO NAME SOME MORE ROBOTS, A TASK I FEEL I'M PRETTY DARN GOOD AT.

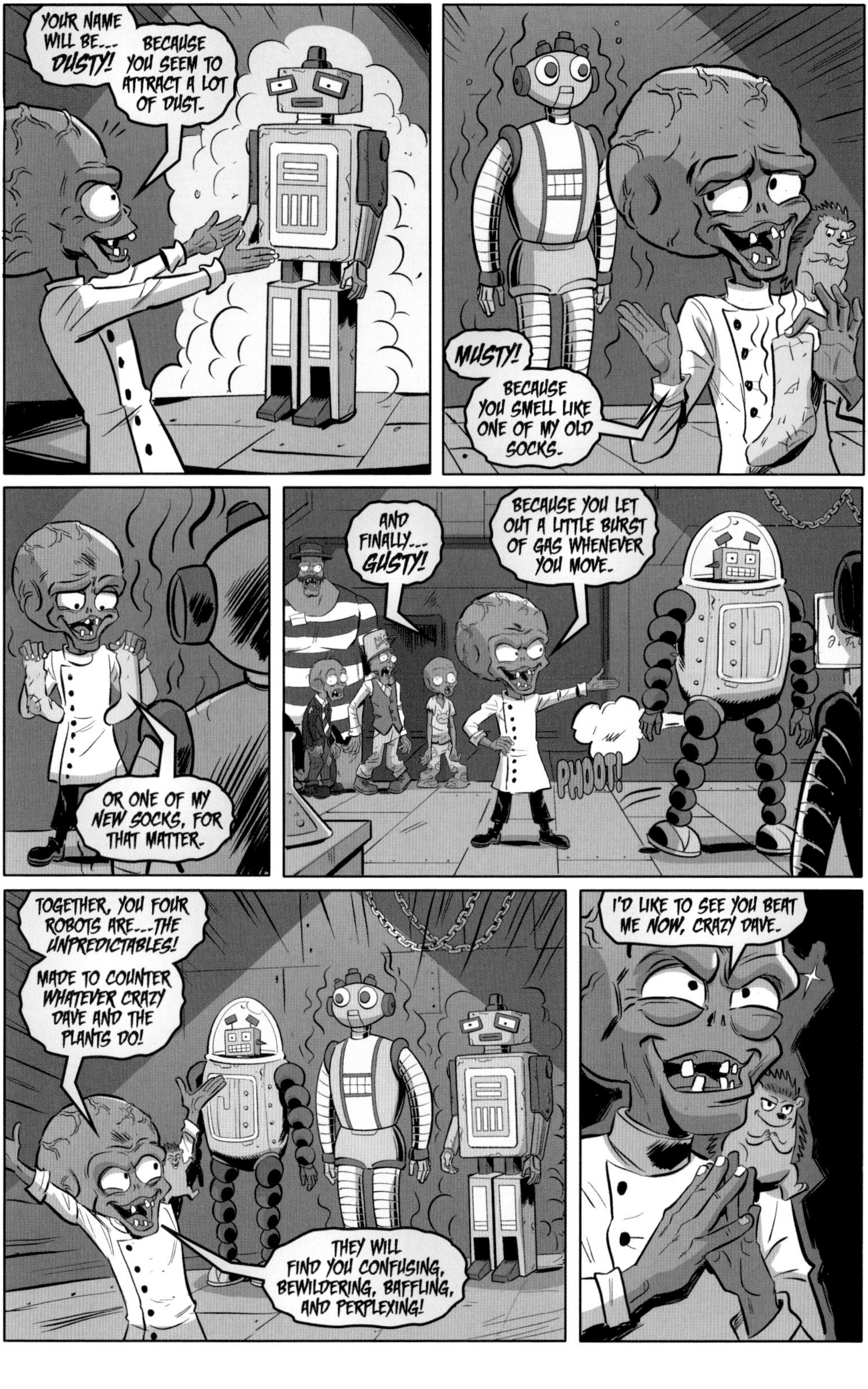
YOUR NAME WILL BE... DUSTY!
BECAUSE YOU SEEM TO ATTRACT A LOT OF DUST.
MUSTY!
BECAUSE YOU SMELL LIKE ONE OF MY OLD SOCKS.
OR ONE OF MY NEW SOCKS, FOR THAT MATTER.
AND FINALLY... GUSTY!
BECAUSE YOU LET OUT A LITTLE BURST OF GAS WHENEVER YOU MOVE.
PHOOT!
TOGETHER, YOU FOUR ROBOTS ARE... THE UNPREDICTABLES!
MADE TO COUNTER WHATEVER CRAZY DAVE AND THE PLANTS DO!
THEY WILL FIND YOU CONFUSING, BEWILDERING, BAFFLING, AND PERPLEXING!
I'D LIKE TO SEE YOU BEAT ME NOW, CRAZY DAVE.

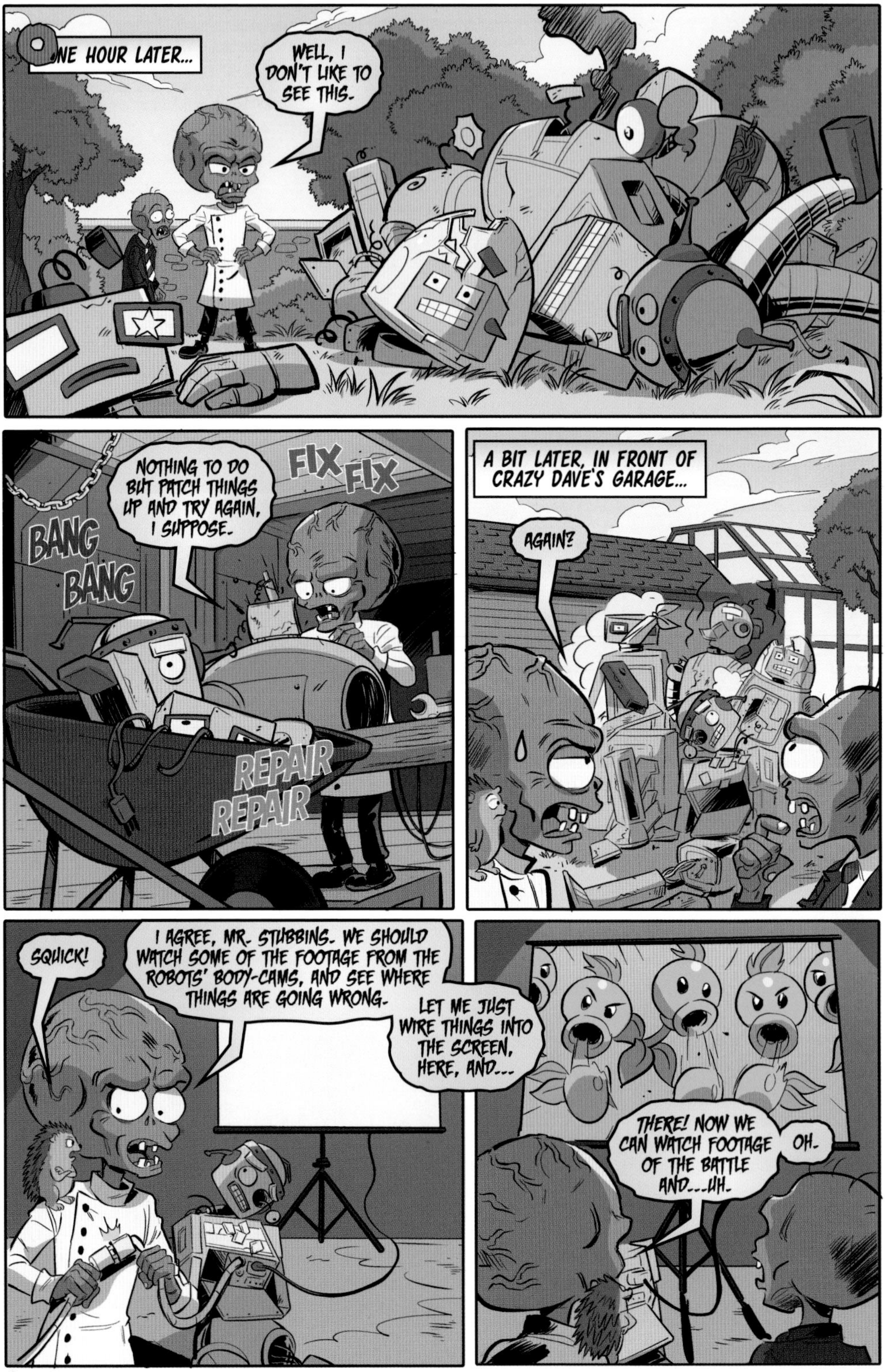
ONE HOUR LATER...
WELL, I DON'T LIKE TO SEE THIS.
NOTHING TO DO BUT PATCH THINGS UP AND TRY AGAIN, I SUPPOSE.
FIX FIX
BANG BANG
REPAIR REPAIR
A BIT LATER, IN FRONT OF CRAZY DAVE'S GARAGE...
AGAIN?
SQUICK!
I AGREE, MR. STUBBINS. WE SHOULD WATCH SOME OF THE FOOTAGE FROM THE ROBOTS' BODY-CAMS, AND SEE WHERE THINGS ARE GOING WRONG.
LET ME JUST WIRE THINGS INTO THE SCREEN, HERE, AND...
THERE! NOW WE CAN WATCH FOOTAGE OF THE BATTLE AND...UH.
OH.

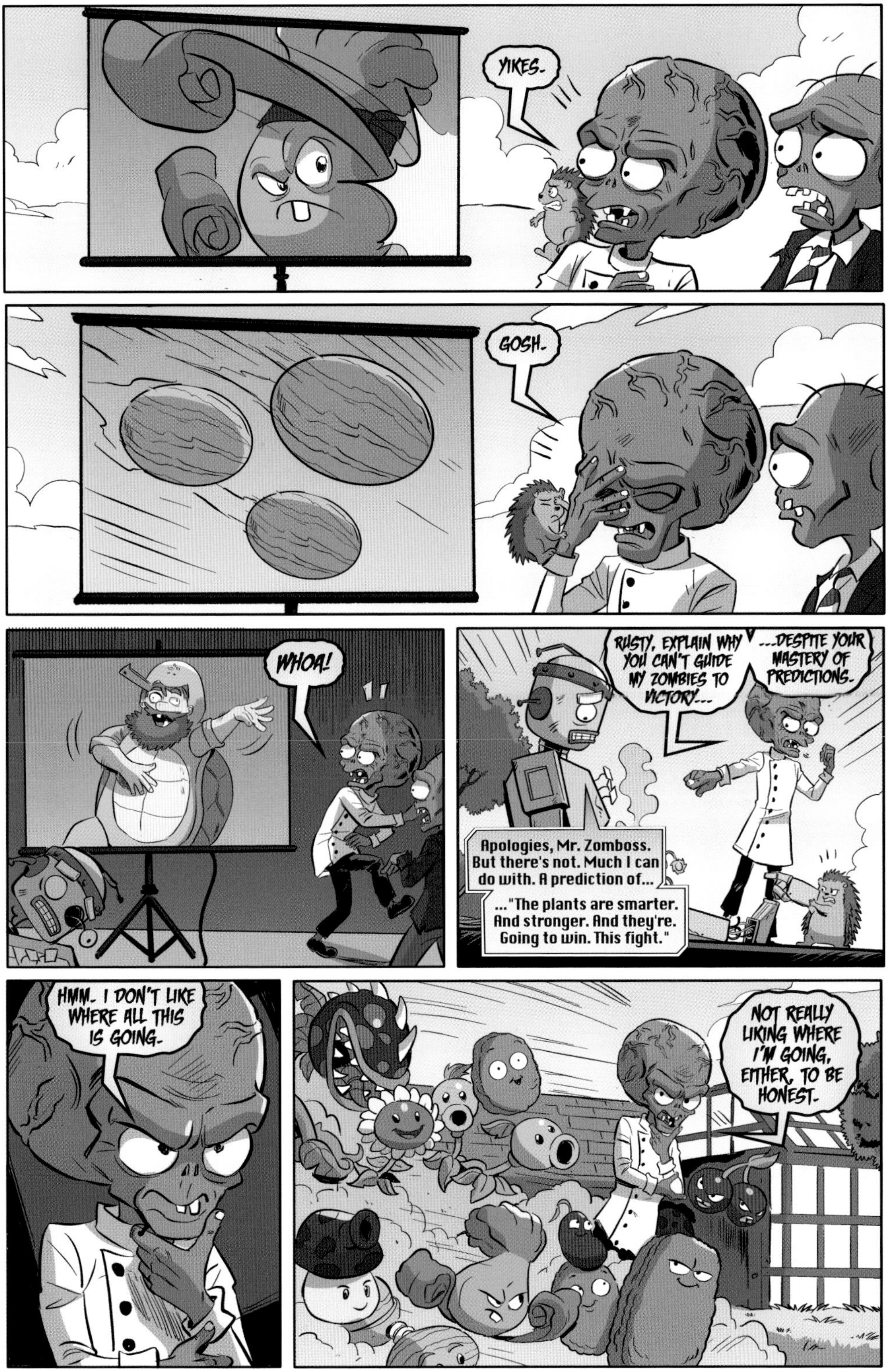
YIKES.
GOSH.
WHOA!
RUSTY, EXPLAIN WHY YOU CAN'T GUIDE MY ZOMBIES TO VICTORY...
...DESPITE YOUR MASTERY OF PREDICTIONS.
Apologies, Mr. Zomboss. But there's not. Much I can do with. A prediction of...
..."The plants are smarter. And stronger. And they're. Going to win. This fight."
HMM. I DON'T LIKE WHERE ALL THIS IS GOING.
NOT REALLY LIKING WHERE I'M GOING, EITHER, TO BE HONEST.

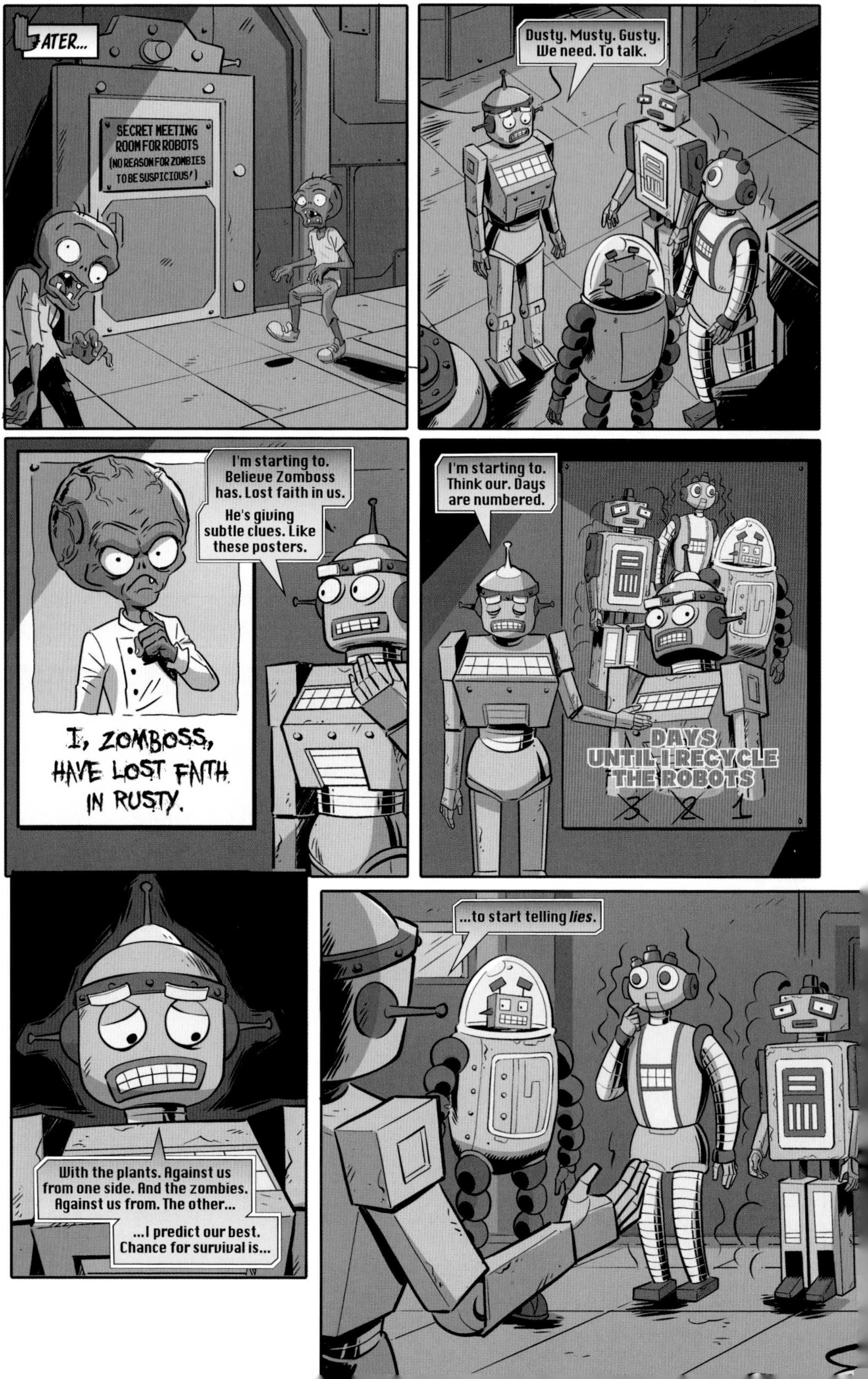
LATER...
SECRET MEETING ROOM FOR ROBOTS (NO REASON FOR ZOMBIES TO BE SUSPICIOUS!)
Dusty. Musty. Gusty. We need. To talk.
I'm starting to. Believe Zomboss has. Lost faith in us.
He's giving subtle clues. Like these posters.
I, ZOMBOSS, HAVE LOST FAITH IN RUSTY.
I'm starting to. Think our. Days are numbered.
DAYS UNTIL I RECYCLE THE ROBOTS
3 2 1
With the plants. Against us from one side. And the zombies. Against us from. The other...
...I predict our best. Chance for survival is...
...to start telling *lies*.

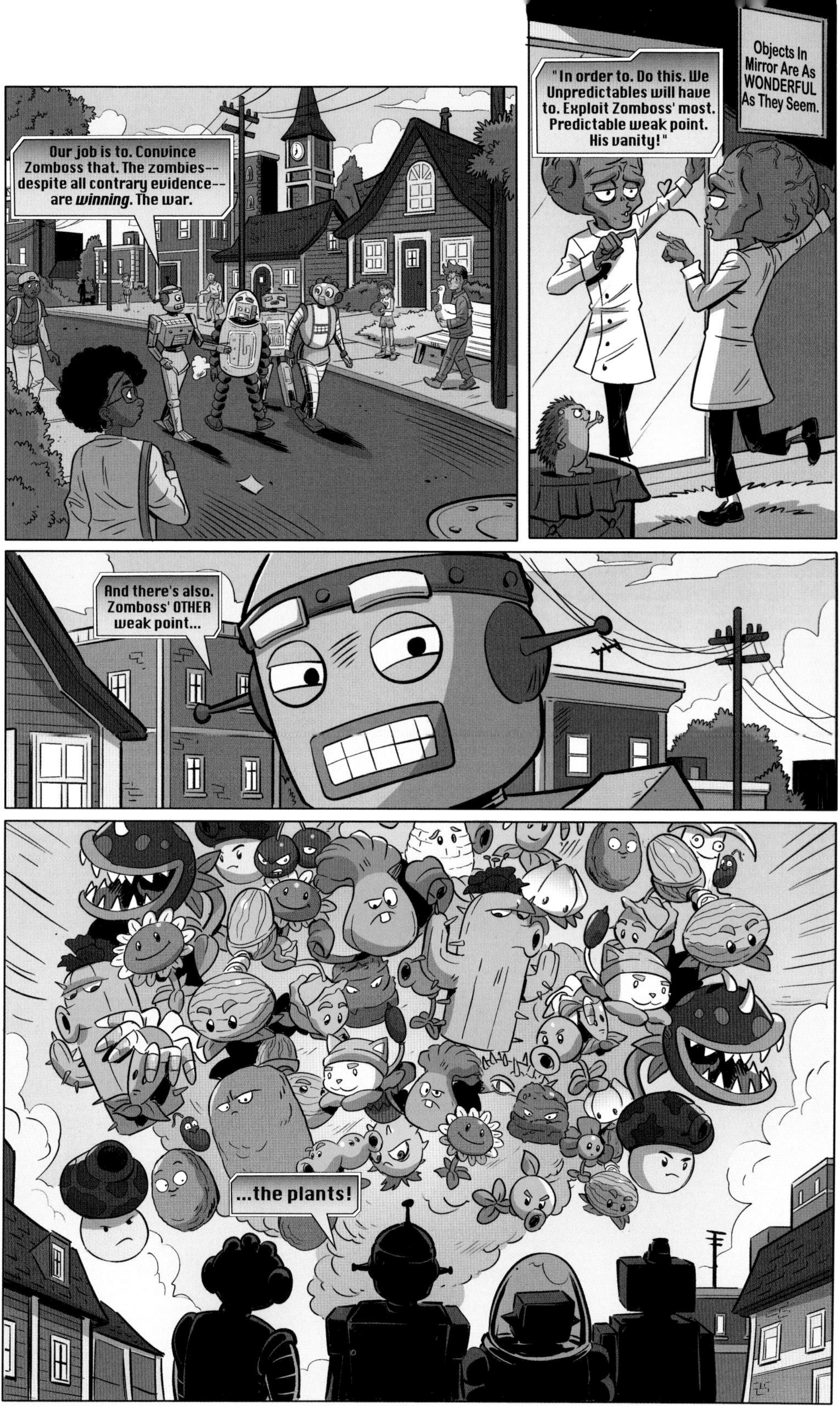
Our job is to. Convince Zomboss that. The zombies--despite all contrary evidence--are *winning*. The war.
Objects In Mirror Are As WONDERFUL As They Seem.
"In order to. Do this. We Unpredictables will have to. Exploit Zomboss' most. Predictable weak point. His vanity!"
And there's also. Zomboss' OTHER weak point...
...the plants!

OON...

LET ME GET THIS STRAIGHT, YOU WANT TO TEAM UP WITH US?

That is correct, Nate Timely. I have calculated it. As vital for. Our self-preservation.

My name is Rusty. I speak for my. Friends. Dusty. Musty. And Gusty.

PHOOT!

OH, OKAY. WELL, I SPEAK FOR MY FRIENDS.

PATRICE BLAZING. GRRWARR-BEAR THE ULTIMATE FACE PUNCHER. CHELSEA CHOMPER. EDGAR ALLAN POTATO MINE. CRAZY DAVE, AND...

...MONSIEUR CARL.

Monsieur Carl?

GROBBLE FLONT!

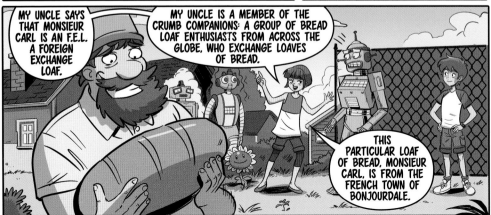

MY UNCLE SAYS THAT MONSIEUR CARL IS AN F.E.L. A FOREIGN EXCHANGE LOAF.

MY UNCLE IS A MEMBER OF THE CRUMB COMPANIONS: A GROUP OF BREAD LOAF ENTHUSIASTS FROM ACROSS THE GLOBE, WHO EXCHANGE LOAVES OF BREAD.

THIS PARTICULAR LOAF OF BREAD, MONSIEUR CARL, IS FROM THE FRENCH TOWN OF BONJOURDALE.

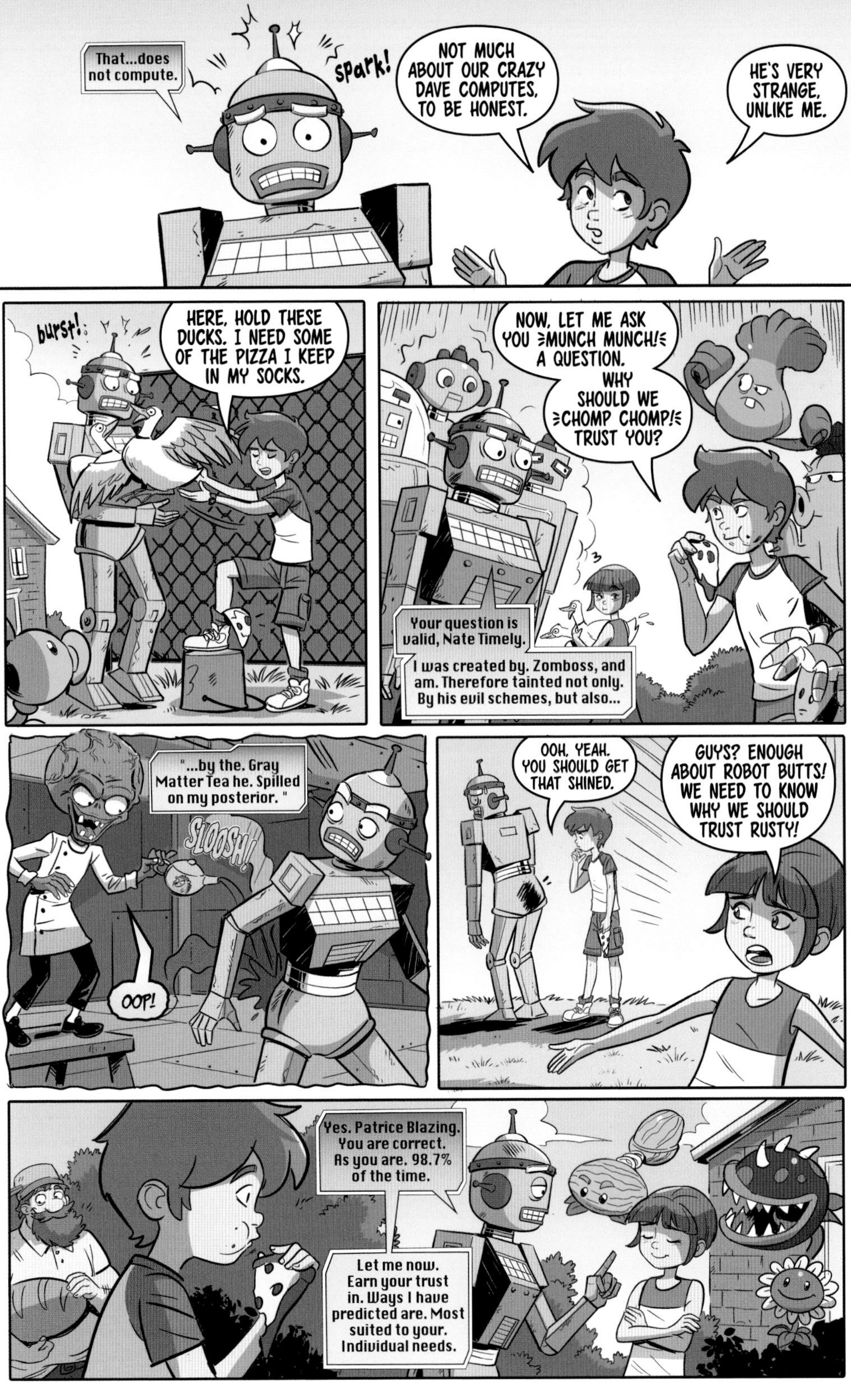
That...does not compute.
spark!
NOT MUCH ABOUT OUR CRAZY DAVE COMPUTES, TO BE HONEST.
HE'S VERY STRANGE, UNLIKE ME.
burst!
HERE, HOLD THESE DUCKS. I NEED SOME OF THE PIZZA I KEEP IN MY SOCKS.
NOW, LET ME ASK YOU ≥MUNCH MUNCH!≤ A QUESTION.
WHY SHOULD WE ≥CHOMP CHOMP!≤ TRUST YOU?
Your question is valid, Nate Timely.
I was created by. Zomboss, and am. Therefore tainted not only. By his evil schemes, but also...
"...by the. Gray Matter Tea he. Spilled on my posterior."
SLOOSH!
OOP!
OOH, YEAH. YOU SHOULD GET THAT SHINED.
GUYS? ENOUGH ABOUT ROBOT BUTTS! WE NEED TO KNOW WHY WE SHOULD TRUST RUSTY!
Yes. Patrice Blazing. You are correct. As you are. 98.7% of the time.
Let me now. Earn your trust in. Ways I have predicted are. Most suited to your. Individual needs.

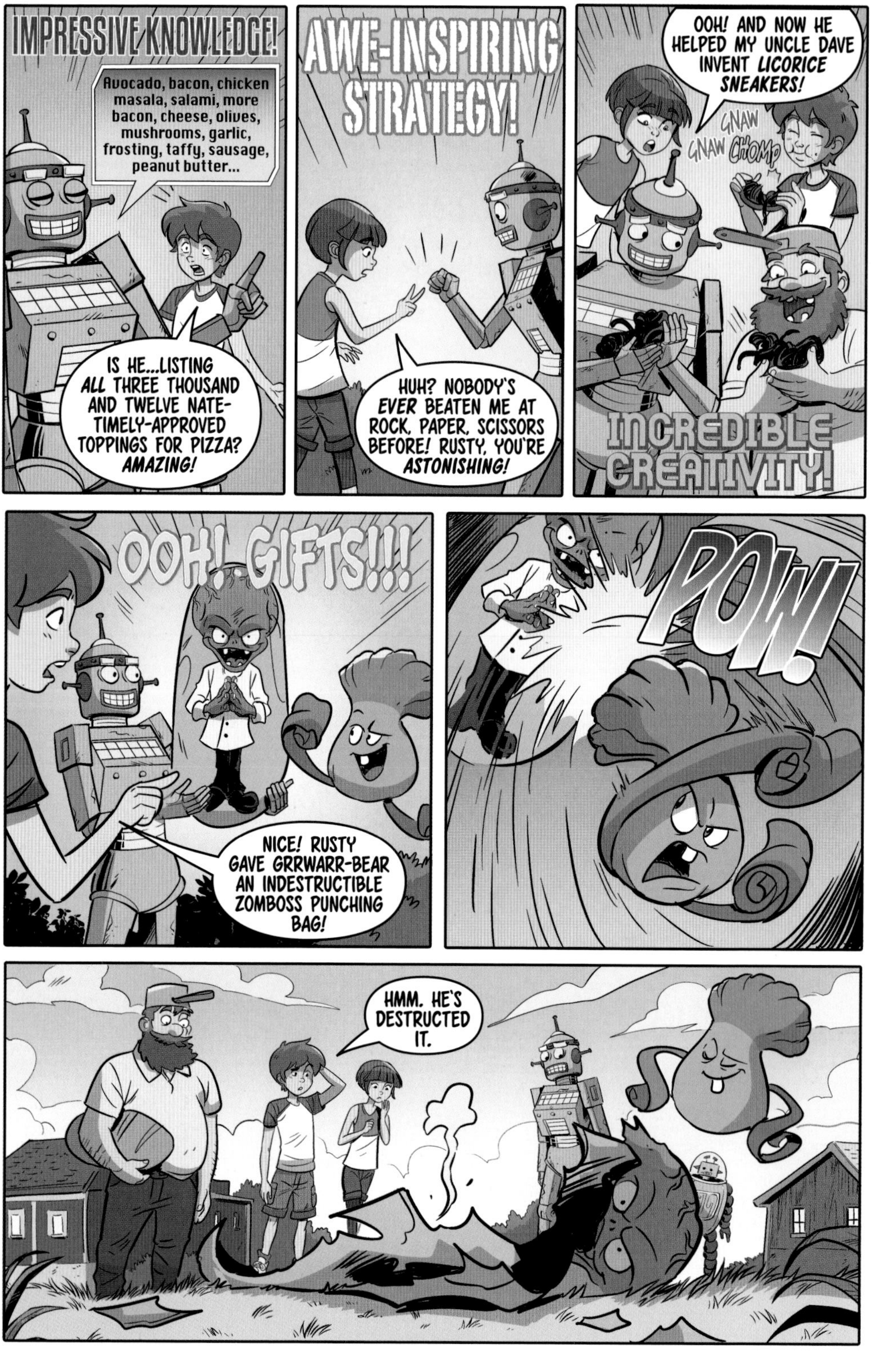
IMPRESSIVE KNOWLEDGE!
Avocado, bacon, chicken masala, salami, more bacon, cheese, olives, mushrooms, garlic, frosting, taffy, sausage, peanut butter...
IS HE...LISTING ALL THREE THOUSAND AND TWELVE NATE-TIMELY-APPROVED TOPPINGS FOR PIZZA? AMAZING!
AWE-INSPIRING STRATEGY!
HUH? NOBODY'S EVER BEATEN ME AT ROCK, PAPER, SCISSORS BEFORE! RUSTY, YOU'RE ASTONISHING!
OOH! AND NOW HE HELPED MY UNCLE DAVE INVENT LICORICE SNEAKERS!
GNAW GNAW CHOMP
INCREDIBLE CREATIVITY!
OOH! GIFTS!!!
NICE! RUSTY GAVE GRRWARR-BEAR AN INDESTRUCTIBLE ZOMBOSS PUNCHING BAG!
POW!
HMM. HE'S DESTRUCTED IT.

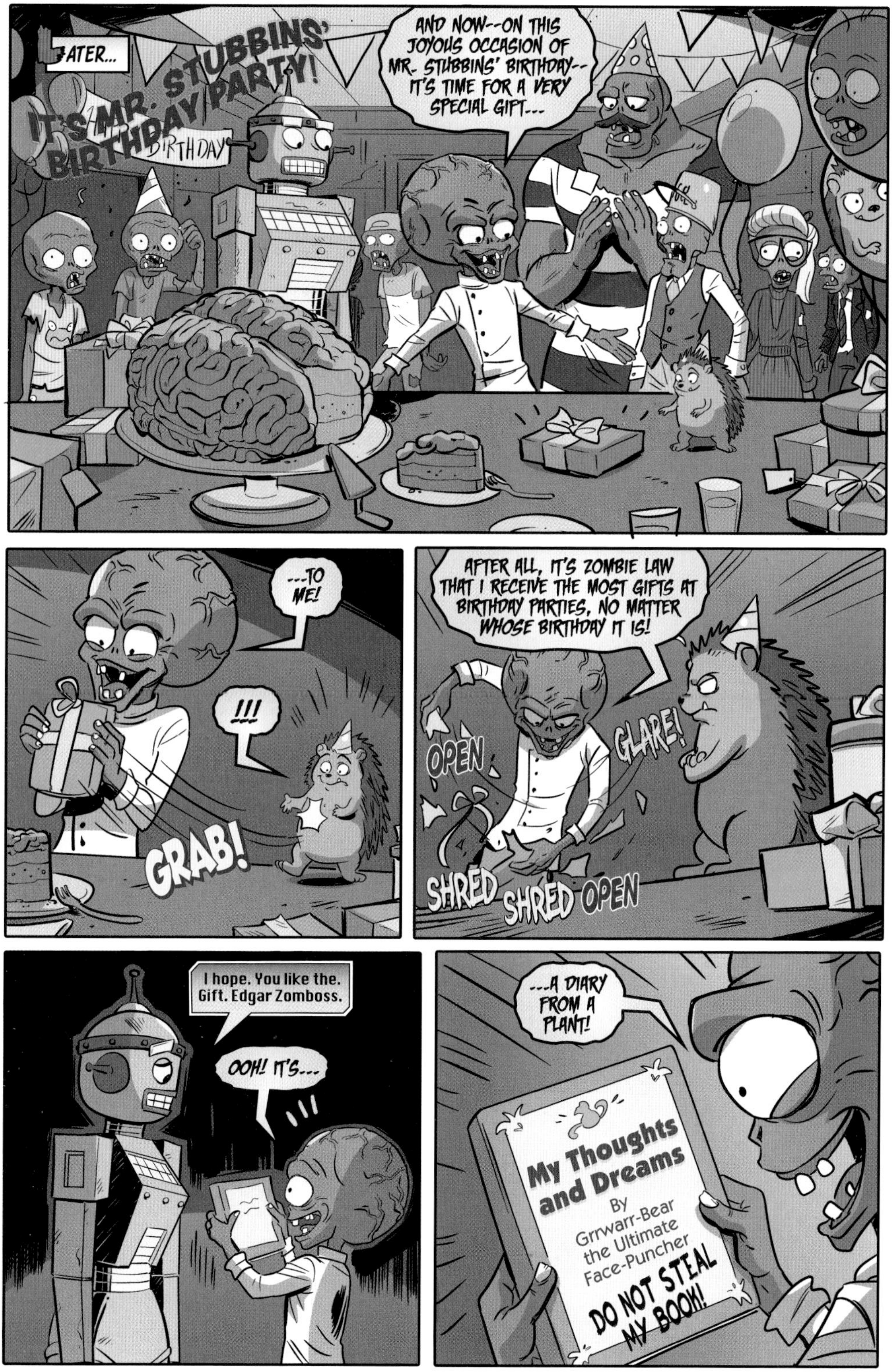
LATER...
IT'S MR. STUBBINS' BIRTHDAY PARTY!
BIRTHDAY
AND NOW--ON THIS JOYOUS OCCASION OF MR. STUBBINS' BIRTHDAY--IT'S TIME FOR A VERY SPECIAL GIFT...
--TO ME!
!!!
GRAB!
AFTER ALL, IT'S ZOMBIE LAW THAT I RECEIVE THE MOST GIFTS AT BIRTHDAY PARTIES, NO MATTER WHOSE BIRTHDAY IT IS!
GLARE!
OPEN
SHRED
SHRED
OPEN
I hope. You like the. Gift. Edgar Zomboss.
OOH! IT'S...
...A DIARY FROM A PLANT!
My Thoughts and Dreams
By Grrwarr-Bear the Ultimate Face-Puncher
DO NOT STEAL MY BOOK!

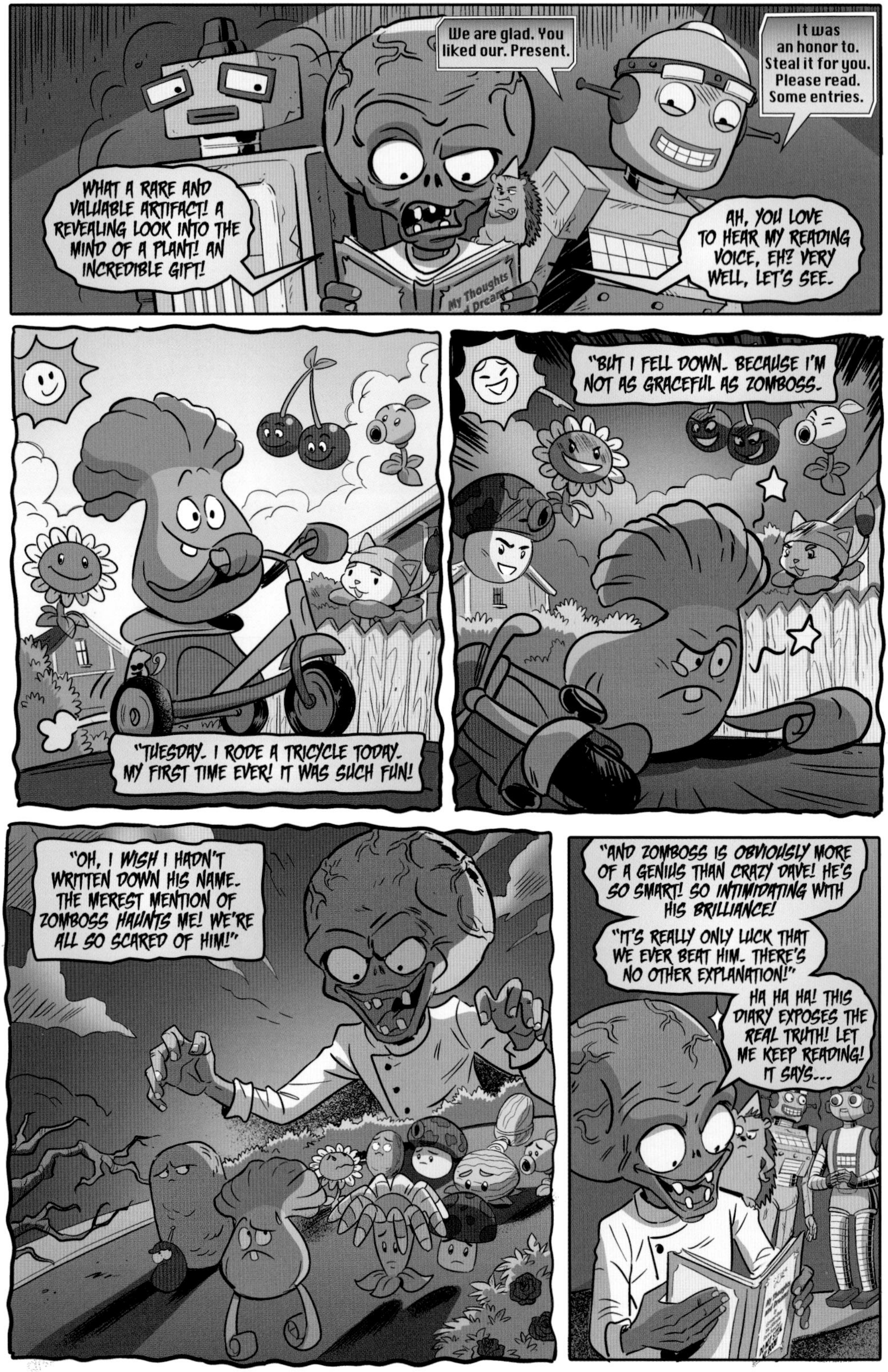
We are glad. You liked our. Present.
It was an honor to. Steal it for you. Please read. Some entries.
WHAT A RARE AND VALUABLE ARTIFACT! A REVEALING LOOK INTO THE MIND OF A PLANT! AN INCREDIBLE GIFT!
AH, YOU LOVE TO HEAR MY READING VOICE, EH? VERY WELL, LET'S SEE.
My Thoughts
"TUESDAY. I RODE A TRICYCLE TODAY. MY FIRST TIME EVER! IT WAS SUCH FUN!
"BUT I FELL DOWN. BECAUSE I'M NOT AS GRACEFUL AS ZOMBOSS.
"OH, I WISH I HADN'T WRITTEN DOWN HIS NAME. THE MEREST MENTION OF ZOMBOSS HAUNTS ME! WE'RE ALL SO SCARED OF HIM!"
"AND ZOMBOSS IS OBVIOUSLY MORE OF A GENIUS THAN CRAZY DAVE! HE'S SO SMART! SO INTIMIDATING WITH HIS BRILLIANCE!
"IT'S REALLY ONLY LUCK THAT WE EVER BEAT HIM. THERE'S NO OTHER EXPLANATION!"
HA HA HA! THIS DIARY EXPOSES THE REAL TRUTH! LET ME KEEP READING! IT SAYS...

"SECRETLY, I HAVE SO MANY POSTERS OF ZOMBOSS ON MY WALLS. AND I LISTEN TO HIS MUSIC AT NIGHT AND...OH! HOW I DANCE!"

IT SAYS, "ZOMBOSS IS SO KIND, AND GENEROUS. AND ELEGANT AND HANDSOME AND CLEVER AND WITTY!"

AND IT SAYS, "ASK ANYONE... ZOMBOSS IS BETTER THAN A THOUSAND POISONOUS SPIDERS!"

We have gone. Overboard with this. Fake diary.

No one could *possibly*. Believe this is true.

ME? BETTER THAN A *THOUSAND* POISONOUS SPIDERS?

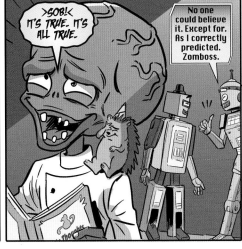

>SOB!< IT'S *TRUE*. IT'S ALL *TRUE*.

No one could believe it. Except for. As I correctly predicted. Zomboss.

43

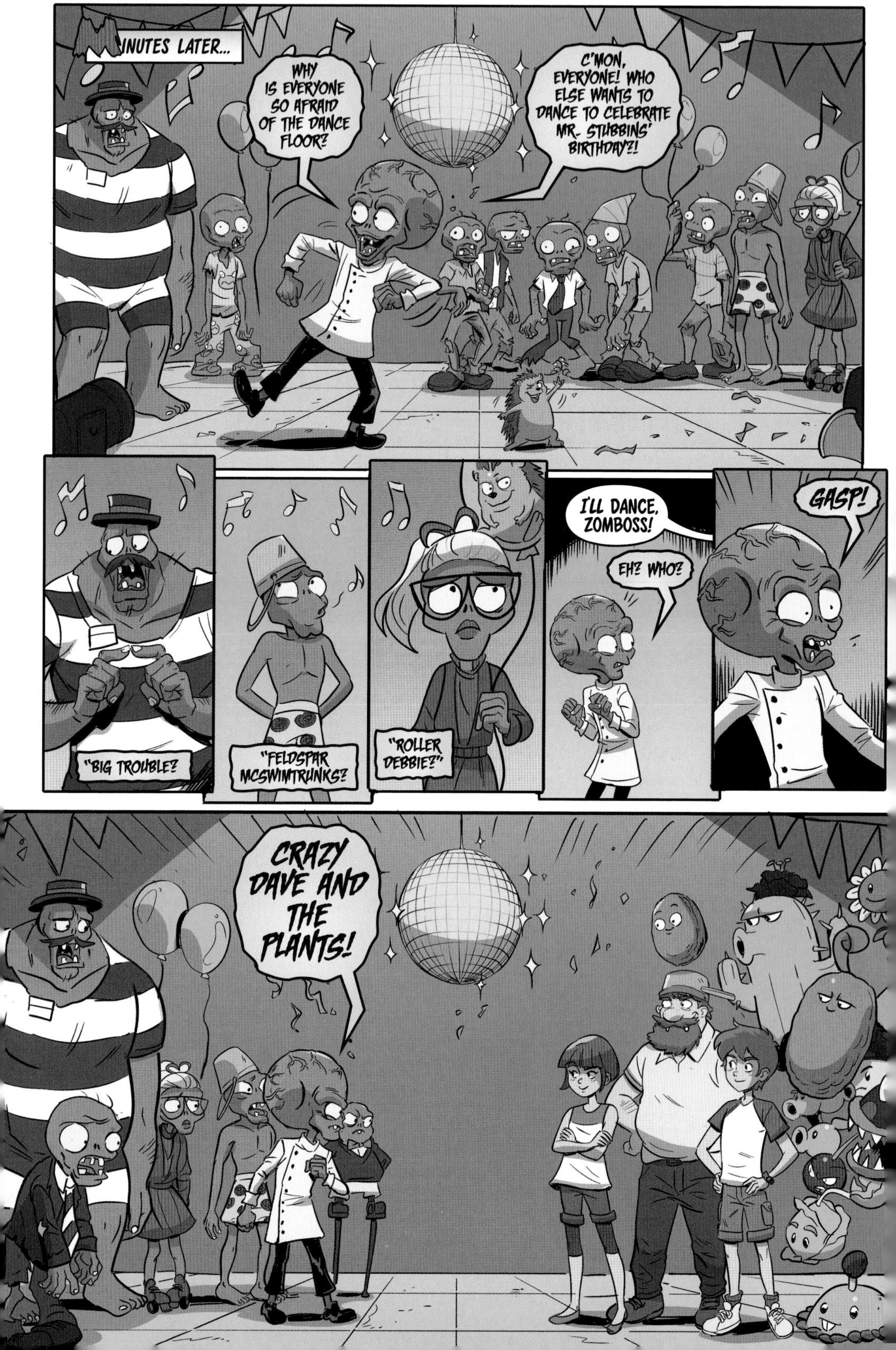
MINUTES LATER...
WHY IS EVERYONE SO AFRAID OF THE DANCE FLOOR?
C'MON, EVERYONE! WHO ELSE WANTS TO DANCE TO CELEBRATE MR. STUBBINS' BIRTHDAY?!
"BIG TROUBLE?
"FELDSPAR MCSWIMTRUNKS?
"ROLLER DEBBIE?"
I'LL DANCE, ZOMBOSS!
EH? WHO?
GASP!
CRAZY DAVE AND THE PLANTS!

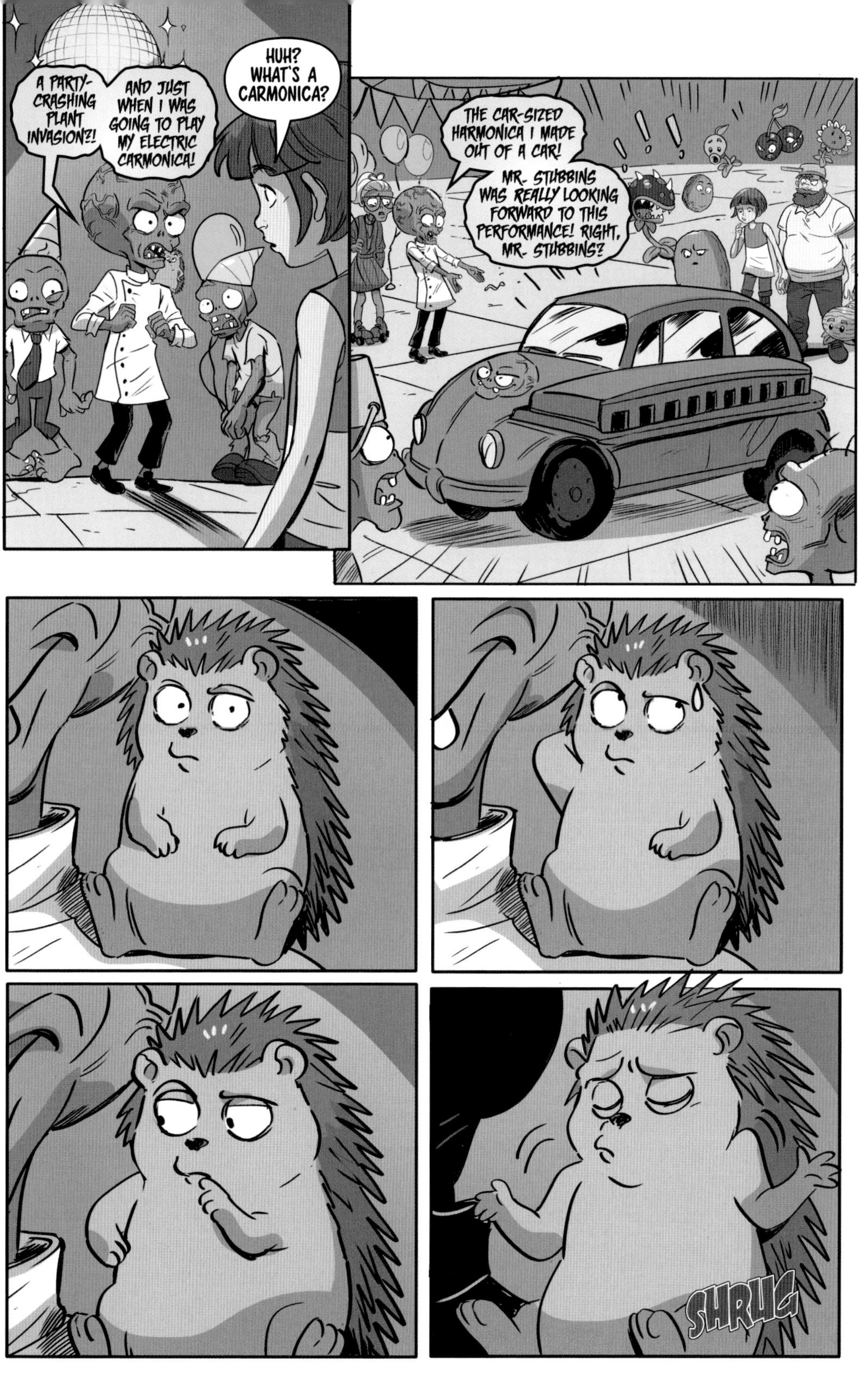
A PARTY-CRASHING PLANT INVASION?!
AND JUST WHEN I WAS GOING TO PLAY MY ELECTRIC CARMONICA!
HUH? WHAT'S A CARMONICA?
THE CAR-SIZED HARMONICA I MADE OUT OF A CAR!
MR. STUBBINS WAS REALLY LOOKING FORWARD TO THIS PERFORMANCE! RIGHT, MR. STUBBINS?
SHRUG

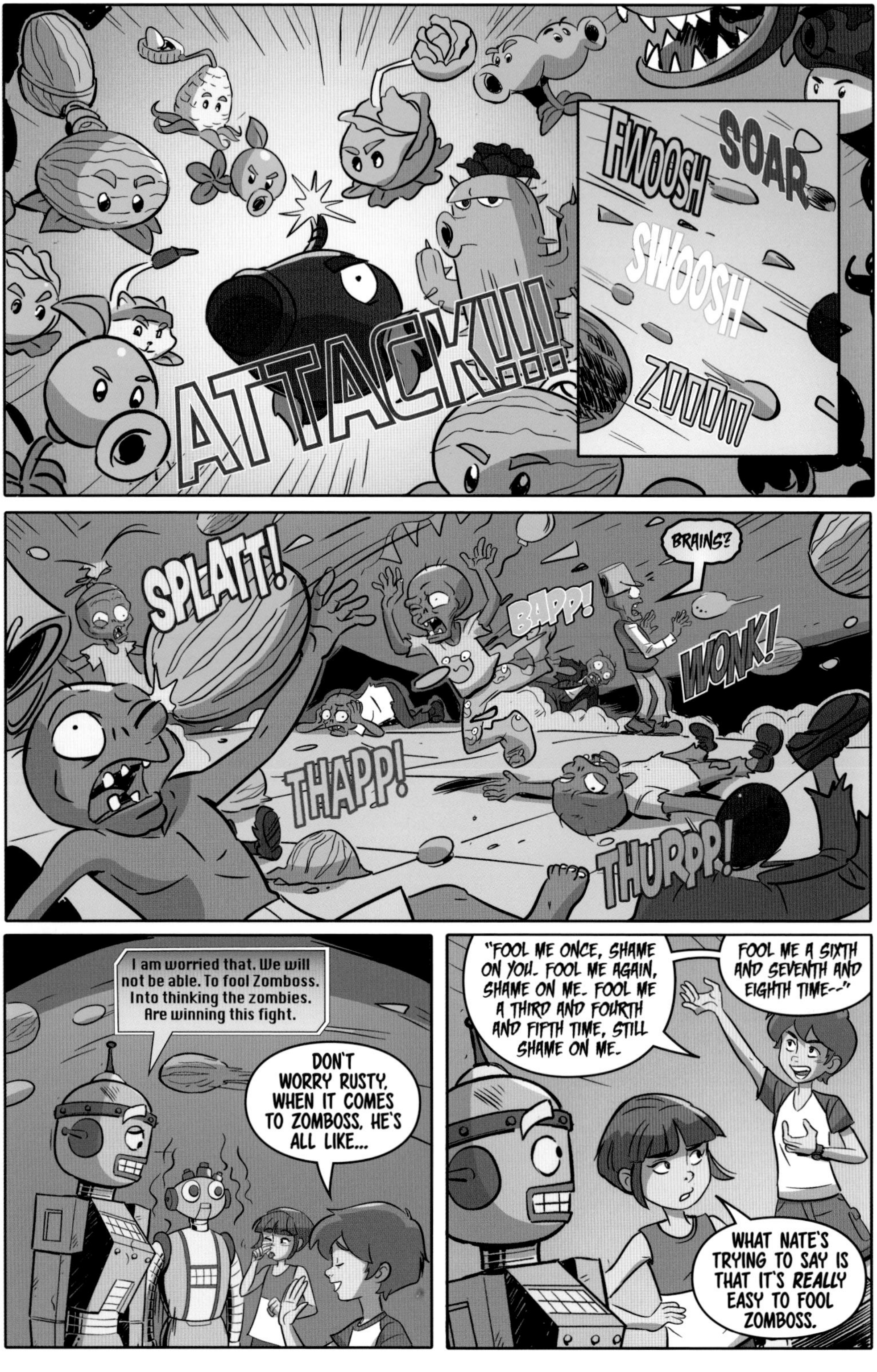
FWOOSH
SOAR
SWOOSH
ZOOOM
ATTACK!!!
SPLATT!
BRAINS?
BAPP!
WONK!
THAPP!
THURPP!
I am worried that. We will not be able. To fool Zomboss. Into thinking the zombies. Are winning this fight.
DON'T WORRY RUSTY, WHEN IT COMES TO ZOMBOSS, HE'S ALL LIKE...
"FOOL ME ONCE, SHAME ON YOU. FOOL ME AGAIN, SHAME ON ME. FOOL ME A THIRD AND FOURTH AND FIFTH TIME, STILL SHAME ON ME.
FOOL ME A SIXTH AND SEVENTH AND EIGHTH TIME--"
WHAT NATE'S TRYING TO SAY IS THAT IT'S *REALLY* EASY TO FOOL ZOMBOSS.

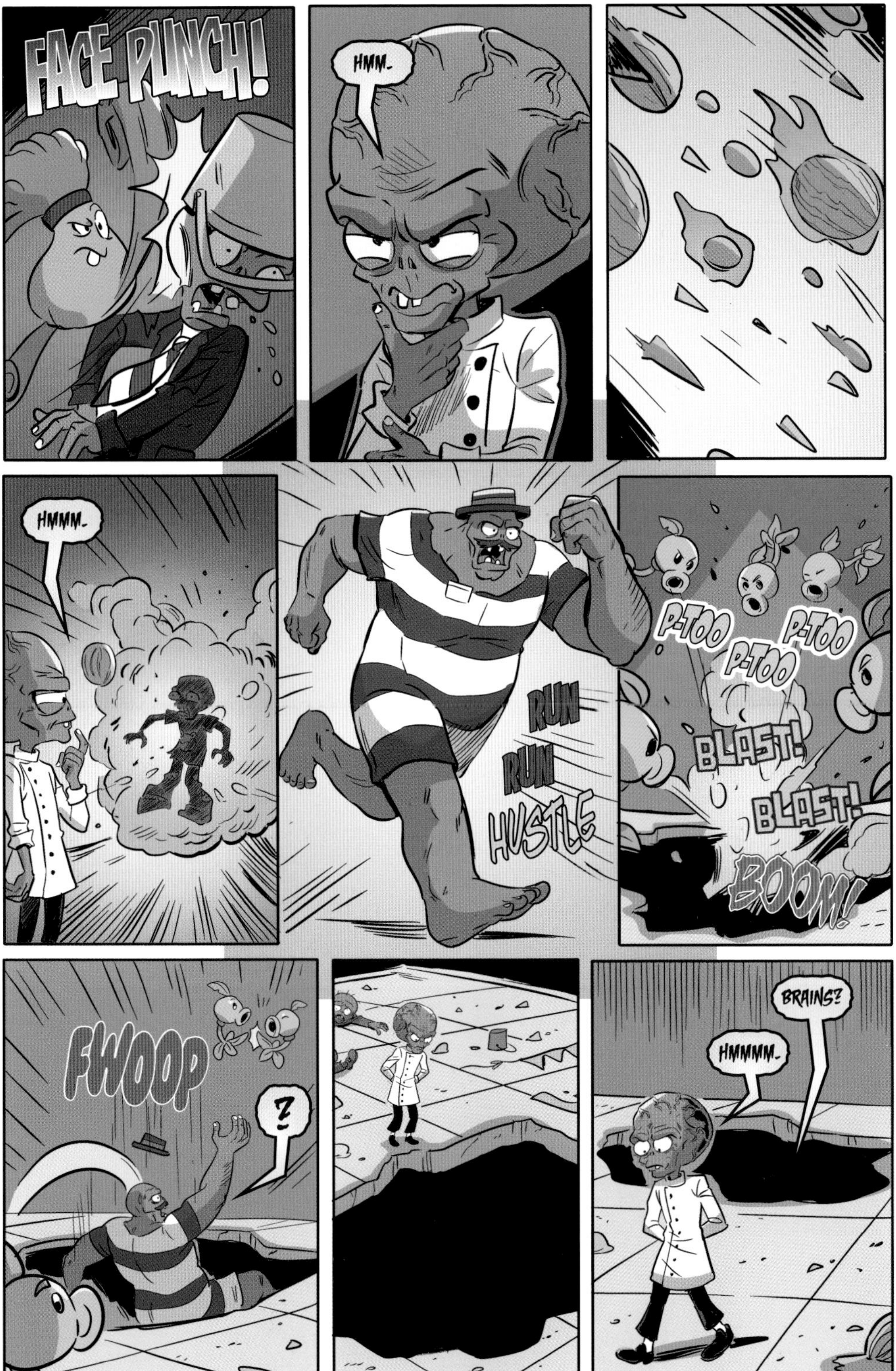
FACE PUNCH!
HMM.
HMMM.
RUN
RUN
HUSTLE
P-TOO
P-TOO
P-TOO
BLAST!
BLAST!
BOOM!
FWOOP
?
HMMMM.
BRAINS?

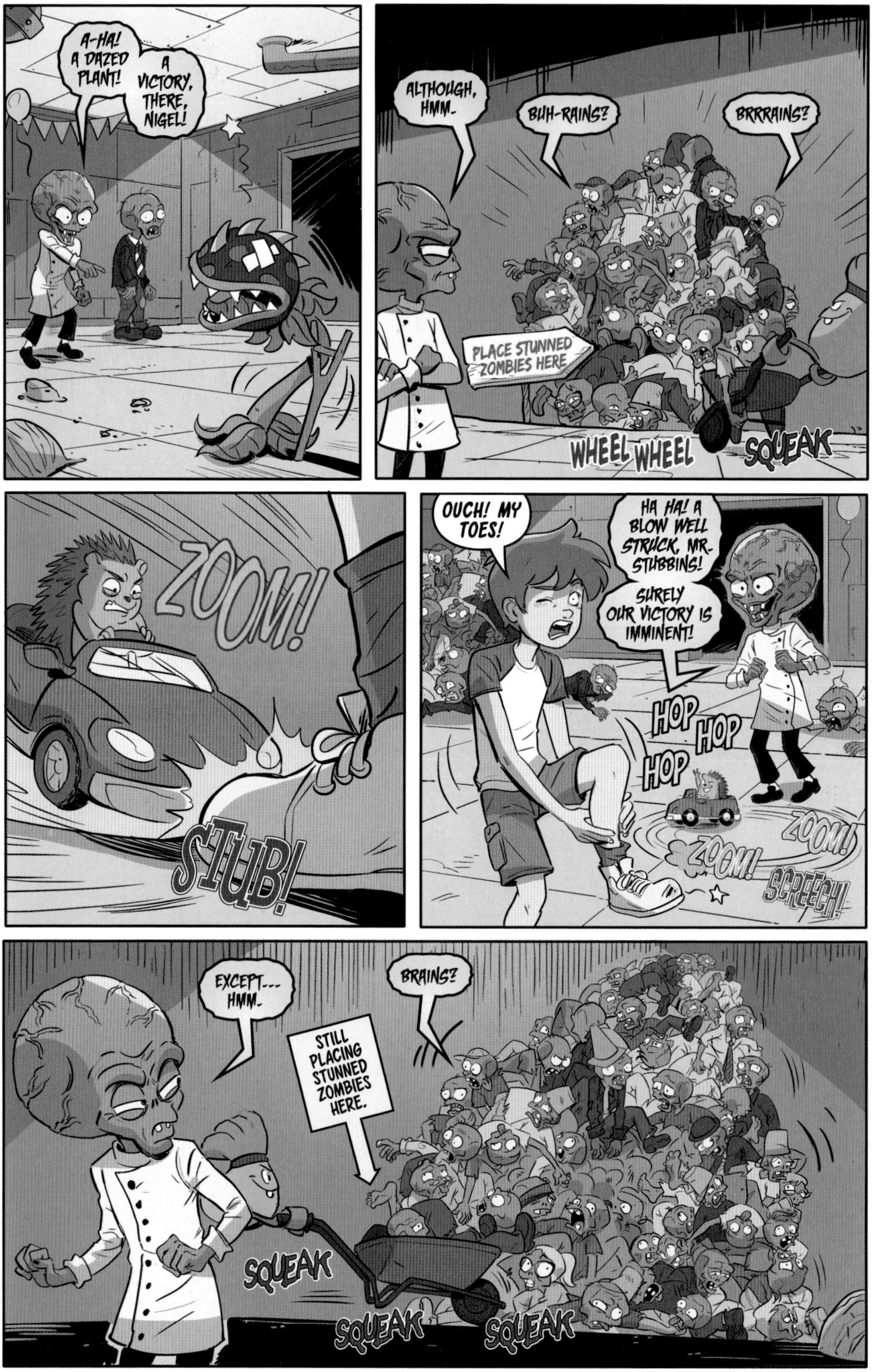
A-HA! A DAZED PLANT!
A VICTORY, THERE, NIGEL!
ALTHOUGH, HMM...
BUH-RAINS?
BRRRAINS?
PLACE STUNNED ZOMBIES HERE
WHEEL WHEEL
SQUEAK
ZOOM!
STUB!
OUCH! MY TOES!
HA HA! A BLOW WELL STRUCK, MR. STUBBINS!
SURELY OUR VICTORY IS IMMINENT!
HOP HOP HOP
ZOOM!
ZOOM!
SCREECH!
EXCEPT... HMM...
BRAINS?
STILL PLACING STUNNED ZOMBIES HERE.
SQUEAK
SQUEAK
SQUEAK

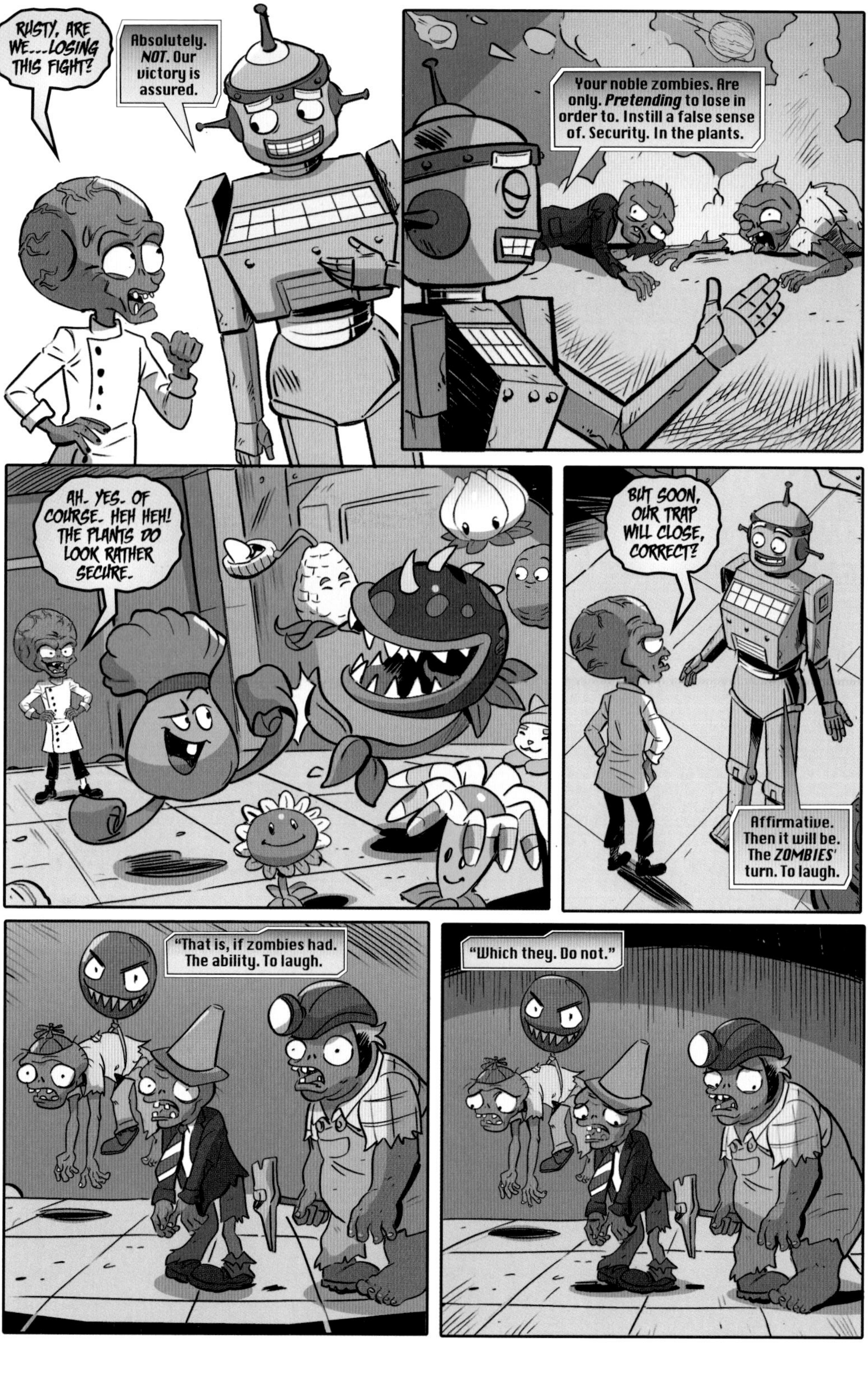
RUSTY, ARE WE...LOSING THIS FIGHT?
Absolutely. NOT. Our victory is assured.
Your noble zombies. Are only. Pretending to lose in order to. Instill a false sense of. Security. In the plants.
AH. YES. OF COURSE. HEH HEH! THE PLANTS DO LOOK RATHER SECURE.
BUT SOON, OUR TRAP WILL CLOSE, CORRECT?
Affirmative. Then it will be. The ZOMBIES' turn. To laugh.
"That is, if zombies had. The ability. To laugh.
"Which they. Do not."

HE NEXT DAY...

SLURP
SLURRRRP
SLURP
SLURRRP
LIQUID GUM: SO YUM!

SLURP
SLURRRP
LIQUID GUM: SO YUM!

HA HA HA! WE CONTINUE TO LURE THEM INTO OUR TRAP!

WHAP PUMMEL! SPAKK!
BRAINS?
THONK PLAPP
PLAPP THONK THWAP
THWAP PLAPP
PUMMEL! WHAP
WHAP SPAKK!
SPAKK! THONK
THWAP PUMMEL!

SLURP
SLURRRRP
CREAM OF MUFFIN SOUP
SLURRRP

YES, INDEED. SOON, THE TRAP WILL BE SPRUNG.

ANNNAY TIME NOW.

BLOOORSH SPLAPP
THAPP FLOOOP!
SPLAPP
THWURKK
FLOOOP! GLORB

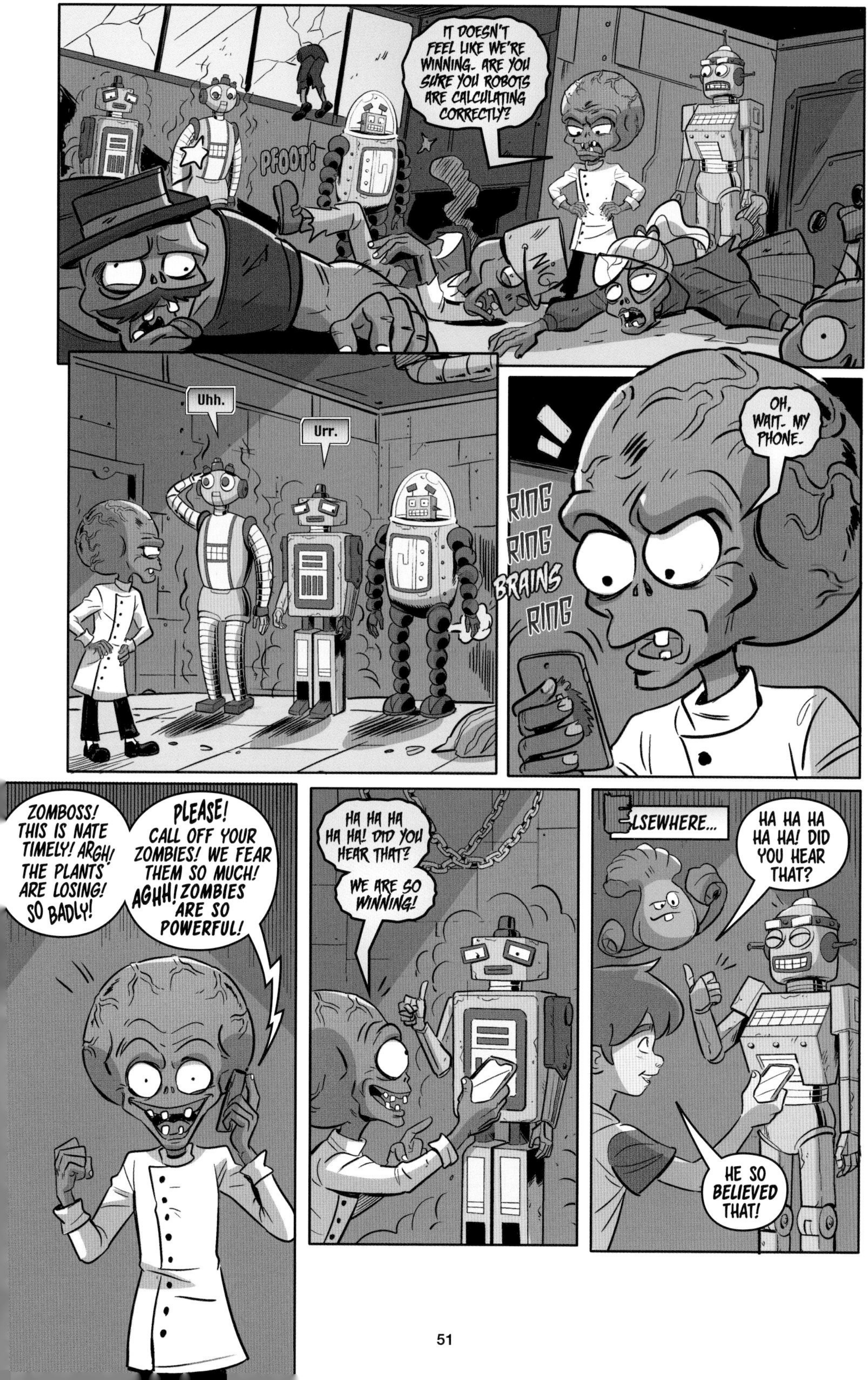

IT DOESN'T FEEL LIKE WE'RE WINNING. ARE YOU SURE YOU ROBOTS ARE CALCULATING CORRECTLY?
PFOOT!
Uhh.
Urr.
RING
RING
BRAINS
RING
OH, WAIT. MY PHONE.
ZOMBOSS! THIS IS NATE TIMELY! ARGH! THE PLANTS ARE LOSING! SO BADLY!
PLEASE! CALL OFF YOUR ZOMBIES! WE FEAR THEM SO MUCH! AGHH! ZOMBIES ARE SO POWERFUL!
HA HA HA HA HA! DID YOU HEAR THAT?
WE ARE SO WINNING!
ELSEWHERE...
HA HA HA HA HA! DID YOU HEAR THAT?
HE SO BELIEVED THAT!

THE NEXT DAY...

I CAN'T SHAKE THIS FEELING THAT SOMETHING'S WRONG.

IF WE'RE WINNING, WHY DO WE KEEP GETTING BEATEN UP?

Perhaps there. Is something. You should see.

HMM. MY PHONE? WHAT HAVE YOU DONE TO MY PHONE?

I have created. A new app. All selfies will now. Look like. Mr. Stubbins.

CLICK

HA HA HA HA! SO WONDERFUL! I LOVE IT!

UMM, WAIT. WHAT WERE WE TALKING ABOUT?

You were saying that. You should eat Pop Smarts. And nap.

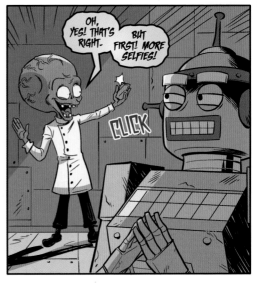

OH, YES! THAT'S RIGHT.

BUT FIRST! MORE SELFIES!

CLICK

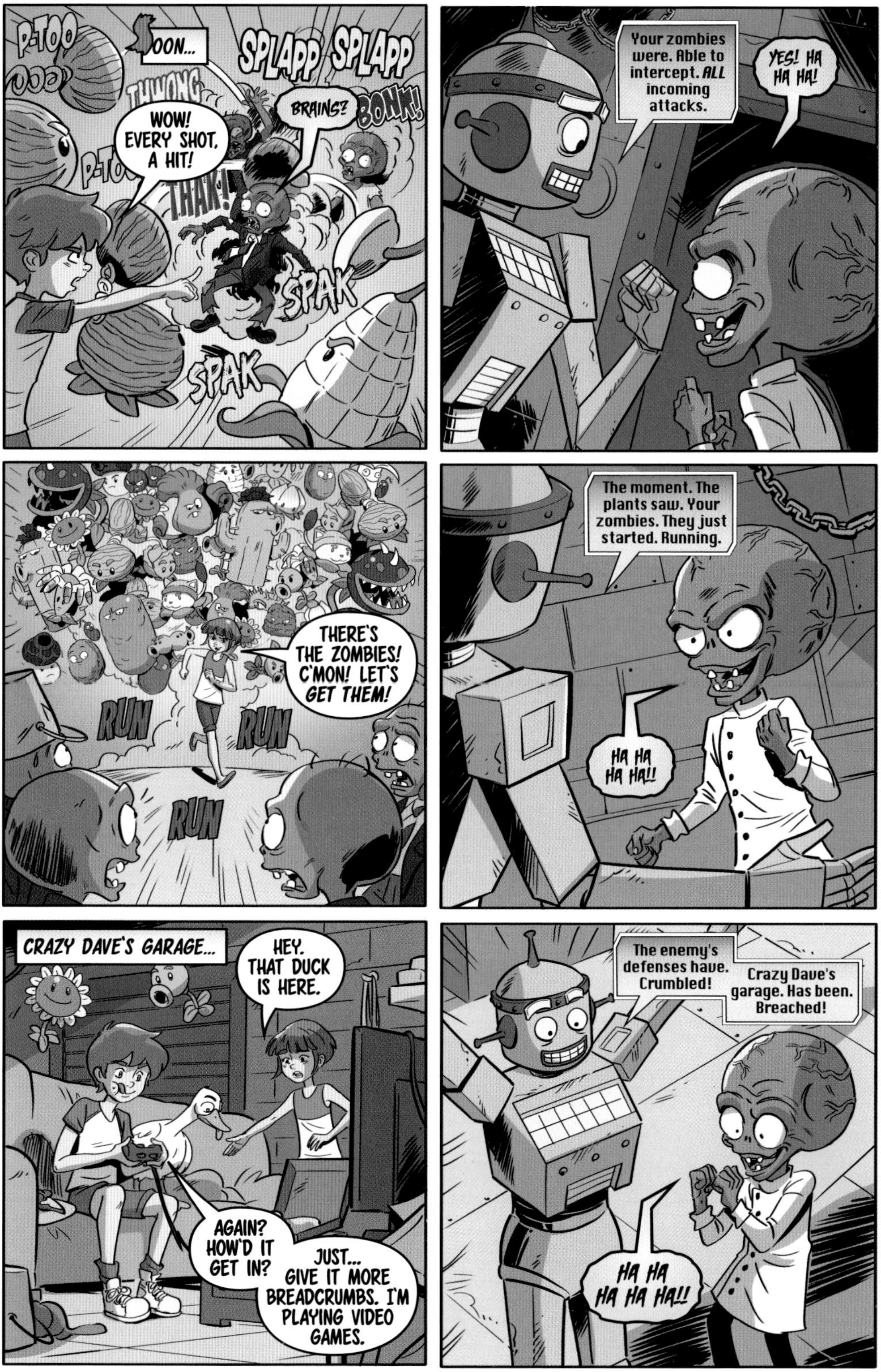
P-TOO
OOON...
SPLAPP SPLAPP
THWONG
BRAINS?
BONK!
WOW! EVERY SHOT, A HIT!
P-TOO
THAK!
SPAK
SPAK
Your zombies were. Able to intercept. ALL incoming attacks.
YES! HA HA HA!
THERE'S THE ZOMBIES! C'MON! LET'S GET THEM!
RUN
RUN
RUN
The moment. The plants saw. Your zombies. They just started. Running.
HA HA HA HA!!
CRAZY DAVE'S GARAGE...
HEY. THAT DUCK IS HERE.
AGAIN? HOW'D IT GET IN?
JUST... GIVE IT MORE BREADCRUMBS. I'M PLAYING VIDEO GAMES.
The enemy's defenses have. Crumbled!
Crazy Dave's garage. Has been. Breached!
HA HA HA HA HA!!

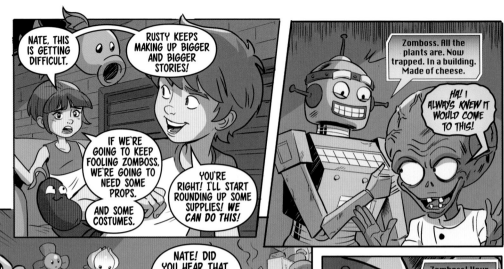

NATE, THIS IS GETTING DIFFICULT.

RUSTY KEEPS MAKING UP BIGGER AND BIGGER STORIES!

IF WE'RE GOING TO KEEP FOOLING ZOMBOSS, WE'RE GOING TO NEED SOME PROPS. AND SOME COSTUMES.

YOU'RE RIGHT! I'LL START ROUNDING UP SOME SUPPLIES! WE CAN DO THIS!

Zomboss. All the plants are. Now trapped. In a building. Made of cheese.

HA! I ALWAYS KNEW IT WOULD COME TO THIS!

NATE! DID YOU HEAR THAT LAST ONE? WHAT'S RUSTY TALKING ABOUT?

URGH! HOW ARE WE GOING TO MAKE THIS BELIEVABLE??!

NO PROBLEM, PATRICE! I ALWAYS HAVE ENOUGH CHEESE!

Zomboss! Your zombies are. So powerful that. They have now chased the plants. To the moon!

OOH!

UGH? THE MOON? REALLY? I WISH RUSTY WOULD KEEP HIS STORIES MORE BELIEVABLE!

IT DOESN'T REALLY MATTER. ZOMBOSS' VANITY IS SO HUGE HE'LL BELIEVE ANYTHING IF HE THINKS IT MAKES HIM LOOK GOOD.

NOW, KEEP FILMING. AND... HURRY!

BECAUSE, UGH, THIS ZOMBIE COSTUME SMELLS LIKE A SKUNK'S ARMPIT AFTER A MUD FIGHT.

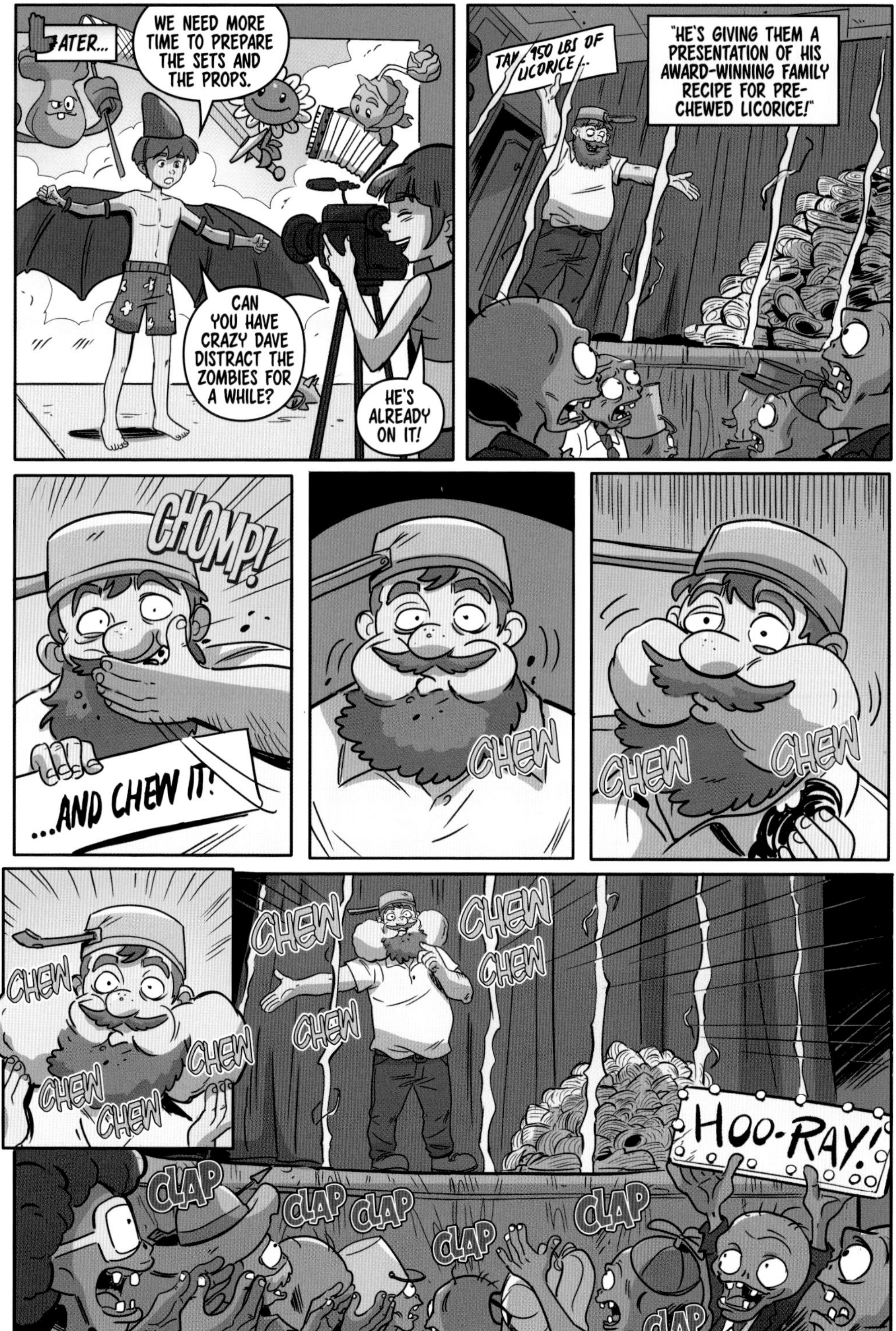
LATER...
WE NEED MORE TIME TO PREPARE THE SETS AND THE PROPS.
CAN YOU HAVE CRAZY DAVE DISTRACT THE ZOMBIES FOR A WHILE?
HE'S ALREADY ON IT!
950 LBS OF LICORICE...
"HE'S GIVING THEM A PRESENTATION OF HIS AWARD-WINNING FAMILY RECIPE FOR PRE-CHEWED LICORICE!"
CHOMP!
...AND CHEW IT!
CHEW
CHEW
CHEW
CHEW
CHEW
CHEW
CHEW
CHEW
CHEW
CHEW
CHEW
HOO-RAY!
CLAP
CLAP
CLAP
CLAP
CLAP
CLAP

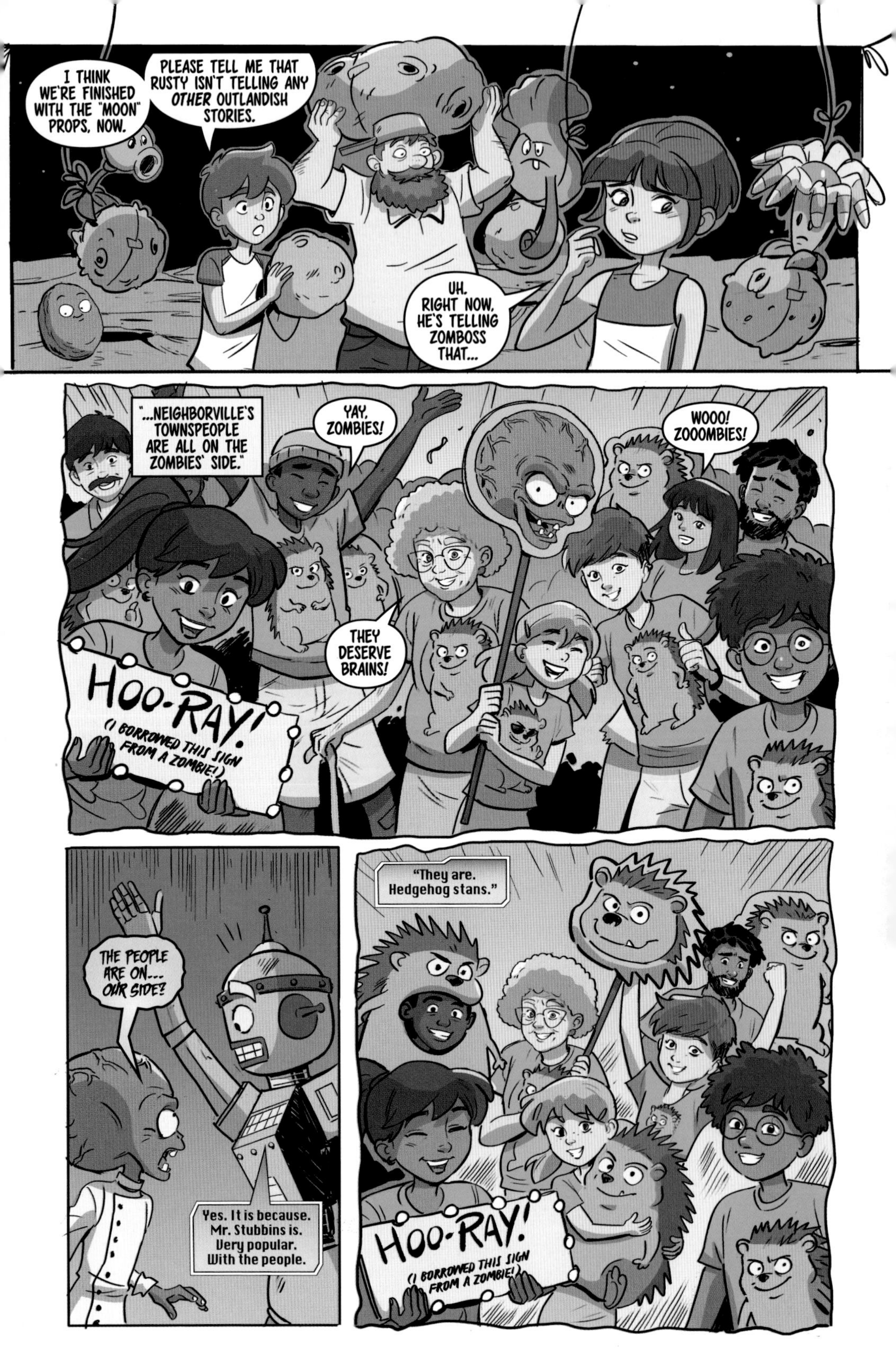
I THINK WE'RE FINISHED WITH THE "MOON" PROPS, NOW.
PLEASE TELL ME THAT RUSTY ISN'T TELLING ANY *OTHER* OUTLANDISH STORIES.
UH. RIGHT NOW, HE'S TELLING ZOMBOSS THAT...
"...NEIGHBORVILLE'S TOWNSPEOPLE ARE ALL ON THE ZOMBIES' SIDE."
YAY, ZOMBIES!
WOOO! ZOOOMBIES!
THEY DESERVE BRAINS!
HOO-RAY! (I BORROWED THIS SIGN FROM A ZOMBIE!)
THE PEOPLE ARE ON... OUR SIDE?
Yes. It is because. Mr. Stubbins is. Very popular. With the people.
"They are. Hedgehog stans."
HOO-RAY! (I BORROWED THIS SIGN FROM A ZOMBIE!)

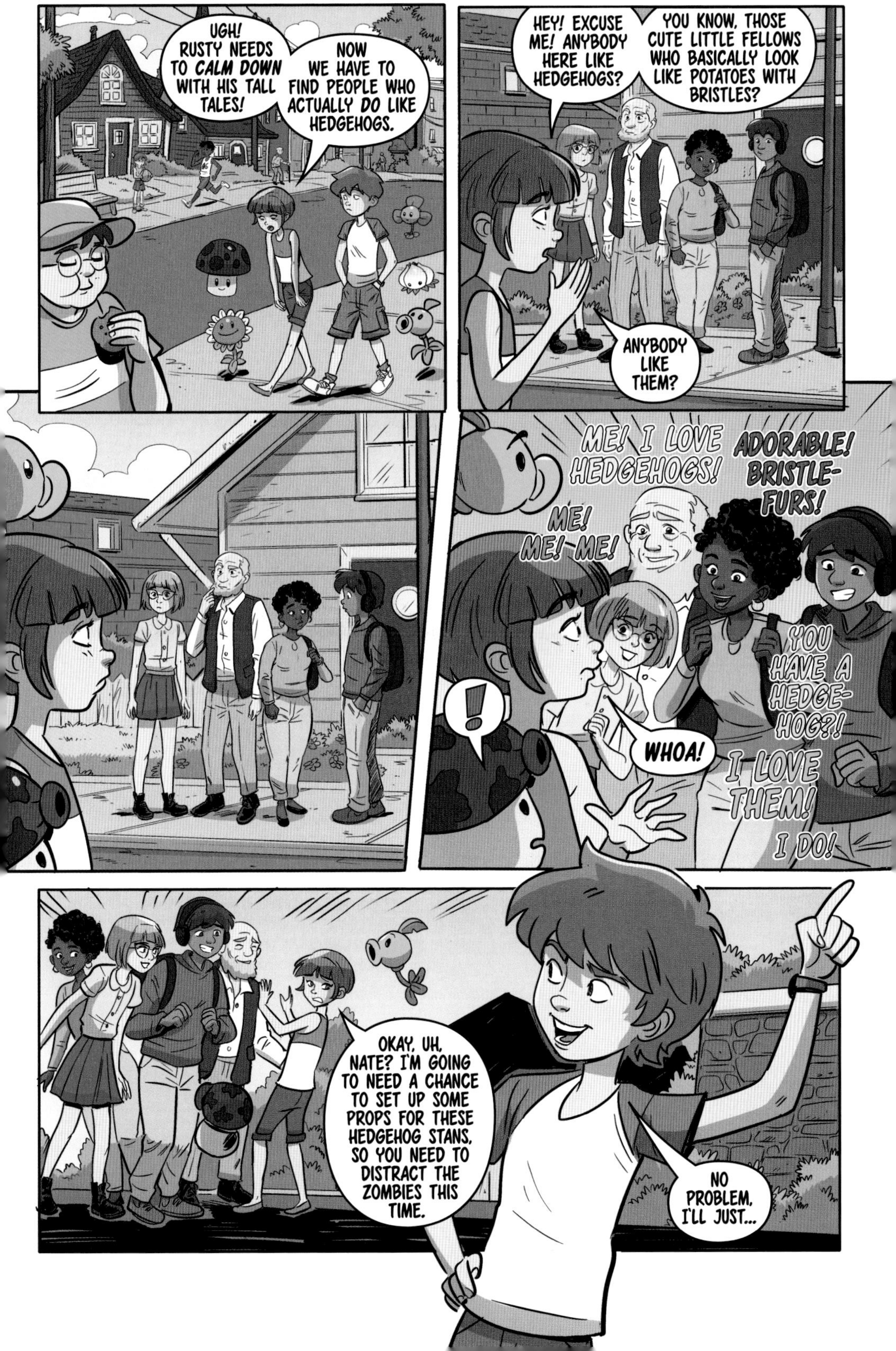
UGH! RUSTY NEEDS TO CALM DOWN WITH HIS TALL TALES!
NOW WE HAVE TO FIND PEOPLE WHO ACTUALLY DO LIKE HEDGEHOGS.
HEY! EXCUSE ME! ANYBODY HERE LIKE HEDGEHOGS?
YOU KNOW, THOSE CUTE LITTLE FELLOWS WHO BASICALLY LOOK LIKE POTATOES WITH BRISTLES?
ANYBODY LIKE THEM?
ME! I LOVE HEDGEHOGS!
ADORABLE! BRISTLE-FURS!
ME! ME! ME!
YOU HAVE A HEDGE-HOG?!
I LOVE THEM!
I DO!
!
WHOA!
OKAY, UH, NATE? I'M GOING TO NEED A CHANCE TO SET UP SOME PROPS FOR THESE HEDGEHOG STANS, SO YOU NEED TO DISTRACT THE ZOMBIES THIS TIME.
NO PROBLEM, I'LL JUST...

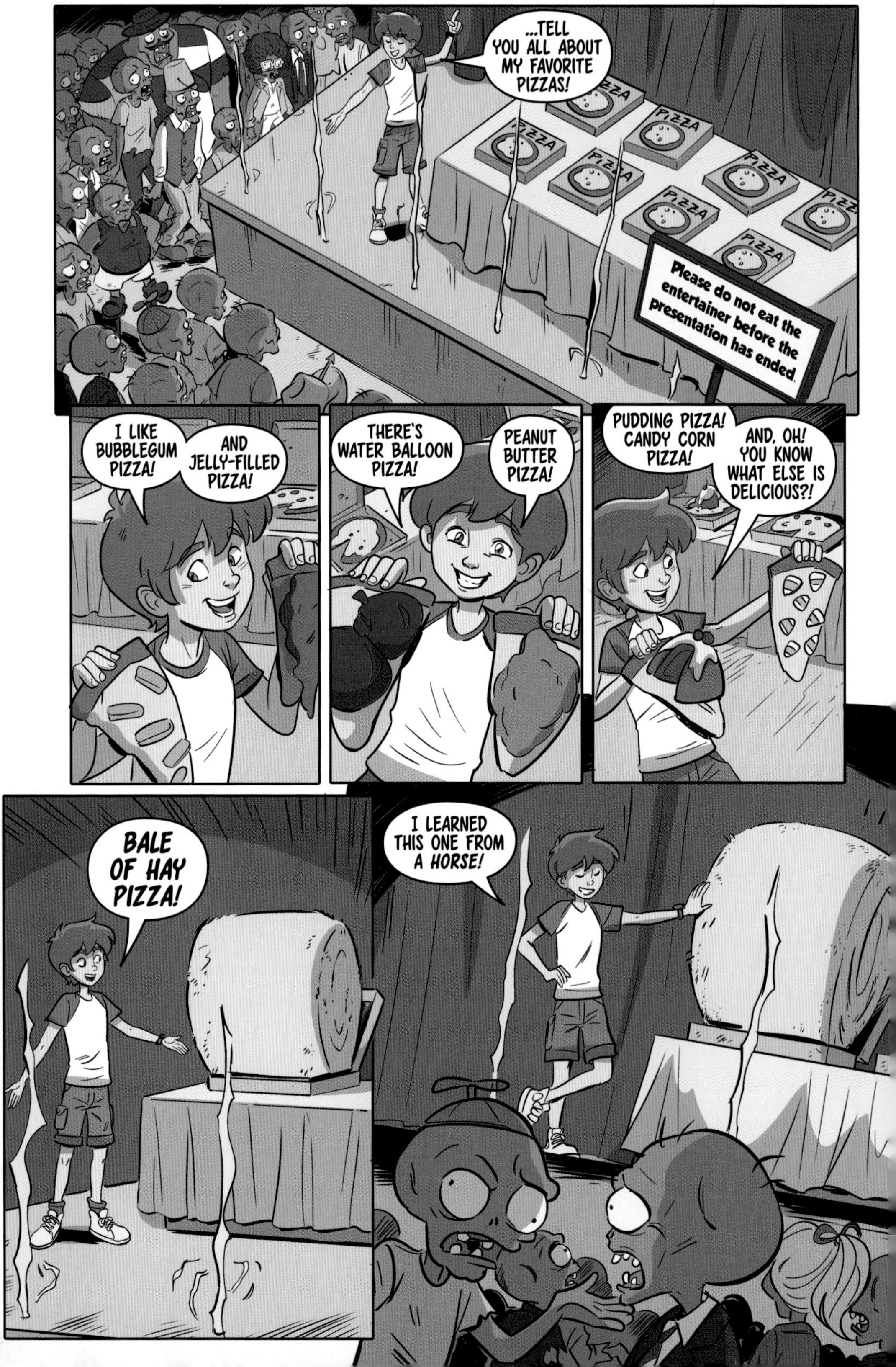
...TELL YOU ALL ABOUT MY FAVORITE PIZZAS!
PIZZA
Please do not eat the entertainer before the presentation has ended.
I LIKE BUBBLEGUM PIZZA!
AND JELLY-FILLED PIZZA!
THERE'S WATER BALLOON PIZZA!
PEANUT BUTTER PIZZA!
PUDDING PIZZA! CANDY CORN PIZZA!
AND, OH! YOU KNOW WHAT ELSE IS DELICIOUS?!
BALE OF HAY PIZZA!
I LEARNED THIS ONE FROM A HORSE!

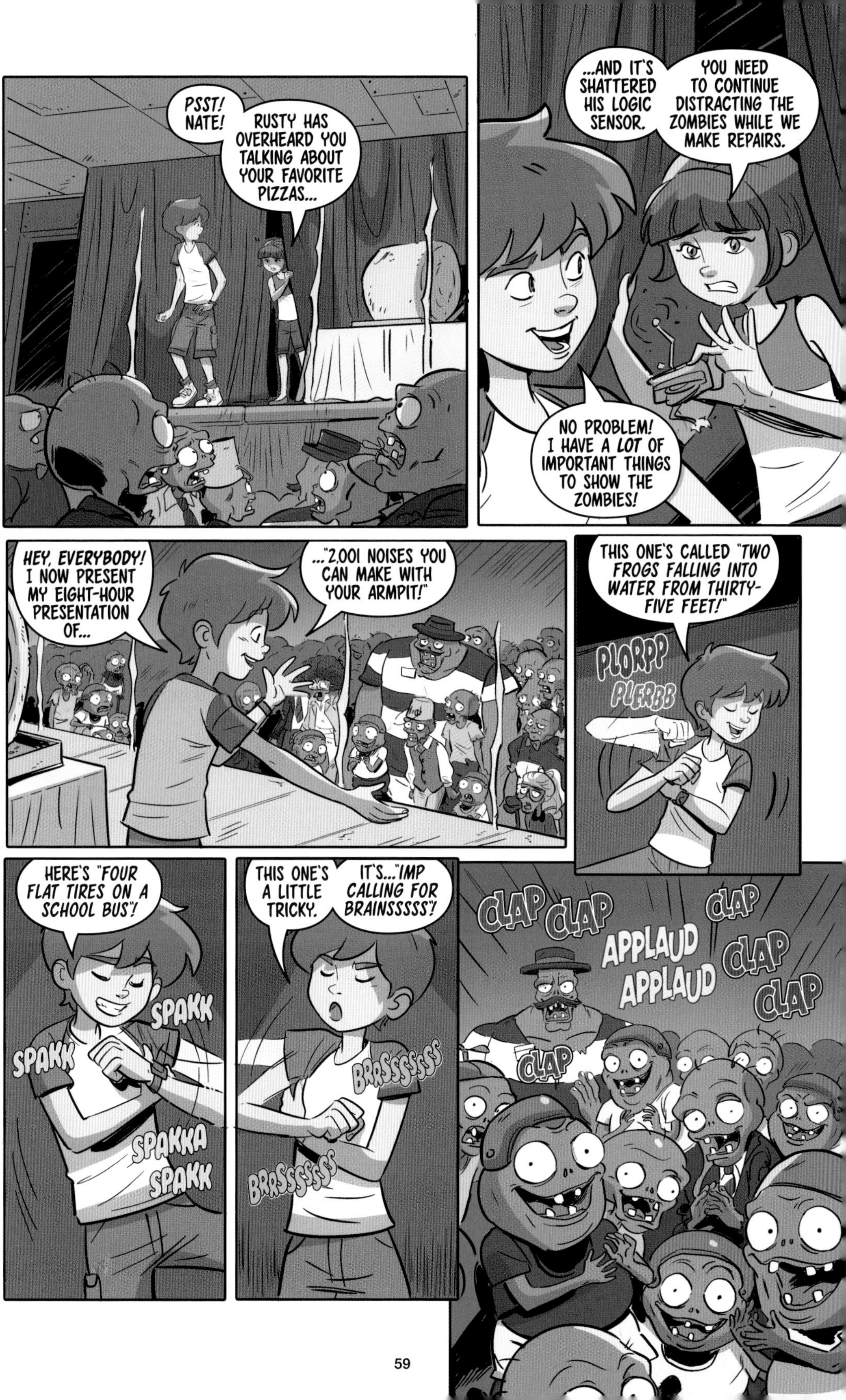

PSST! NATE!
RUSTY HAS OVERHEARD YOU TALKING ABOUT YOUR FAVORITE PIZZAS...
...AND IT'S SHATTERED HIS LOGIC SENSOR.
YOU NEED TO CONTINUE DISTRACTING THE ZOMBIES WHILE WE MAKE REPAIRS.
NO PROBLEM! I HAVE A LOT OF IMPORTANT THINGS TO SHOW THE ZOMBIES!
HEY, EVERYBODY! I NOW PRESENT MY EIGHT-HOUR PRESENTATION OF...
..."2,001 NOISES YOU CAN MAKE WITH YOUR ARMPIT!"
THIS ONE'S CALLED "TWO FROGS FALLING INTO WATER FROM THIRTY-FIVE FEET!"
PLORPP
PLERBB
HERE'S "FOUR FLAT TIRES ON A SCHOOL BUS"!
SPAKK
SPAKK
SPAKKA
SPAKK
THIS ONE'S A LITTLE TRICKY.
IT'S..."IMP CALLING FOR BRAINSSSSS"!
BRRSSSSSSS
BRRSSSSSSS
CLAP CLAP
CLAP
APPLAUD
CLAP
APPLAUD
CLAP
CLAP

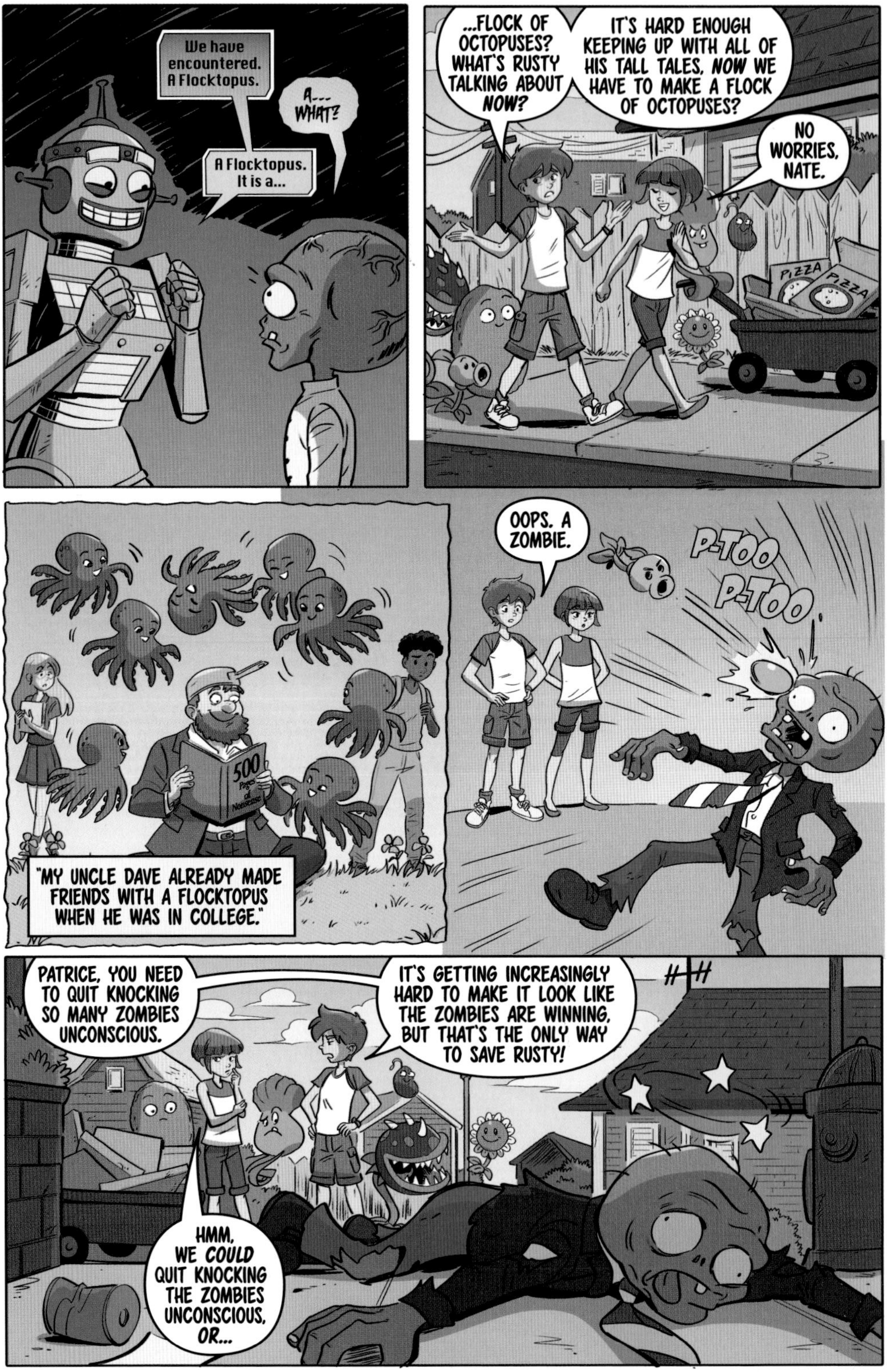
We have encountered. A Flocktopus.
A--- WHAT?
A Flocktopus. It is a...
...FLOCK OF OCTOPUSES? WHAT'S RUSTY TALKING ABOUT NOW?
IT'S HARD ENOUGH KEEPING UP WITH ALL OF HIS TALL TALES, NOW WE HAVE TO MAKE A FLOCK OF OCTOPUSES?
NO WORRIES, NATE.
PIZZA
PIZZA
500 Pages of Nonsense
"MY UNCLE DAVE ALREADY MADE FRIENDS WITH A FLOCKTOPUS WHEN HE WAS IN COLLEGE."
OOPS. A ZOMBIE.
P-TOO
P-TOO
PATRICE, YOU NEED TO QUIT KNOCKING SO MANY ZOMBIES UNCONSCIOUS.
IT'S GETTING INCREASINGLY HARD TO MAKE IT LOOK LIKE THE ZOMBIES ARE WINNING, BUT THAT'S THE ONLY WAY TO SAVE RUSTY!
HMM, WE COULD QUIT KNOCKING THE ZOMBIES UNCONSCIOUS, OR...

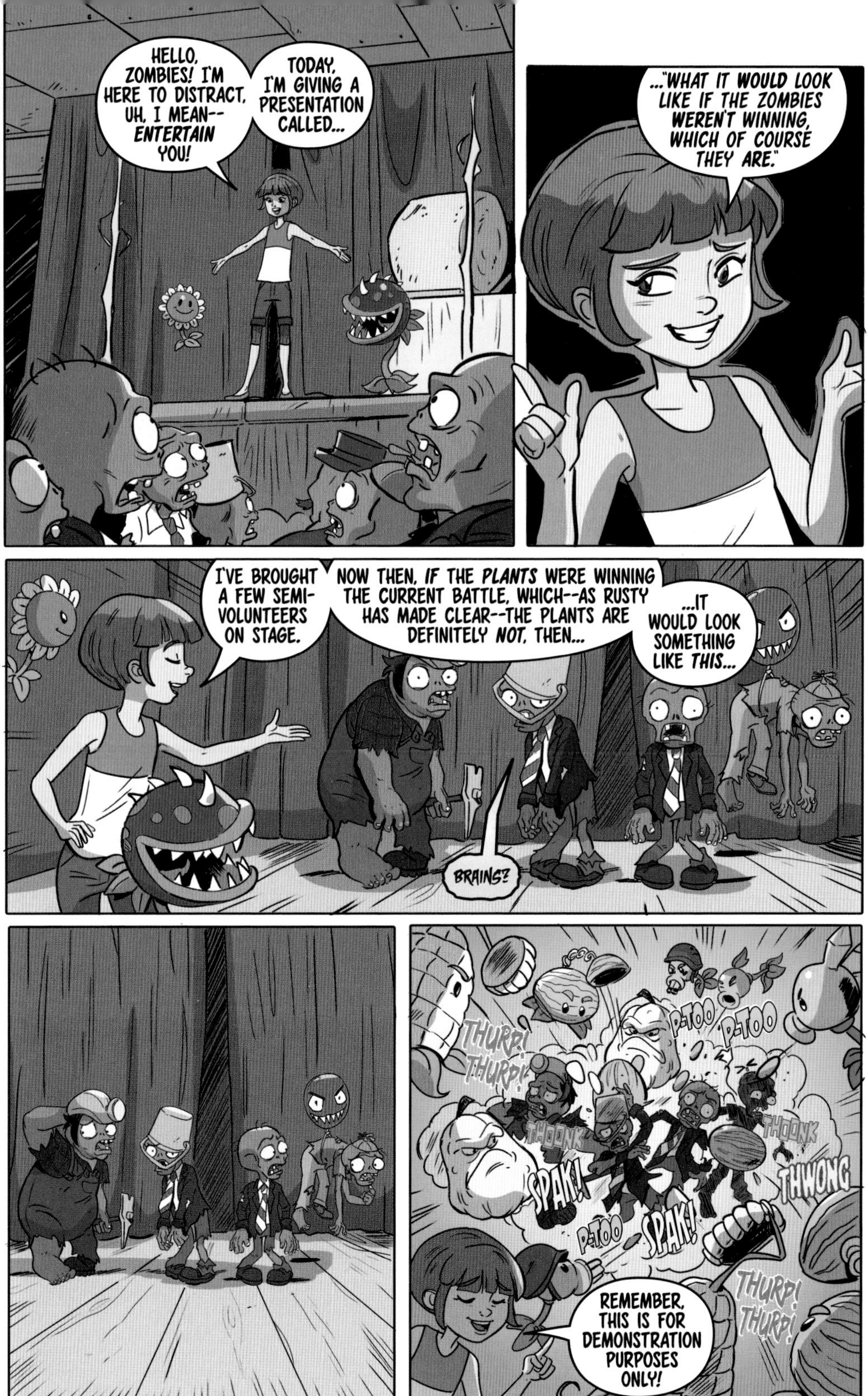

HELLO, ZOMBIES! I'M HERE TO DISTRACT, UH, I MEAN-- ENTERTAIN YOU!
TODAY, I'M GIVING A PRESENTATION CALLED...
..."WHAT IT WOULD LOOK LIKE IF THE ZOMBIES WEREN'T WINNING, WHICH OF COURSE THEY ARE."
I'VE BROUGHT A FEW SEMI-VOLUNTEERS ON STAGE.
NOW THEN, IF THE PLANTS WERE WINNING THE CURRENT BATTLE, WHICH--AS RUSTY HAS MADE CLEAR--THE PLANTS ARE DEFINITELY NOT, THEN...
...IT WOULD LOOK SOMETHING LIKE THIS...
BRAINS?
THURP! THURP!
P-TOO
P-TOO
THOONK
THOONK
THWONG
SPAK!
P-TOO
SPAK!
THURP! THURP!
REMEMBER, THIS IS FOR DEMONSTRATION PURPOSES ONLY!

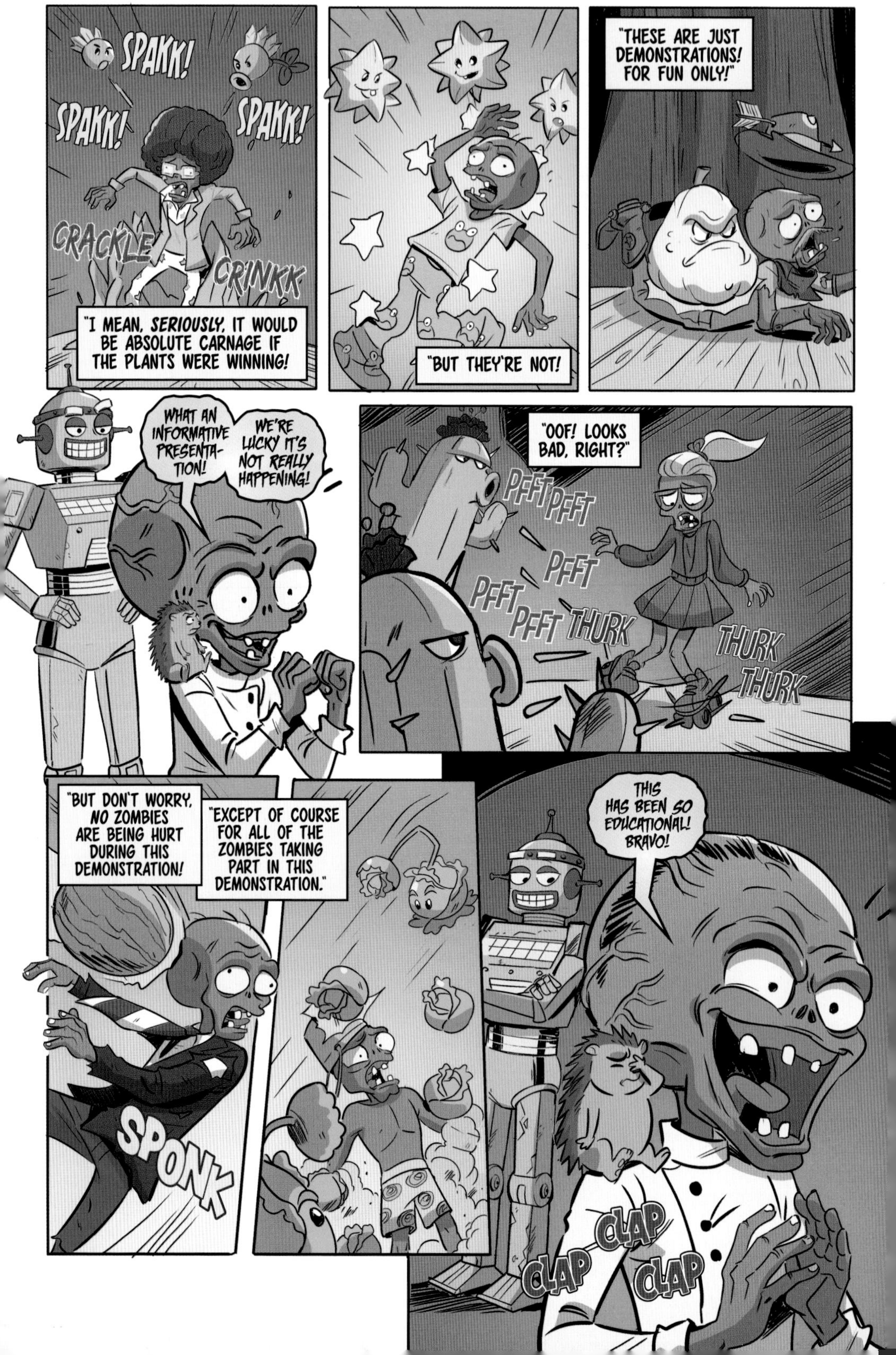
SPAKK!
SPAKK!
SPAKK!
CRACKLE
CRINKK
"I MEAN, *SERIOUSLY*, IT WOULD BE ABSOLUTE CARNAGE IF THE PLANTS WERE WINNING!
"BUT THEY'RE NOT!
"THESE ARE JUST DEMONSTRATIONS! FOR FUN ONLY!"
WHAT AN INFORMATIVE PRESENTA-TION!
WE'RE LUCKY IT'S NOT REALLY HAPPENING!
"OOF! LOOKS BAD, RIGHT?"
PFFT PFFT
PFFT
PFFT
PFFT
THURK
THURK
THURK
"BUT DON'T WORRY, *NO ZOMBIES* ARE BEING HURT DURING THIS DEMONSTRATION!
"EXCEPT OF COURSE FOR ALL OF THE ZOMBIES TAKING PART IN THIS DEMONSTRATION."
SPONK
THIS HAS BEEN SO EDUCATIONAL! BRAVO!
CLAP
CLAP
CLAP

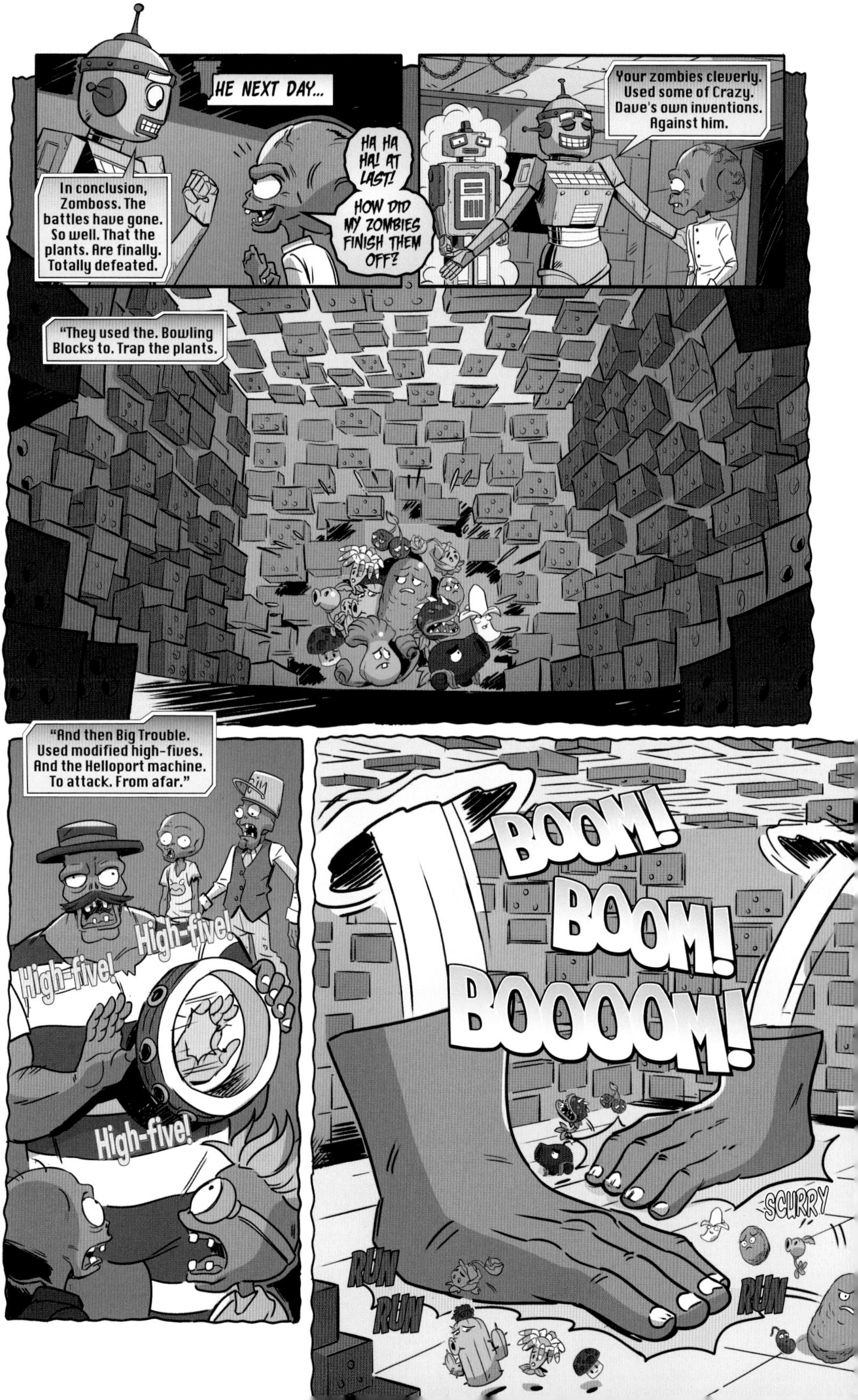
THE NEXT DAY...
In conclusion, Zomboss. The battles have gone. So well. That the plants. Are finally. Totally defeated.
HA HA HA! AT LAST!
HOW DID MY ZOMBIES FINISH THEM OFF?
Your zombies cleverly. Used some of Crazy. Dave's own inventions. Against him.
"They used the. Bowling Blocks to. Trap the plants.
"And then Big Trouble. Used modified high-fives. And the Helloport machine. To attack. From afar."
High-five!
High-five!
High-five!
BOOM! BOOM! BOOOOM!
SCURRY
RUN
RUN
RUN

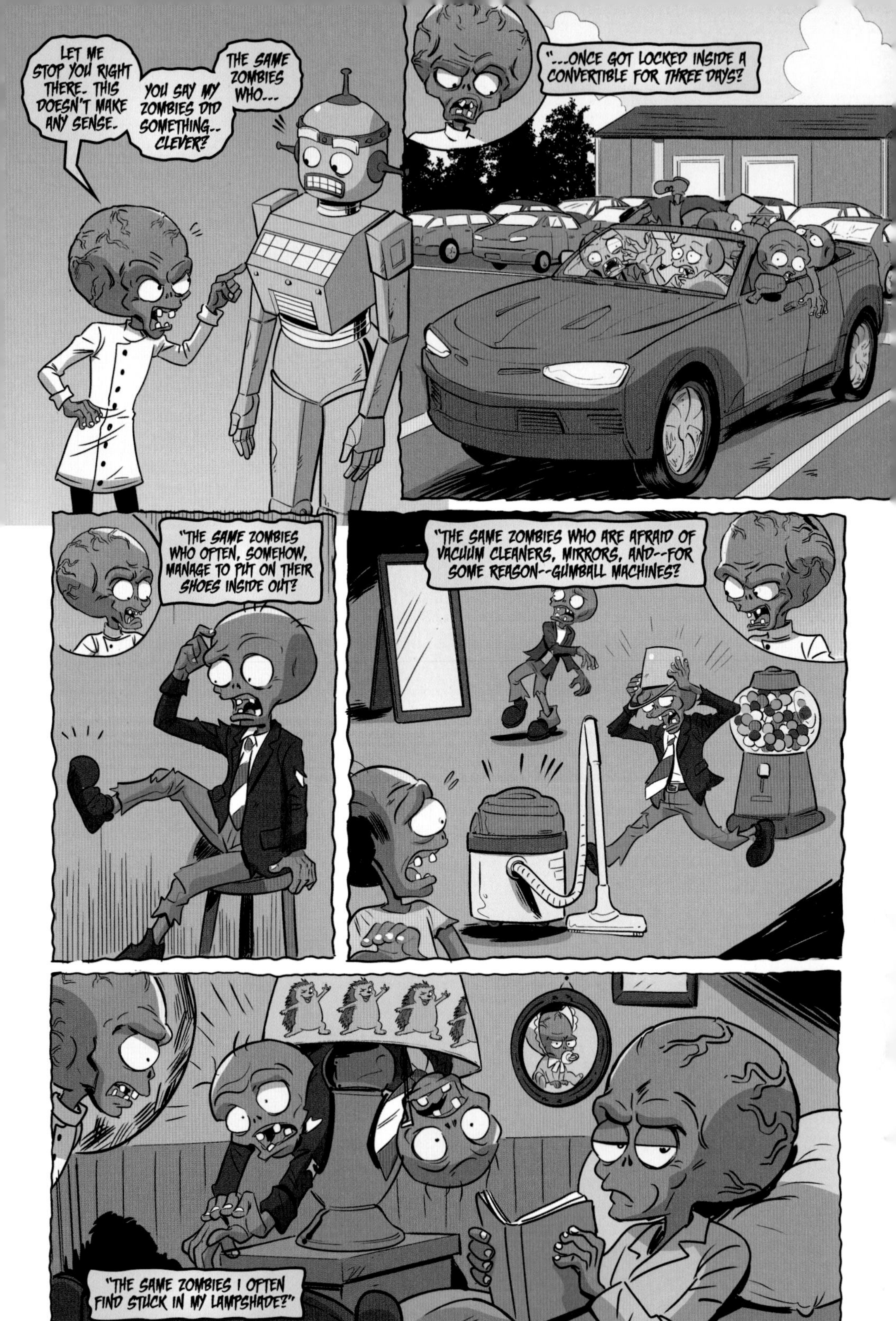
LET ME STOP YOU RIGHT THERE. THIS DOESN'T MAKE ANY SENSE.
YOU SAY MY ZOMBIES DID SOMETHING-- CLEVER?
THE SAME ZOMBIES WHO...
"...ONCE GOT LOCKED INSIDE A CONVERTIBLE FOR THREE DAYS?
"THE SAME ZOMBIES WHO OFTEN, SOMEHOW, MANAGE TO PUT ON THEIR SHOES INSIDE OUT?
"THE SAME ZOMBIES WHO ARE AFRAID OF VACUUM CLEANERS, MIRRORS, AND--FOR SOME REASON--GUMBALL MACHINES?
"THE SAME ZOMBIES I OFTEN FIND STUCK IN MY LAMPSHADE?"

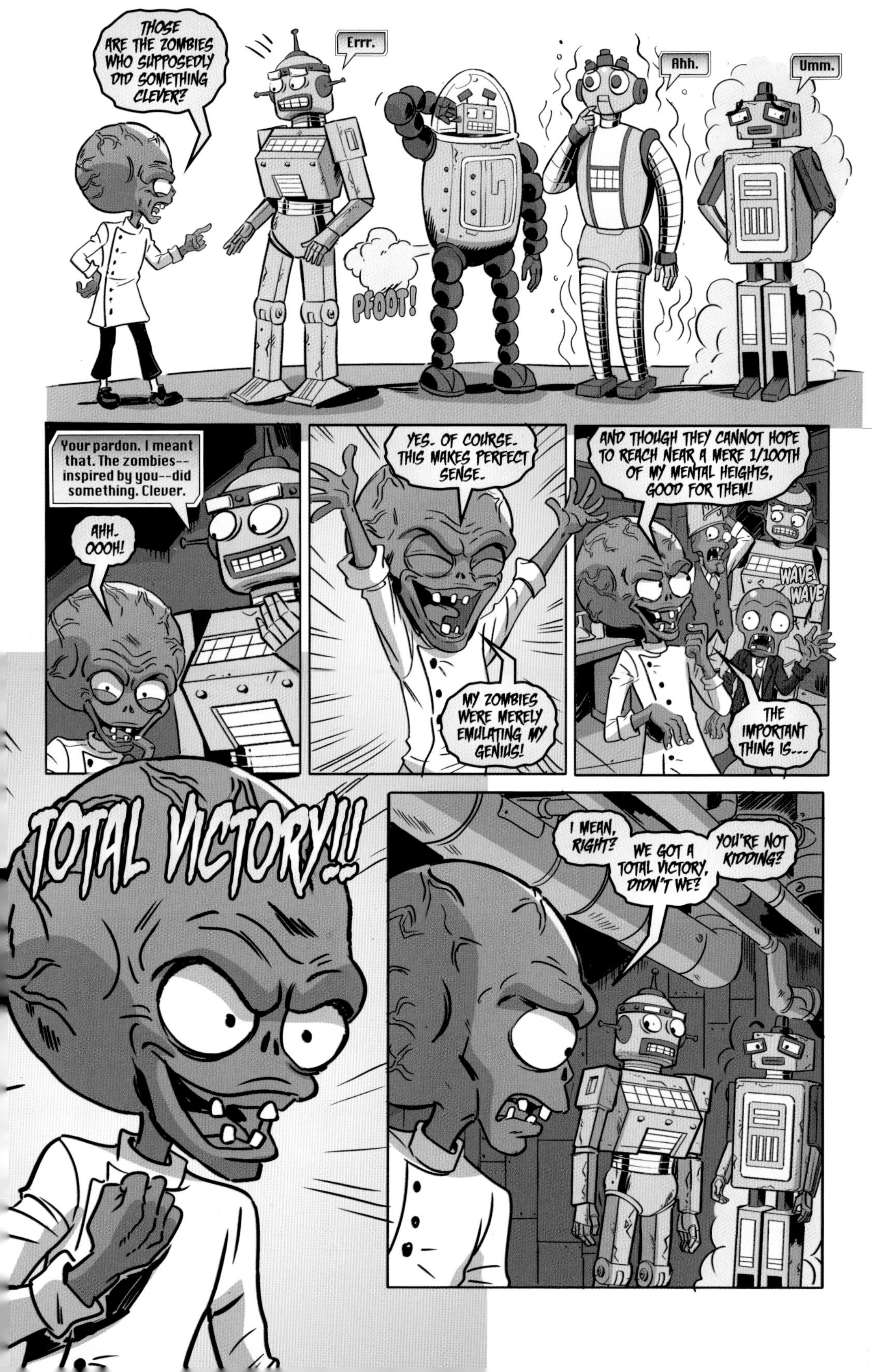
THOSE ARE THE ZOMBIES WHO SUPPOSEDLY DID SOMETHING CLEVER?
Errr.
PFOOT!
Ahh.
Umm.
Your pardon. I meant that. The zombies--inspired by you--did something. Clever.
AHH. OOOH!
YES. OF COURSE. THIS MAKES PERFECT SENSE.
MY ZOMBIES WERE MERELY EMULATING MY GENIUS!
AND THOUGH THEY CANNOT HOPE TO REACH NEAR A MERE 1/100TH OF MY MENTAL HEIGHTS, GOOD FOR THEM!
WAVE WAVE
THE IMPORTANT THING IS...
TOTAL VICTORY!!
I MEAN, RIGHT?
WE GOT A TOTAL VICTORY, DIDN'T WE?
YOU'RE NOT KIDDING?

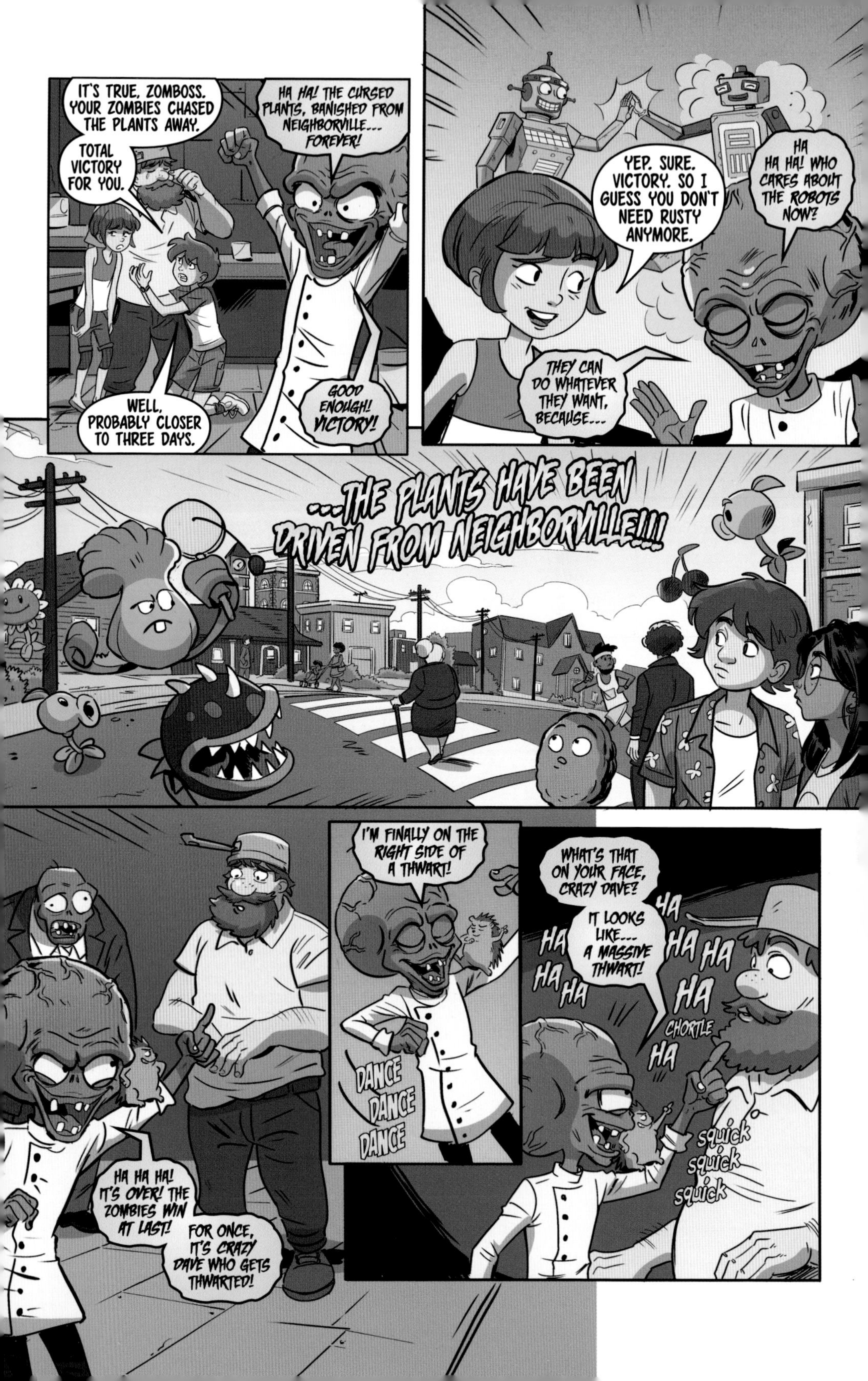
IT'S TRUE, ZOMBOSS. YOUR ZOMBIES CHASED THE PLANTS AWAY.
TOTAL VICTORY FOR YOU.
HA HA! THE CURSED PLANTS, BANISHED FROM NEIGHBORVILLE... FOREVER!
WELL, PROBABLY CLOSER TO THREE DAYS.
GOOD ENOUGH! VICTORY!
YEP. SURE. VICTORY. SO I GUESS YOU DON'T NEED RUSTY ANYMORE.
HA HA HA! WHO CARES ABOUT THE ROBOTS NOW?
THEY CAN DO WHATEVER THEY WANT, BECAUSE...
...THE PLANTS HAVE BEEN DRIVEN FROM NEIGHBORVILLE!!!!
HA HA HA! IT'S OVER! THE ZOMBIES WIN AT LAST!
FOR ONCE, IT'S CRAZY DAVE WHO GETS THWARTED!
I'M FINALLY ON THE RIGHT SIDE OF A THWART!
DANCE
DANCE
DANCE
WHAT'S THAT ON YOUR FACE, CRAZY DAVE?
IT LOOKS LIKE... A MASSIVE THWART!
HA HA HA HA HA HA HA HA
CHORTLE
HA
squick
squick
squick

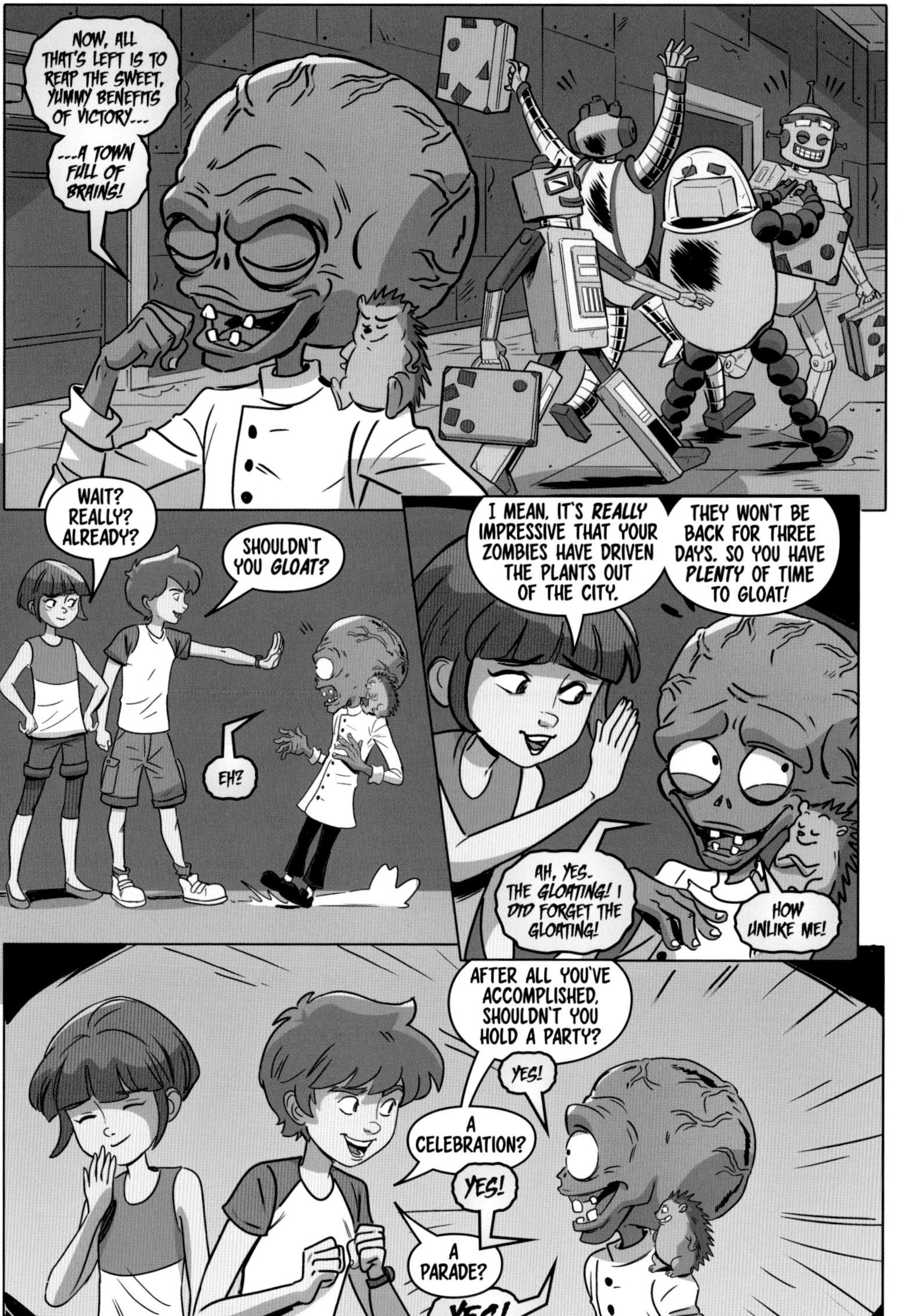

NOW, ALL THAT'S LEFT IS TO REAP THE SWEET, YUMMY BENEFITS OF VICTORY---
---A TOWN FULL OF BRAINS!
WAIT? REALLY? ALREADY?
SHOULDN'T YOU GLOAT?
EH?
I MEAN, IT'S REALLY IMPRESSIVE THAT YOUR ZOMBIES HAVE DRIVEN THE PLANTS OUT OF THE CITY.
THEY WON'T BE BACK FOR THREE DAYS. SO YOU HAVE PLENTY OF TIME TO GLOAT!
AH, YES. THE GLOATING! I DID FORGET THE GLOATING!
HOW UNLIKE ME!
AFTER ALL YOU'VE ACCOMPLISHED, SHOULDN'T YOU HOLD A PARTY?
YES!
A CELEBRATION?
YES!
A PARADE?
YES!

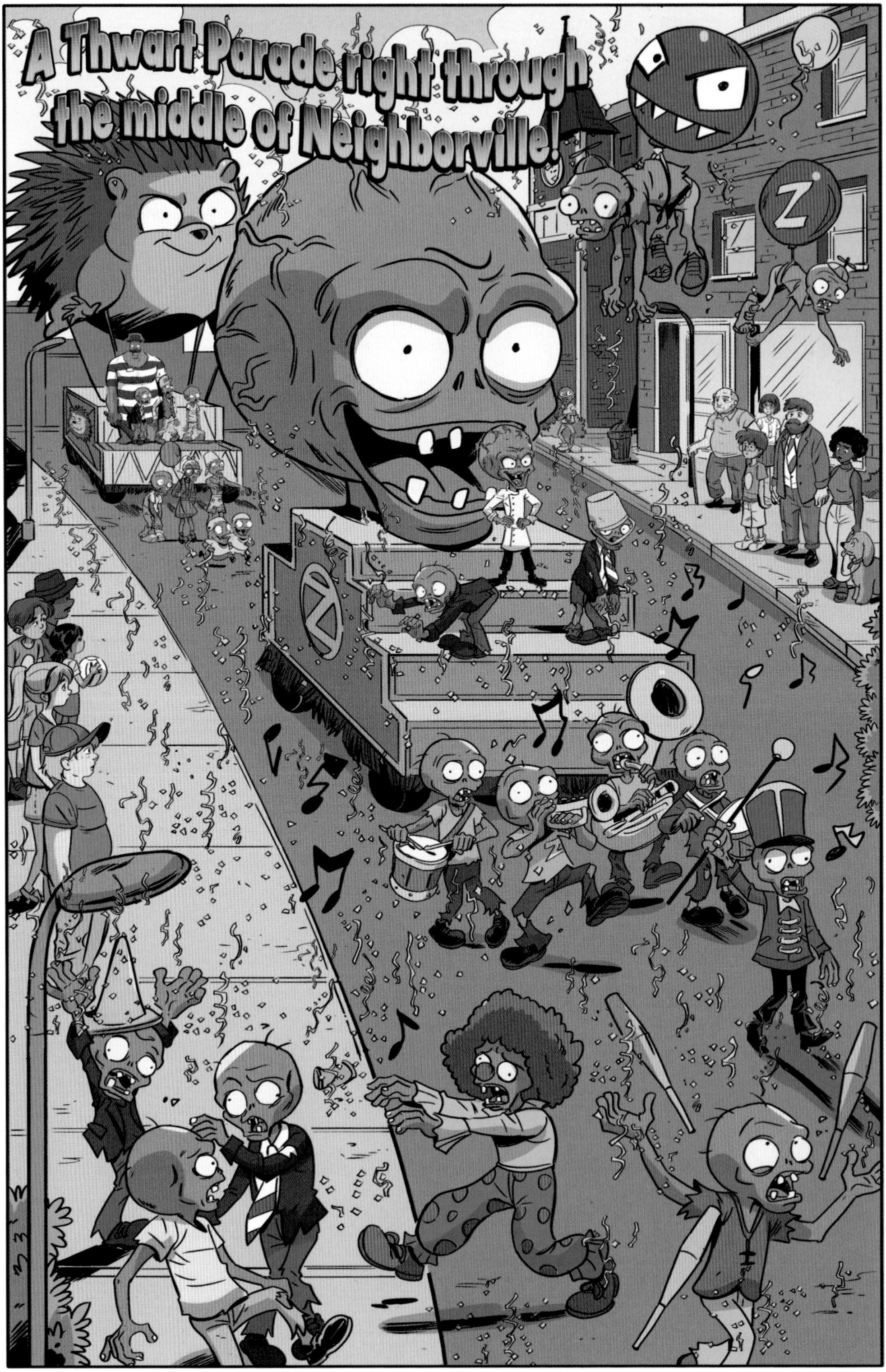
A Thwart Parade right through the middle of Neighborville!
Z

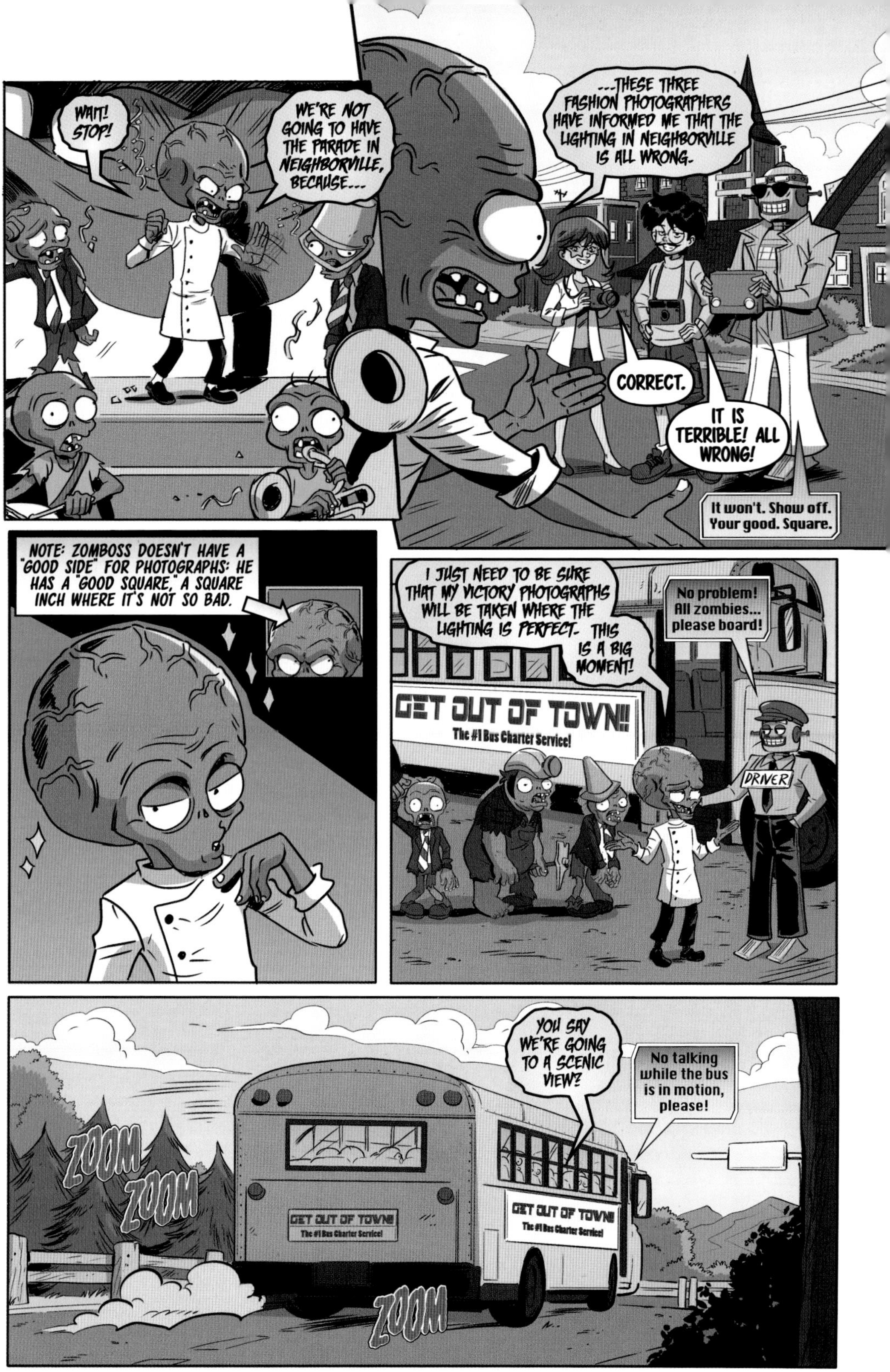
WAIT! STOP!
WE'RE NOT GOING TO HAVE THE PARADE IN NEIGHBORVILLE, BECAUSE...
...THESE THREE FASHION PHOTOGRAPHERS HAVE INFORMED ME THAT THE LIGHTING IN NEIGHBORVILLE IS ALL WRONG.
CORRECT.
IT IS TERRIBLE! ALL WRONG!
It won't. Show off. Your good. Square.
NOTE: ZOMBOSS DOESN'T HAVE A "GOOD SIDE" FOR PHOTOGRAPHS: HE HAS A "GOOD SQUARE," A SQUARE INCH WHERE IT'S NOT SO BAD.
I JUST NEED TO BE SURE THAT MY VICTORY PHOTOGRAPHS WILL BE TAKEN WHERE THE LIGHTING IS PERFECT.
THIS IS A BIG MOMENT!
No problem! All zombies... please board!
GET OUT OF TOWN!!
The #1 Bus Charter Service!
DRIVER
YOU SAY WE'RE GOING TO A SCENIC VIEW?
No talking while the bus is in motion, please!
ZOOM
ZOOM
GET OUT OF TOWN!!
The #1 Bus Charter Service!
GET OUT OF TOWN!!
The #1 Bus Charter Service!
ZOOM

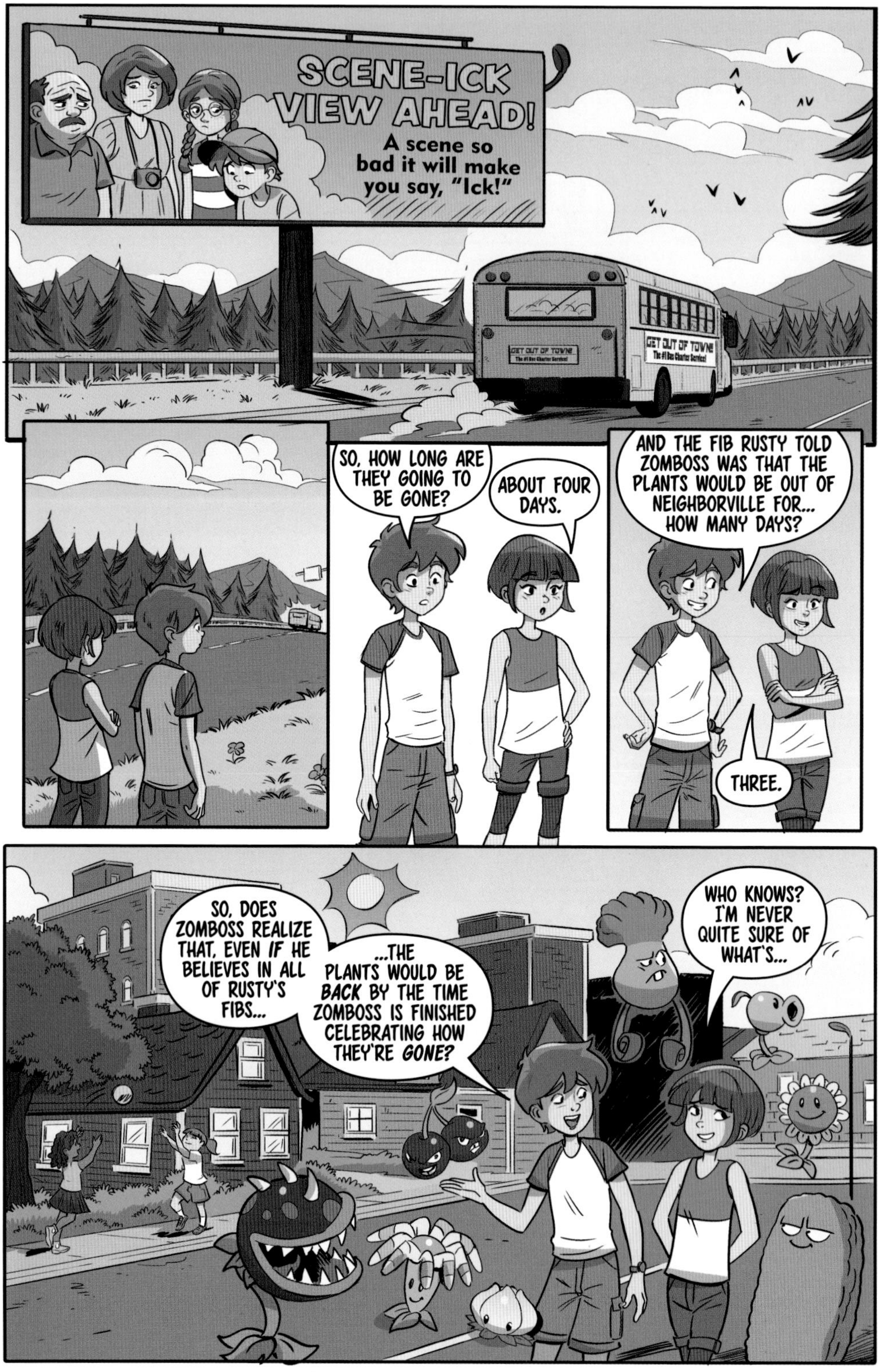
SCENE-ICK VIEW AHEAD!
A scene so bad it will make you say, "Ick!"
GET OUT OF TOWN!
GET OUT OF TOWN! The #1 Bus Charter Service!
SO, HOW LONG ARE THEY GOING TO BE GONE?
ABOUT FOUR DAYS.
AND THE FIB RUSTY TOLD ZOMBOSS WAS THAT THE PLANTS WOULD BE OUT OF NEIGHBORVILLE FOR... HOW MANY DAYS?
THREE.
SO, DOES ZOMBOSS REALIZE THAT, EVEN *IF* HE BELIEVES IN ALL OF RUSTY'S FIBS...
...THE PLANTS WOULD BE *BACK* BY THE TIME ZOMBOSS IS FINISHED CELEBRATING HOW THEY'RE *GONE*?
WHO KNOWS? I'M NEVER QUITE SURE OF WHAT'S...

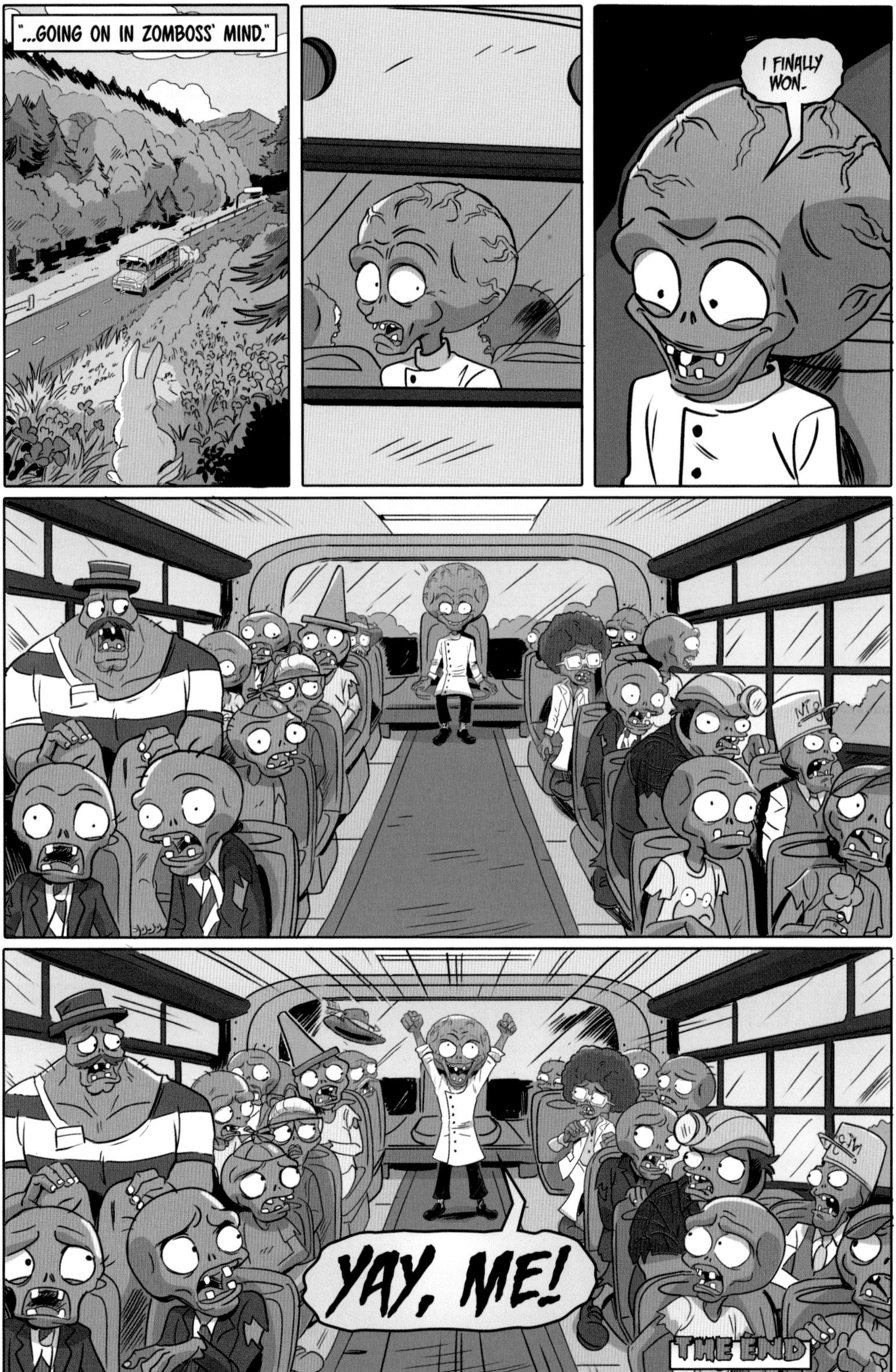
"...GOING ON IN ZOMBOSS' MIND."
I FINALLY WON.
YAY, ME!
THE END

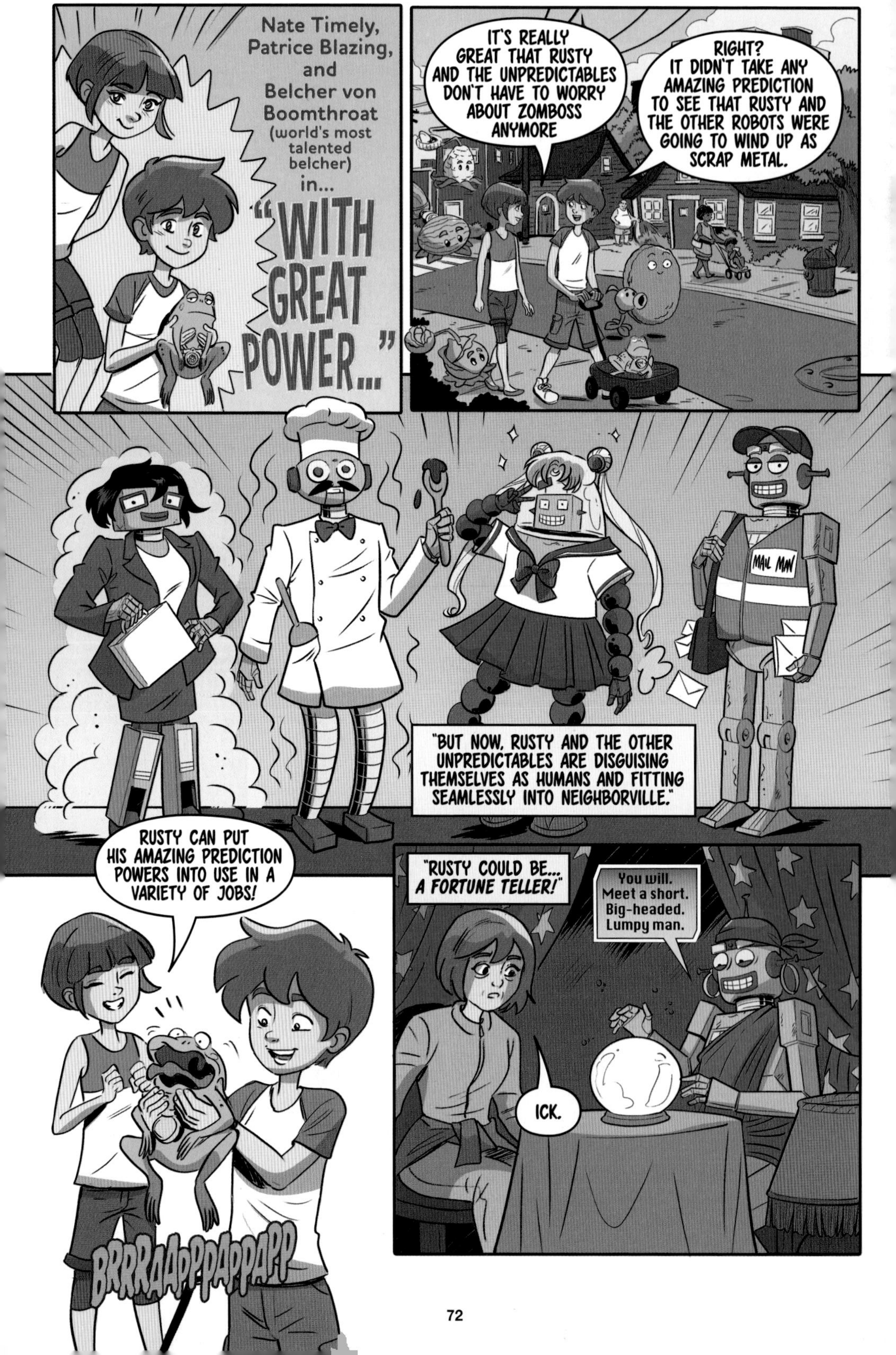
Nate Timely, Patrice Blazing, and Belcher von Boomthroat (world's most talented belcher) in...
"WITH GREAT POWER..."
IT'S REALLY GREAT THAT RUSTY AND THE UNPREDICTABLES DON'T HAVE TO WORRY ABOUT ZOMBOSS ANYMORE
RIGHT? IT DIDN'T TAKE ANY AMAZING PREDICTION TO SEE THAT RUSTY AND THE OTHER ROBOTS WERE GOING TO WIND UP AS SCRAP METAL.
MAIL MAN
"BUT NOW, RUSTY AND THE OTHER UNPREDICTABLES ARE DISGUISING THEMSELVES AS HUMANS AND FITTING SEAMLESSLY INTO NEIGHBORVILLE."
RUSTY CAN PUT HIS AMAZING PREDICTION POWERS INTO USE IN A VARIETY OF JOBS!
BRRRAAPPPAPPAPP
"RUSTY COULD BE... A FORTUNE TELLER!"
You will. Meet a short. Big-headed. Lumpy man.
ICK.

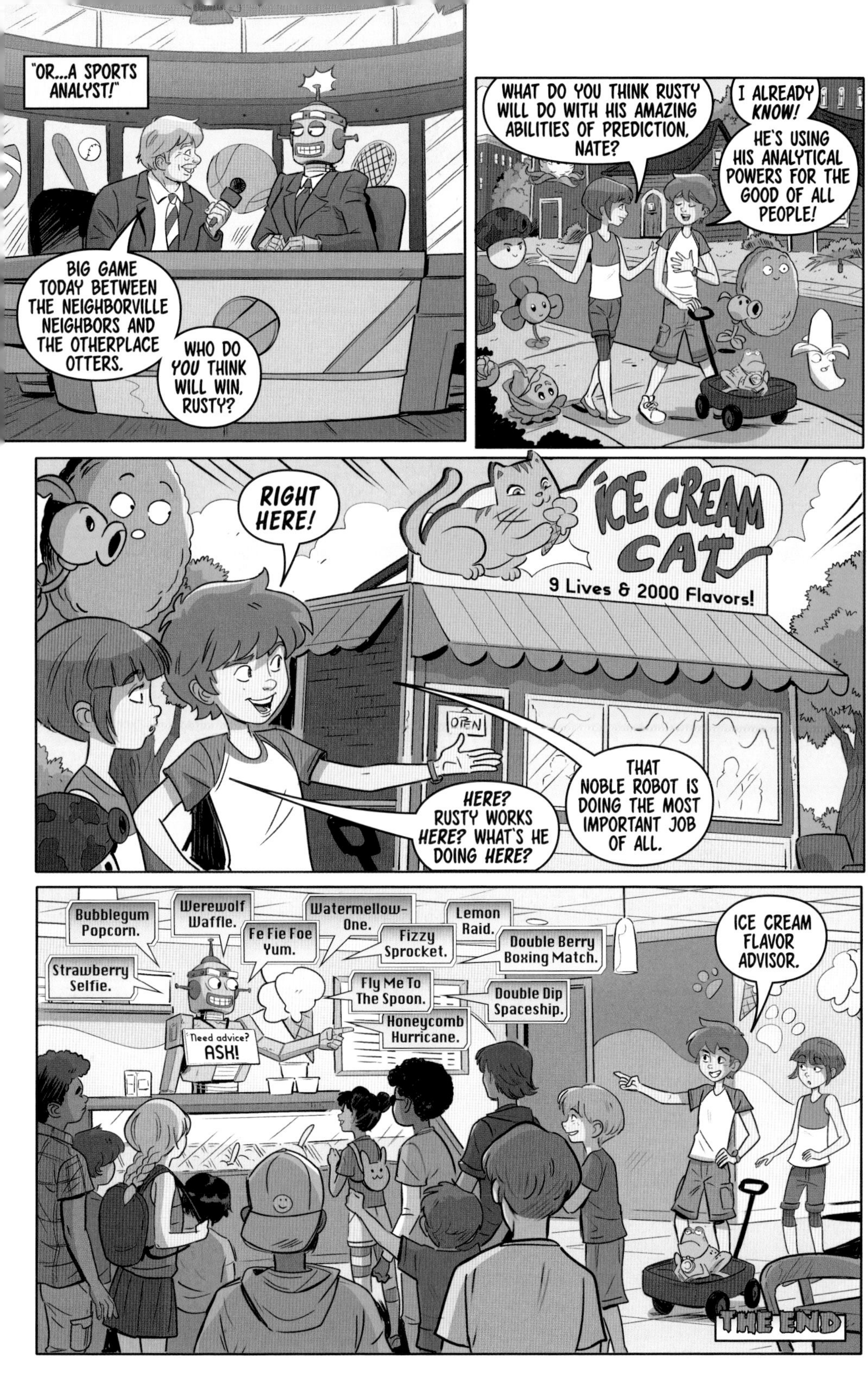
"OR...A SPORTS ANALYST!"
BIG GAME TODAY BETWEEN THE NEIGHBORVILLE NEIGHBORS AND THE OTHERPLACE OTTERS.
WHO DO *YOU* THINK WILL WIN, RUSTY?
WHAT DO YOU THINK RUSTY WILL DO WITH HIS AMAZING ABILITIES OF PREDICTION, NATE?
I ALREADY *KNOW!*
HE'S USING HIS ANALYTICAL POWERS FOR THE GOOD OF ALL PEOPLE!
ICE CREAM CAT
9 Lives & 2000 Flavors!
RIGHT HERE!
OPEN
HERE? RUSTY WORKS *HERE?* WHAT'S HE DOING *HERE?*
THAT NOBLE ROBOT IS DOING THE MOST IMPORTANT JOB OF ALL.
Bubblegum Popcorn.
Werewolf Waffle.
Watermellow-One.
Lemon Raid.
Strawberry Selfie.
Fe Fie Foe Yum.
Fizzy Sprocket.
Double Berry Boxing Match.
Fly Me To The Spoon.
Double Dip Spaceship.
Honeycomb Hurricane.
Need advice? ASK!
ICE CREAM FLAVOR ADVISOR.
THE END

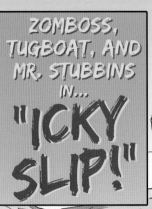

ZOMBOSS, TUGBOAT, AND MR. STUBBINS IN...

"ICKY SLIP!"

SCENE-ICK VIEW AHEAD!

A scene so bad it will make you say, "Ick!"

THIS IS WHERE WE'RE SUPPOSED TO HOLD OUR PARADE? NOBODY WILL SEE US HERE!

WHEN WE'RE THIS FAR OUT OF TOWN, CAN ANYBODY EVEN HEAR ME RANT?

ARGH! I WANT TO--!

Z

EH? TUGBOAT?

QUIT STEALING MY POP SMARTS!

ANTI-THWART CREAM!

STOMP

STOMP STOMP

BLURK!!

SKLURTCH!!

SQUICK?

GAHH!

FWIP

SLIP!

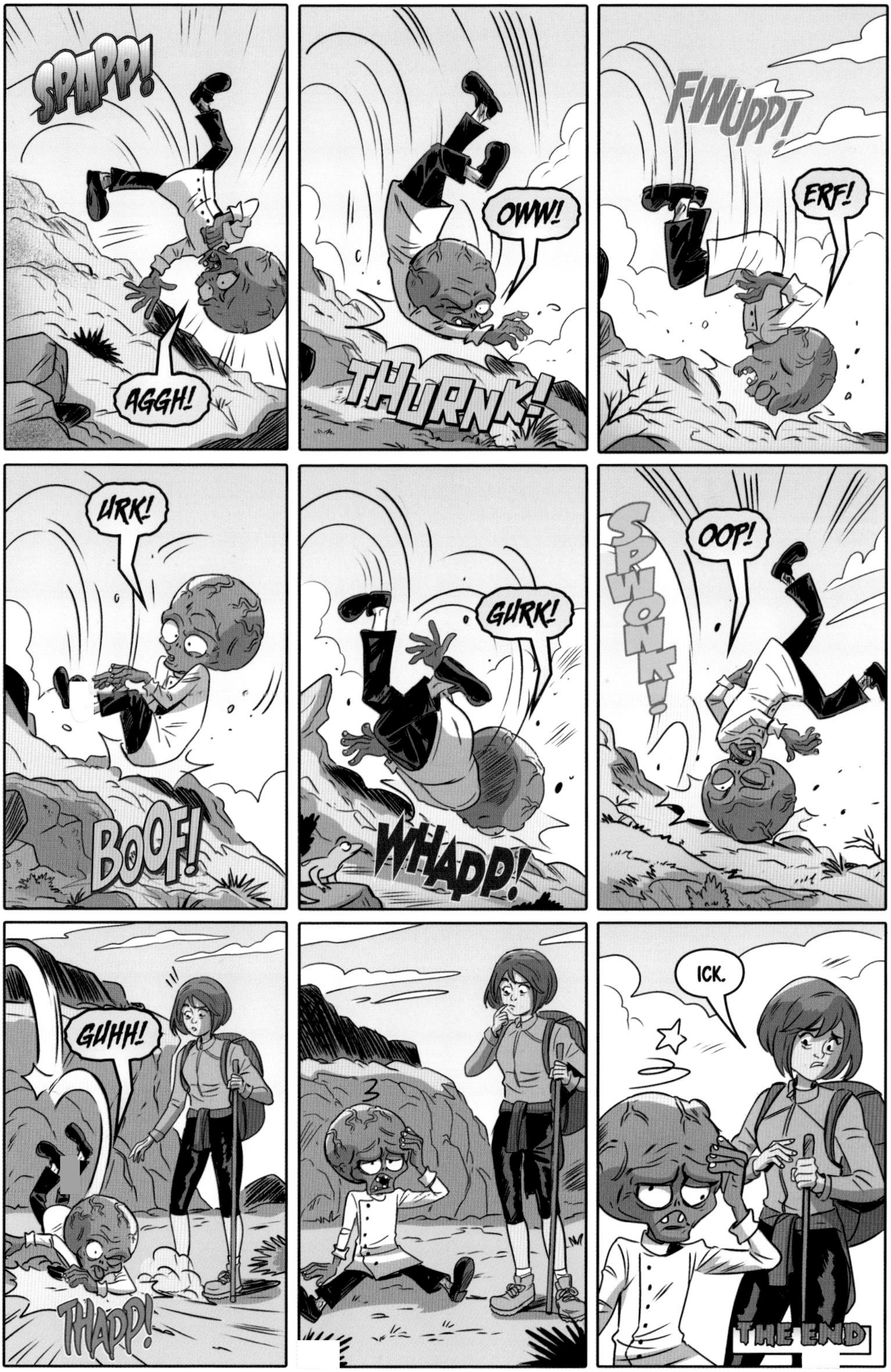
SPAPP!
AGGH!
OWW!
THURNK!
FWUPP!
ERF!
URK!
BOOF!
GURK!
WHAPP!
OOP!
SPWONK!
GUHH!
THAPP!
ICK.
THE END

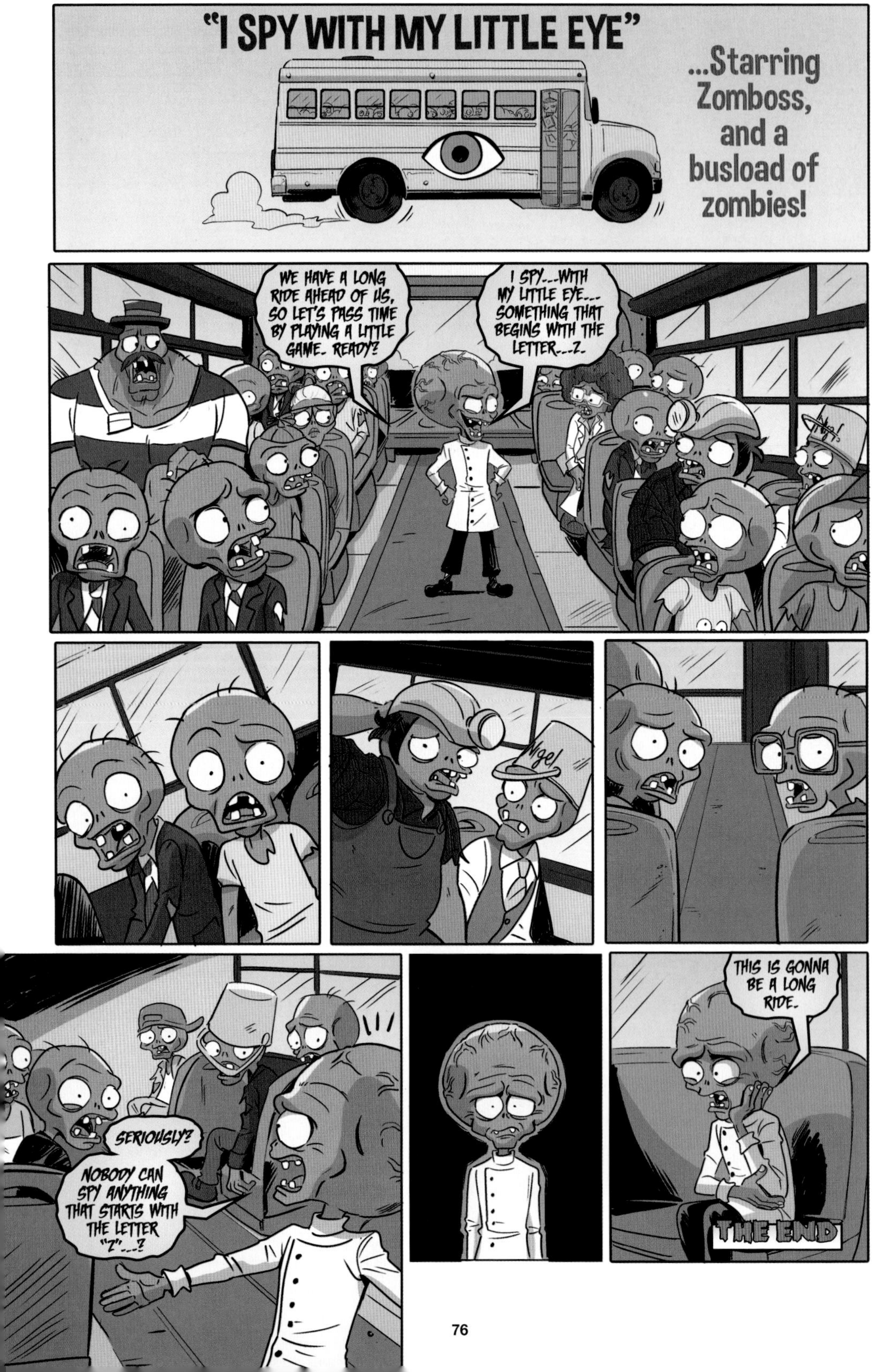
"I SPY WITH MY LITTLE EYE"
...Starring Zomboss, and a busload of zombies!
WE HAVE A LONG RIDE AHEAD OF US, SO LET'S PASS TIME BY PLAYING A LITTLE GAME. READY?
I SPY...WITH MY LITTLE EYE... SOMETHING THAT BEGINS WITH THE LETTER...Z.
Nigel
SERIOUSLY?
NOBODY CAN SPY ANYTHING THAT STARTS WITH THE LETTER "Z"...?
THIS IS GONNA BE A LONG RIDE.
THE END

COVER CONCEPTS FOR *PLANTS VS. ZOMBIES: THE UNPREDICTABLES*, FROM JESSE HAMM'S SKETCHBOOK.

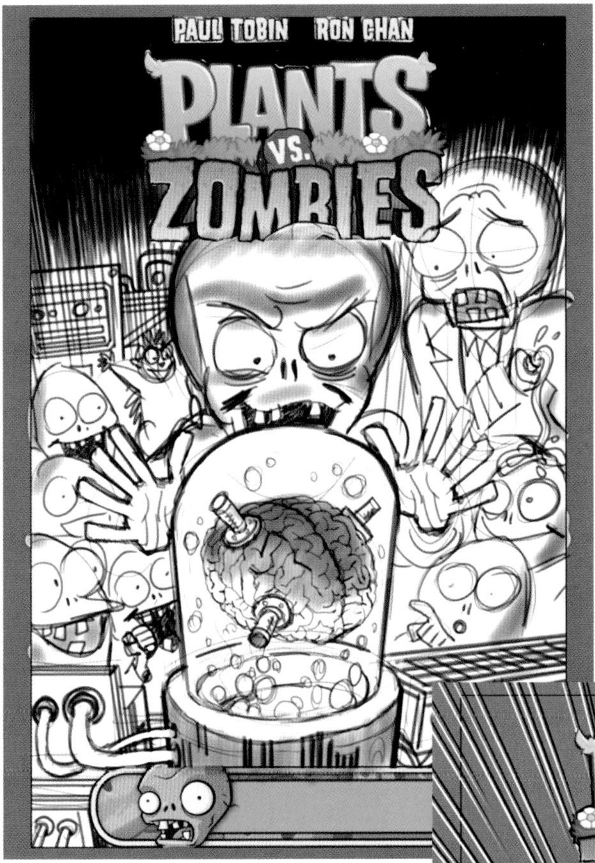
PAUL TOBIN RON CHAN
PLANTS VS. ZOMBIES

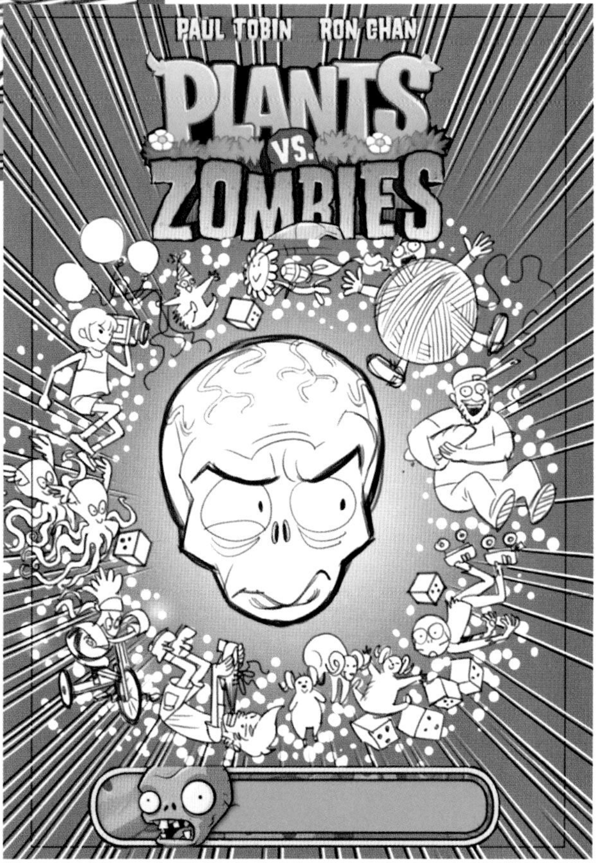
PAUL TOBIN RON CHAN
PLANTS VS. ZOMBIES

THIS PAGE—COVER PENCILS BY JESSE HAMM. FACING PAGE—JESSE'S INKED COVER.

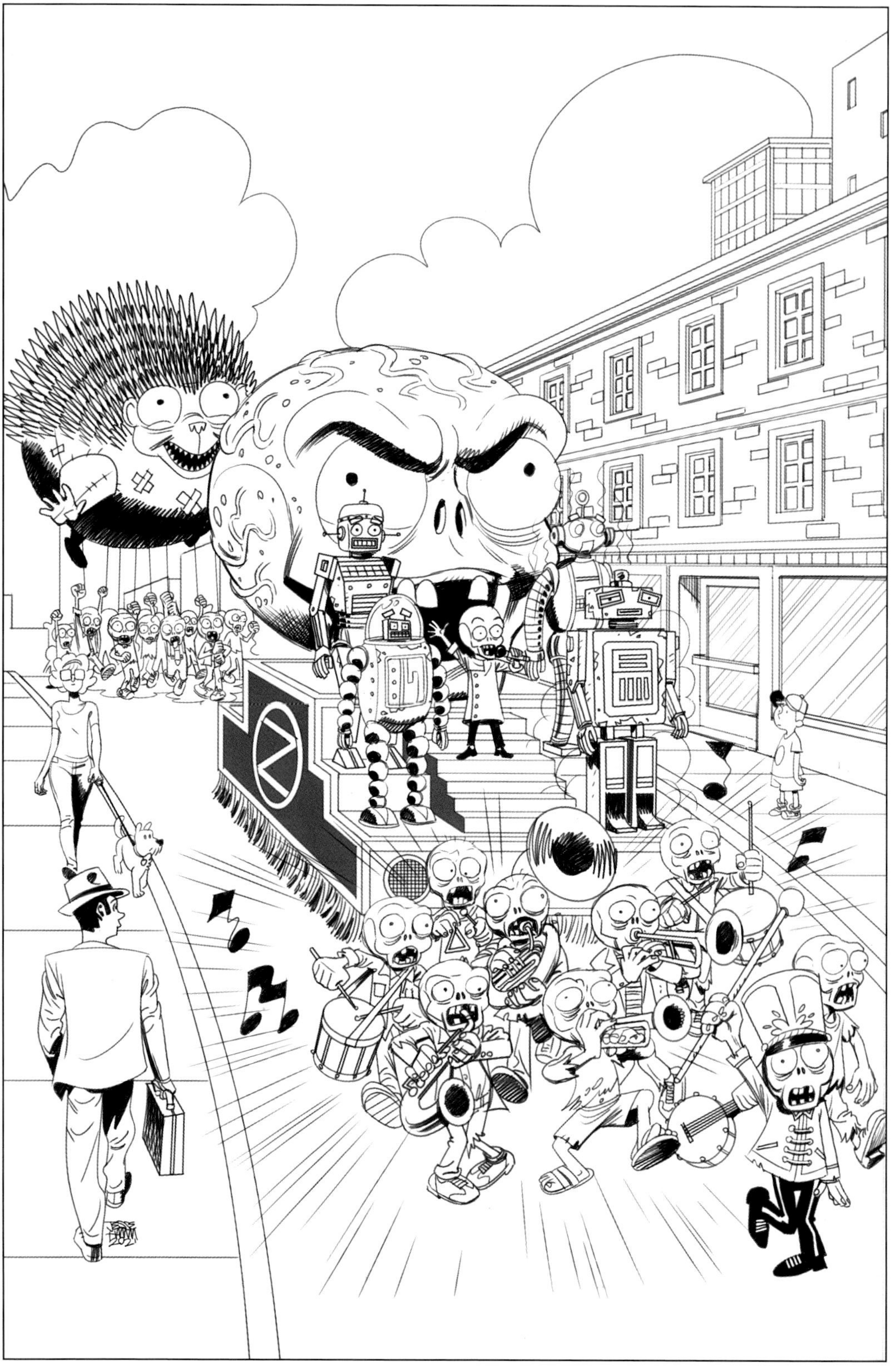

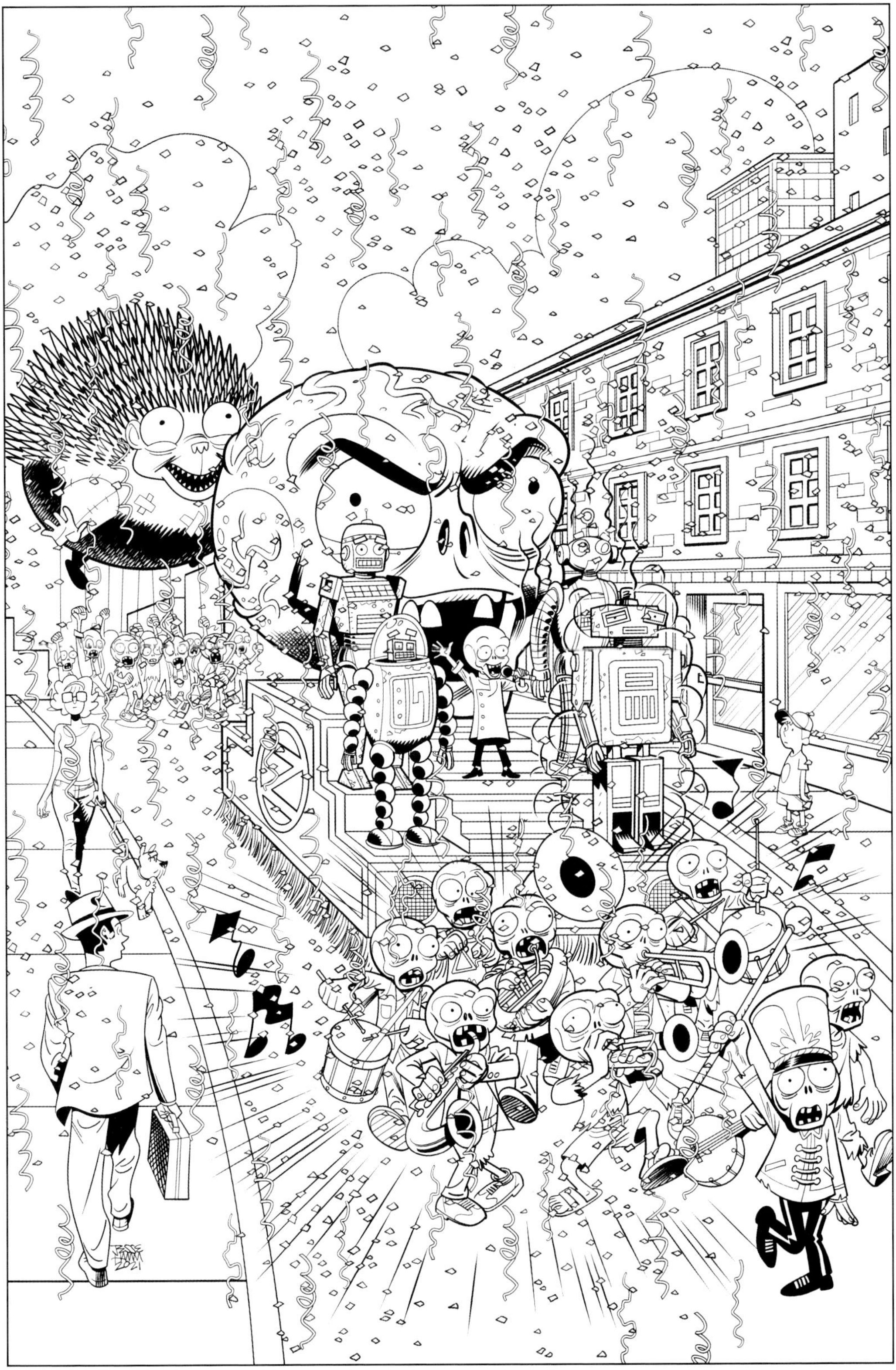
JESSE HAMM 2021

PLANTS VS. ZOMBIES: THE UNPREDICTABLES **LINE ART GALLERY!**

ALL PAGES BY JESSE HAMM

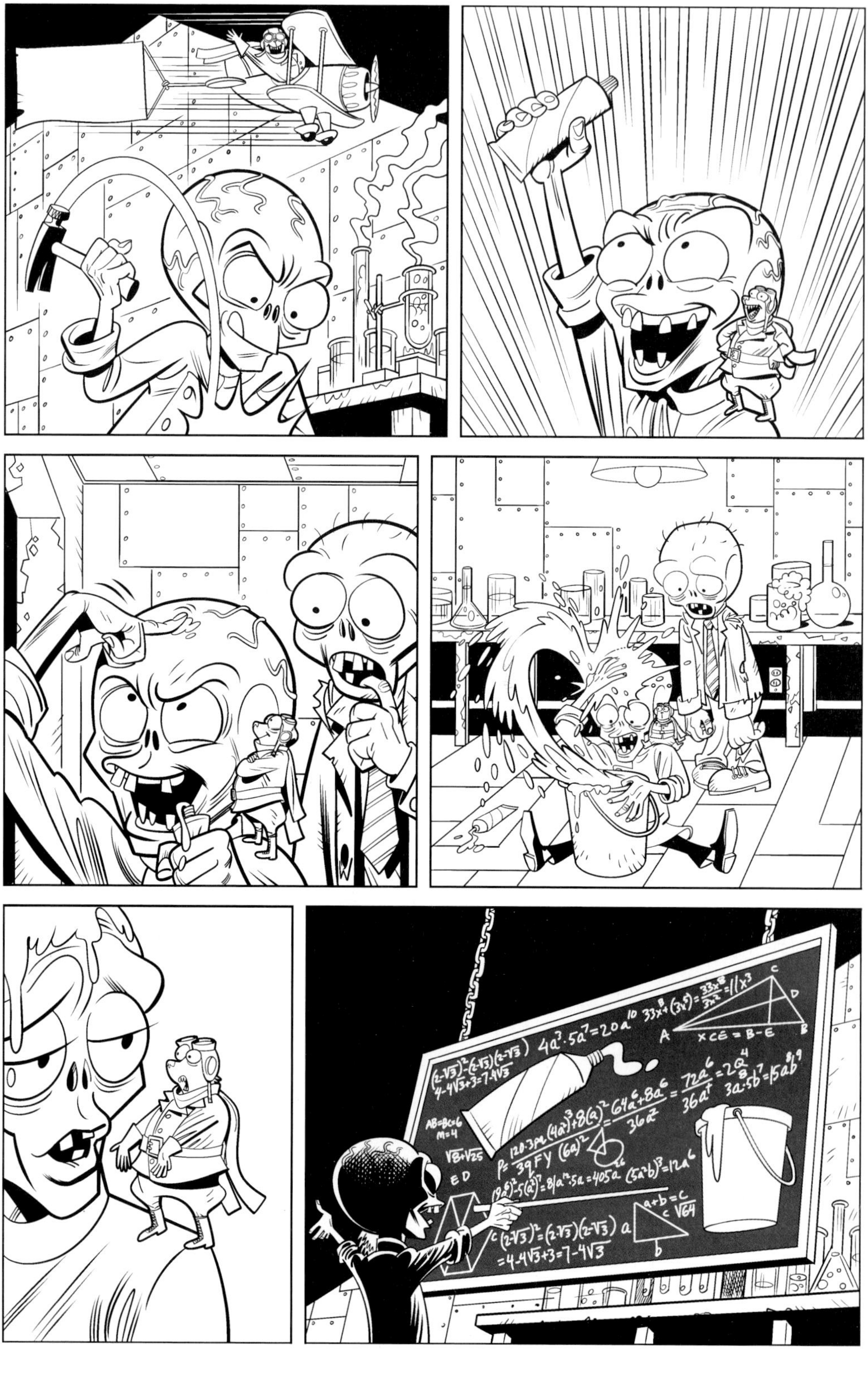

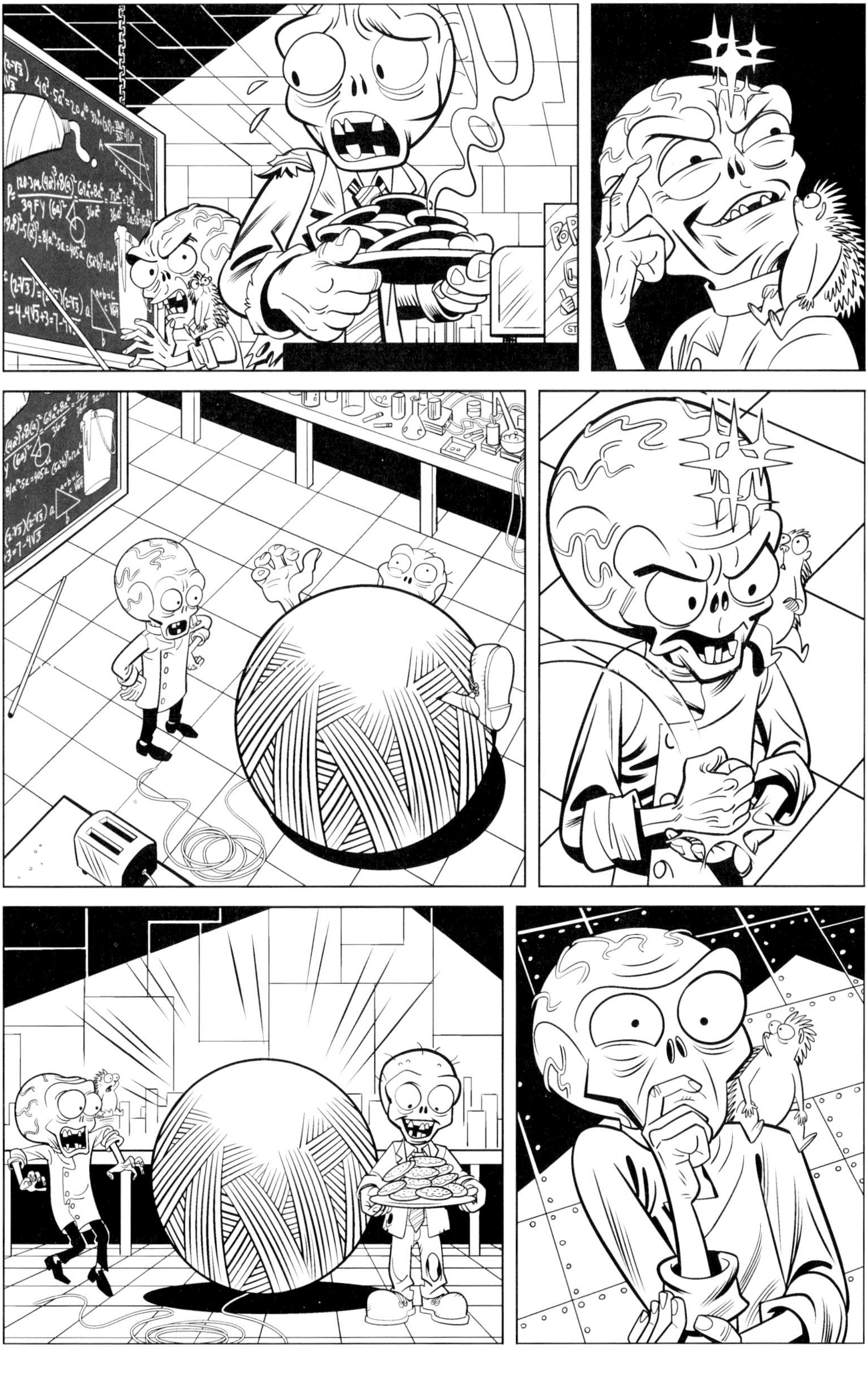

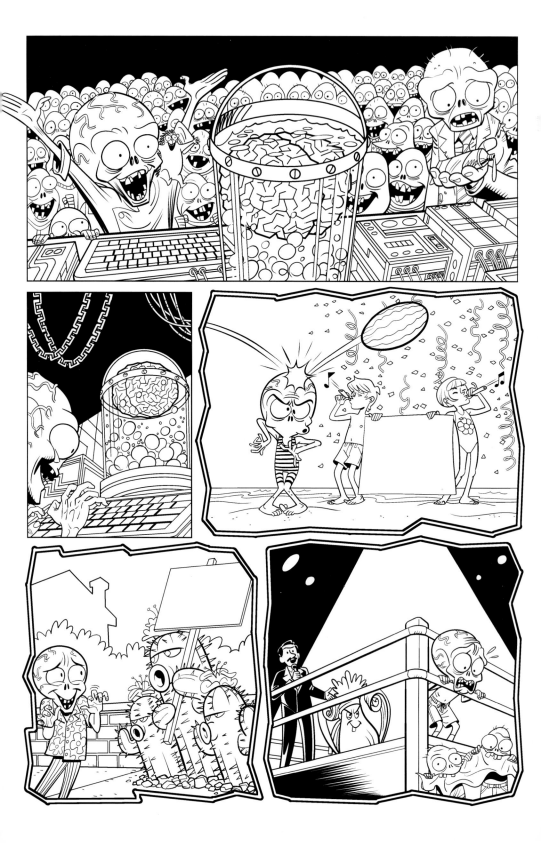

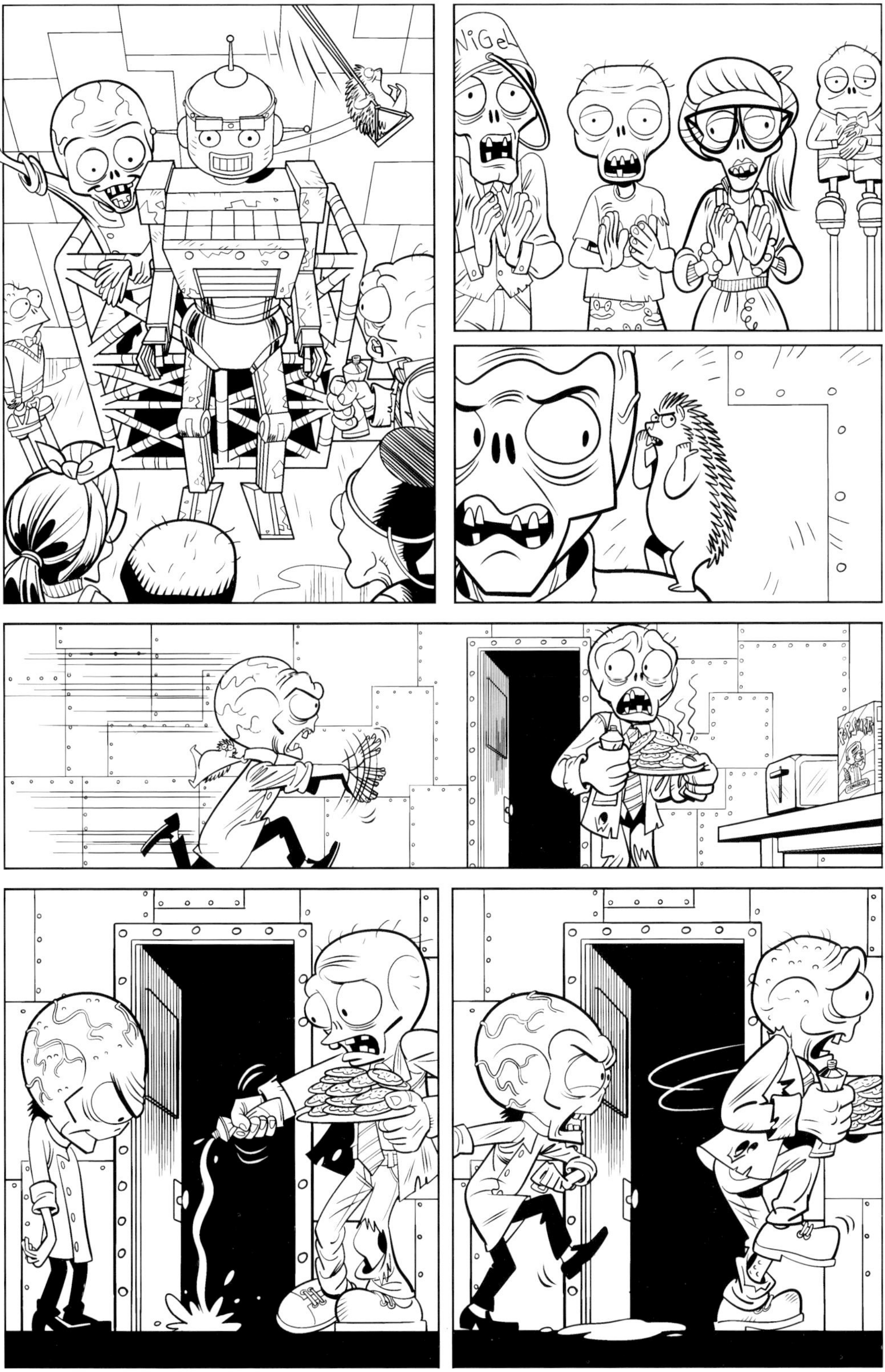
NiGeL

CREATOR BIOS

PAUL TOBIN is a 12th level writer and a 15th level cookie eater. He begins each morning in the manner we all do, by battling those zombies that have strayed too close to his pillow fort. Between writing all the *Plants vs. Zombies* comics and taking four naps a day, he's also found time to write the *Genius Factor* series of novels, the ape-filled *Banana Sunday* graphic novel, the award-winning *Bandette* series, the upcoming *Wrassle Castle* and *Earth Boy* graphic novels, and many other works. He has ridden a giant turtle and an elephant on purpose, and a tornado by accident.

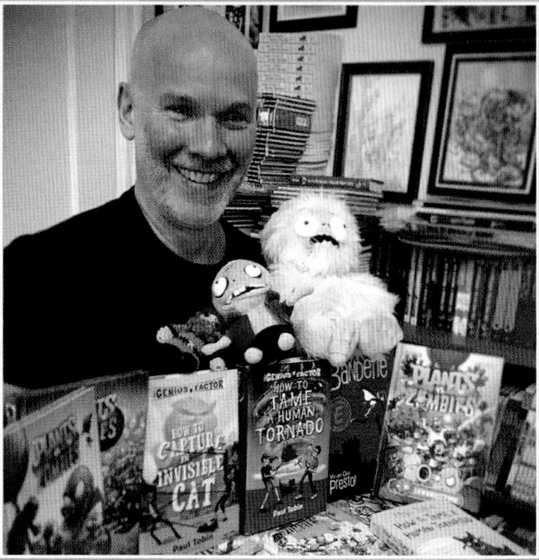

GENIUS FACTOR
HOW TO CAPTURE AN INVISIBLE CAT
Paul Tobin
GENIUS FACTOR
HOW TO TAME A HUMAN TORNADO
Paul Tobin
Bandette
PLANTS vs. ZOMBIES

Paul Tobin

JESSE HAMM (1975–2021) was a cartoonist, illustrator, essayist, and educator who worked on characters such as Batman, Hawkeye, Flash Gordon, Prince Valiant, and The Phantom, as well as his own projects, including the graphic novel *Good as Lily*, with Derek Kirk Kim. He was a brilliant and perceptive writer about the art and craft of cartooning, and much of his work can be found archived at the @Hamm_Tips account on Twitter. Jesse was the artist for *Plants vs. Zombies: Constructionary Tales*.

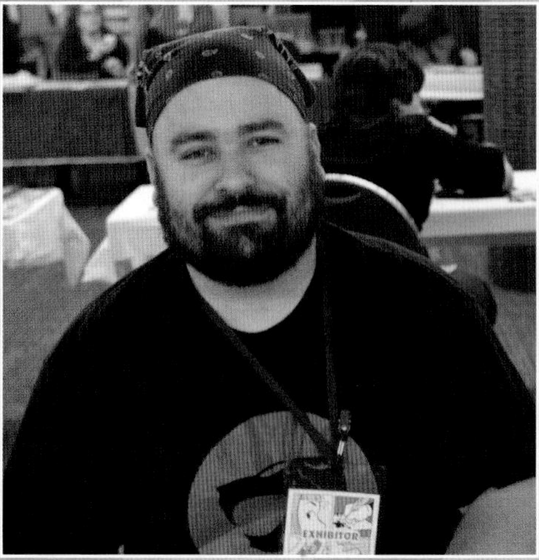

EXHIBITOR

Jesse Hamm

Luisa Russo

LUISA RUSSO is an Italian comic book artist. She lives in Italy, but for almost ten years she has published comics books only in France and the United States! For Dark Horse, she has worked on covers for Disney's *Frozen* series, and she has drawn comics for European publishers, such as Glénat. Her other works include short stories for Z2 Comics and Mad Cave Studios and game card art for Upper Deck featuring Marvel characters. Luisa wants to adopt a cattail and maybe a sunflower to keep her company while she draws!

Heather Breckel

HEATHER BRECKEL went to the Columbus College of Art and Design for animation. She decided animation wasn't for her, so she switched to comics. She's been working as a colorist for nearly ten years and has worked for nearly every major comics publisher out there. When she's not burning the midnight oil in a deadline crunch, she's either dying a bunch in videogames or telling her cats to stop running around at two in the morning.

Steve Dutro

STEVE DUTRO is a pinball fan and an Eisner Award-nominated comic book letterer from Redding, California, who can also drive a tractor. He graduated from the Kubert School and has been lettering comics since the days when foil-embossed covers were cool, working for Dark Horse (*The Fifth Beatle*, *I Am a Hero*, *StarCraft*, *Star Wars*, *Witcher*), Viz, Marvel, and DC Comics. He has submitted a request to the Department of Homeland Security that in the event of a zombie apocalypse he be put in charge of all digital freeway signs so citizens can be alerted to avoid nearby brain-eatings and the like. He finds the *Plants vs. Zombies* game to be a real stress-fest, but highly recommends the *Plants vs. Zombies* table on *Pinball FX2* for game-room hipsters.

ALSO AVAILABLE FROM DARK HORSE!

THE HIT VIDEO GAME CONTINUES ITS COMIC BOOK INVASION!

THE ART OF PLANTS VS. ZOMBIES
Part zombie memoir, part celebration of zombie triumphs, and part anti-plant screed, *The Art of Plants vs. Zombies* is a treasure trove of never-before-seen concept art, character sketches, and surprises from PopCap's popular *Plants vs. Zombies* games!
ISBN 978-1-61655-331-9 | $10.99

PLANTS VS. ZOMBIES: GARDEN WARFARE TRILOGY
Based on the hit video game series, these graphic novels tie in with the events in *Plants vs. Zombies: Garden Warfare 1* and *2* and *Plants vs. Zombies: Battle for Neighborville*!
VOLUME 1 ISBN 978-1-61655-946-5 | $10.99
VOLUME 2 ISBN 978-1-50670-548-4 | $10.99
VOLUME 3 ISBN 978-1-50670-837-9 | $10.99

PLANTS VS. ZOMBIES: LAWNMAGEDDON
Crazy Dave—the babbling-yet-brilliant inventor and top-notch neighborhood defender—helps young adventurer Nate fend off a zombie invasion that threatens to overrun the peaceful town of Neighborville. Their only hope is a brave army of chomping, squashing, and pea-shooting plants!
ISBN 978-1-61655-192-6 | $10.99

PLANTS VS. ZOMBIES: TIMEPOCALYPSE
Dr. Zomboss attacks throughout different timelines, keeping Crazy Dave, Patrice, Nate, and their powerful plant army busy!
ISBN 978-1-61655-621-1 | $10.99

PLANTS VS. ZOMBIES: BULLY FOR YOU
Patrice and Nate are ready to investigate a strange college campus to keep the streets safe from zombies!
ISBN 978-1-61655-889-5 | $10.99

PLANTS VS. ZOMBIES: GROWN SWEET HOME
With newfound knowledge of humanity, Dr. Zomboss strikes at the heart of Neighborville . . . sparking a series of plant-versus-zombie brawls!
ISBN 978-1-61655-971-7 | $10.99

PLANTS VS. ZOMBIES: PETAL TO THE METAL
Crazy Dave takes on the tough *Don't Blink* video game—and challenges Dr. Zomboss to a race to determine the future of Neighborville!
ISBN 978-1-61655-999-1 | $10.99

PLANTS VS. ZOMBIES: BOOM BOOM MUSHROOM
The gang discover Zomboss' secret plan for swallowing the city of Neighborville whole! A rare mushroom must be found in order to save the humans aboveground!
ISBN 978-1-50670-037-3 | $10.99

PLANTS VS. ZOMBIES: BATTLE EXTRAVAGONZO
Zomboss is back, hoping to buy the same factory that Crazy Dave is eyeing! Will Crazy Dave and his intelligent plants beat Zomboss and his zombie army to the punch?
ISBN 978-1-50670-189-9 | $10.99

PLANTS VS. ZOMBIES: LAWN OF DOOM
With Zomboss filling everyone's yards with traps and special soldiers, will he and his zombie army turn Halloween into their zanier Lawn of Doom celebration?!
ISBN 978-1-50670-204-9 | $10.99

PLANTS VS. ZOMBIES: THE GREATEST SHOW UNEARTHED
Dr. Zomboss believes that all humans hold a secret desire to run away and join the circus, so he aims to use his "Big Z's Adequately Amazing Flytrap Circus" to lure Neighborville's citizens to their doom!
ISBN 978-1-50670-298-8 | $10.99

PLANTS VS. ZOMBIES: RUMBLE AT LAKE GUMBO
The battle for clean water begins! Nate, Patrice, and Crazy Dave spot trouble and grab all the Tangle Kelp and Party Crabs they can to quell another zombie attack!
ISBN 978-1-50670-497-5 | $10.99

PLANTS VS. ZOMBIES: WAR AND PEAS
When Dr. Zomboss and Crazy Dave find themselves members of the same book club, a literary war is inevitable! The position of leader of the book club opens up and Zomboss and Crazy Dave compete for the top spot in a scholarly scuffle for the ages!
ISBN 978-1-50670-677-1 | $10.99

PLANTS VS. ZOMBIES: DINO-MIGHT
Dr. Zomboss sets his sights on destroying the yards in town and rendering the plants homeless—and his plans include dogs, cats, rabbits, hammock sloths, and, somehow, dinosaurs . . . !
ISBN 978-1-50670-838-6 | $10.99

PLANTS VS. ZOMBIES: SNOW THANKS
Dr. Zomboss invents a Cold Crystal capable of freezing Neighborville, burying the town in snow and ice! It's up to the humans and the fieriest plants to save Neighborville—with the help of pirates!
ISBN 978-1-50670-839-3 | $10.99

PLANTS VS. ZOMBIES: A LITTLE PROBLEM
Will an invasion of teeny-tiny miniature zombies mean the party for Crazy Dave's two-hundred-year-old pants gets canceled?
ISBN 978-1-50670-840-9 | $10.99

PLANTS VS. ZOMBIES: BETTER HOMES AND GUARDENS
Nate and Patrice try thwarting zombie attacks by putting defending "Guardens" plants *inside* homes as well as in yards! But as soon as Dr. Zomboss finds out, he's determined to circumvent this plan with an epically evil one of his own . . .
ISBN 978-1-50671-305-2 | $10.99

PLANTS VS. ZOMBIES: THE GARDEN PATH
You get to decide the fate of Neighborville in this new *Plants vs. Zombies* choose-your-own-adventure with multiple endings!
ISBN 978-1-50671-306-9 | $10.99

PLANTS VS. ZOMBIES: MULTI-BALL-ISTIC
Dr. Zomboss turns the entirety of Neighborville into a giant, fully functional pinball machine! Nate, Patrice, and their plant posse must find a way to halt this uniquely horrifying zombie invasion.
ISBN 978-1-50671-307-6 | $10.99

PLANTS VS. ZOMBIES: CONSTRUCTIONARY TALES
A behind-the-scenes look at the secret schemes and craziest contraptions concocted by Zomboss, as he proudly leads around a film crew from the Zombie Broadcasting Network!
ISBN 978-1-50672-091-3 | $10.99

PLANTS VS. ZOMBIES: DREAM A LITTLE SCHEME
Dr. Zomboss invents a machine that allows him to enter the dreams of Neighborville's citizens!
ISBN 978-1-50672-092-0 | $10.99

PLANTS VS. ZOMBIES: FAULTY FABLES
Dr. Zomboss sets out to lull the town to sleep with strange-yet-tedious fables of his own creation!
ISBN 978-1-50672-846-9 | $10.99

PLANTS VS. ZOMBIES: IMPFESTATION
With a seemingly endless infestation of zombie imps aboard his ship, pirate Chestbeard sails to Neighborville Harbor and enlists Patrice, Nate, and Crazy Dave in clearing out the impfestation!
ISBN 978-1-50672-847-6 | $10.99

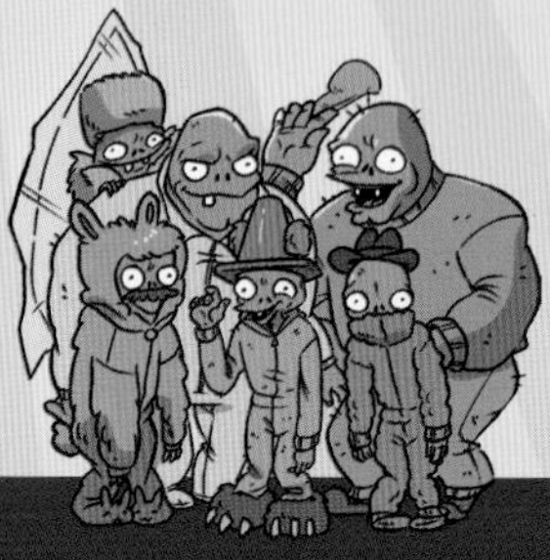

AVAILABLE AT YOUR LOCAL COMICS SHOP OR BOOKSTORE
To find a comics shop in your area, visit comicshoplocator.com. For more information or to order direct, visit **DarkHorse.com**

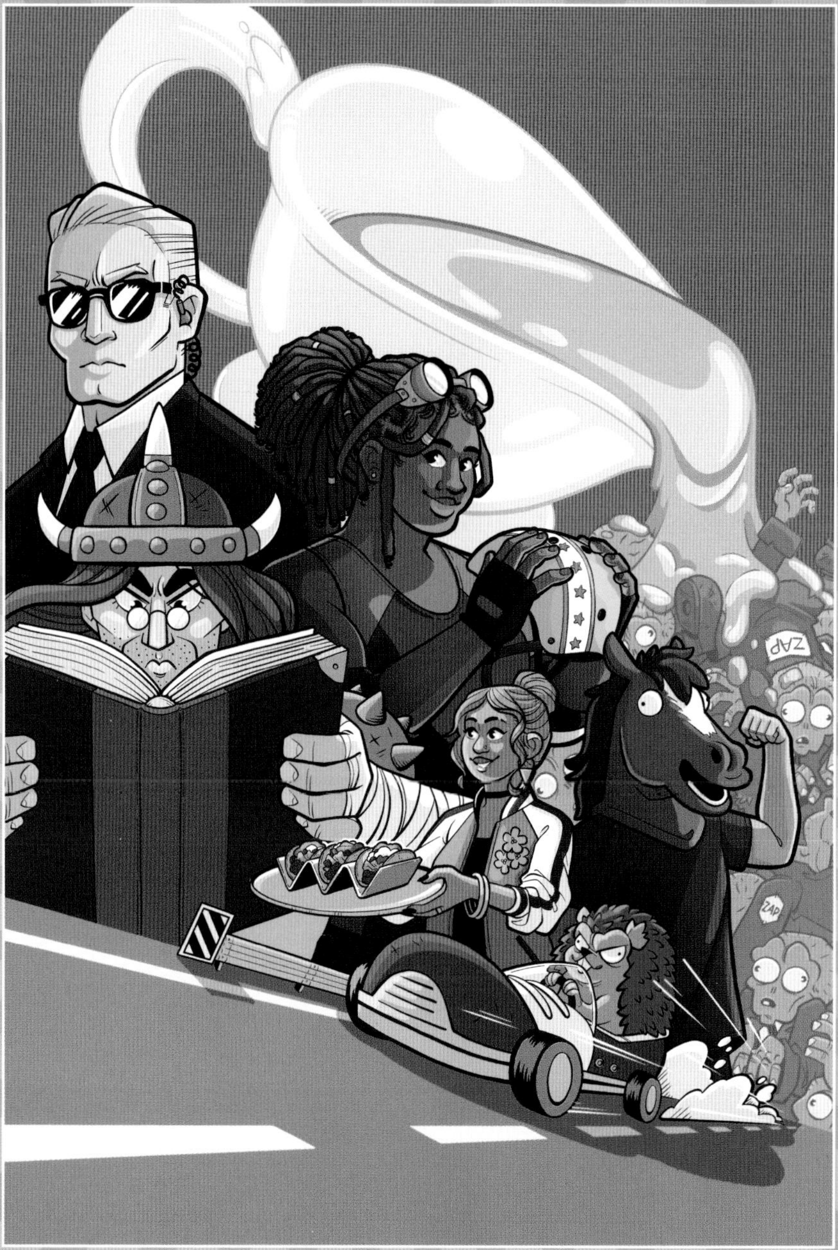
ZAP

IN OUR NEXT EXCITING VOLUME!

More and more custard pies and zombies are appearing seemingly out of thin air every day! The custard pies are pretty nice, but these zombies are becoming a real problem! It's almost as if these Zombies are Automatically Produced, so Patrice, Nate, and Crazy Dave will have to get to the bottom of things before Neighborville is "Zapped" beyond recovery! Eisner Award-winning writer Paul Tobin collaborates with the amazing artist Christianne Gillenardo-Goudreau for a brand-new *Plants vs. Zombies* original graphic novel, with lavish lettering by Eisner-nominated Steve Dutro and gorgeous colors by Heather Breckel!

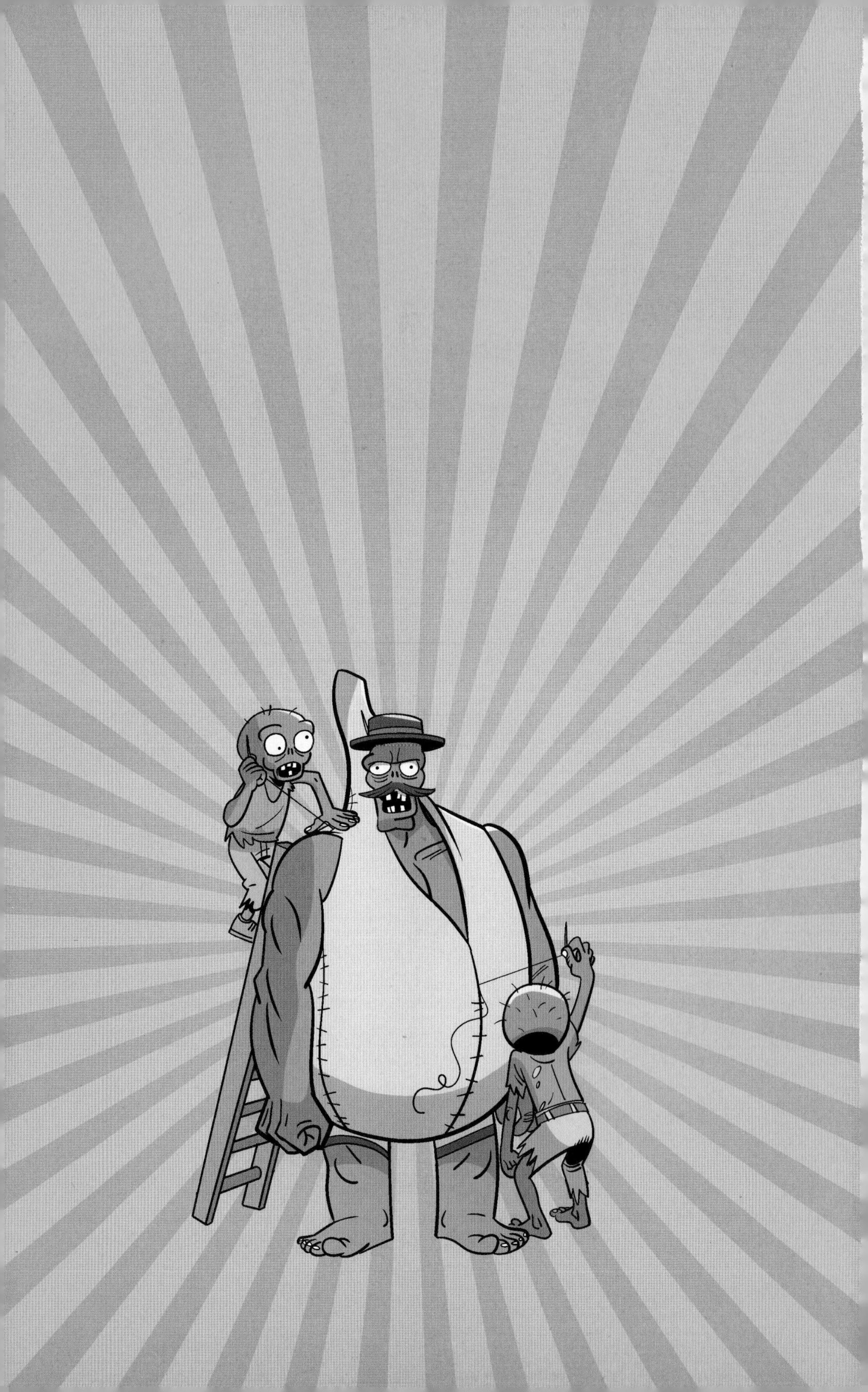

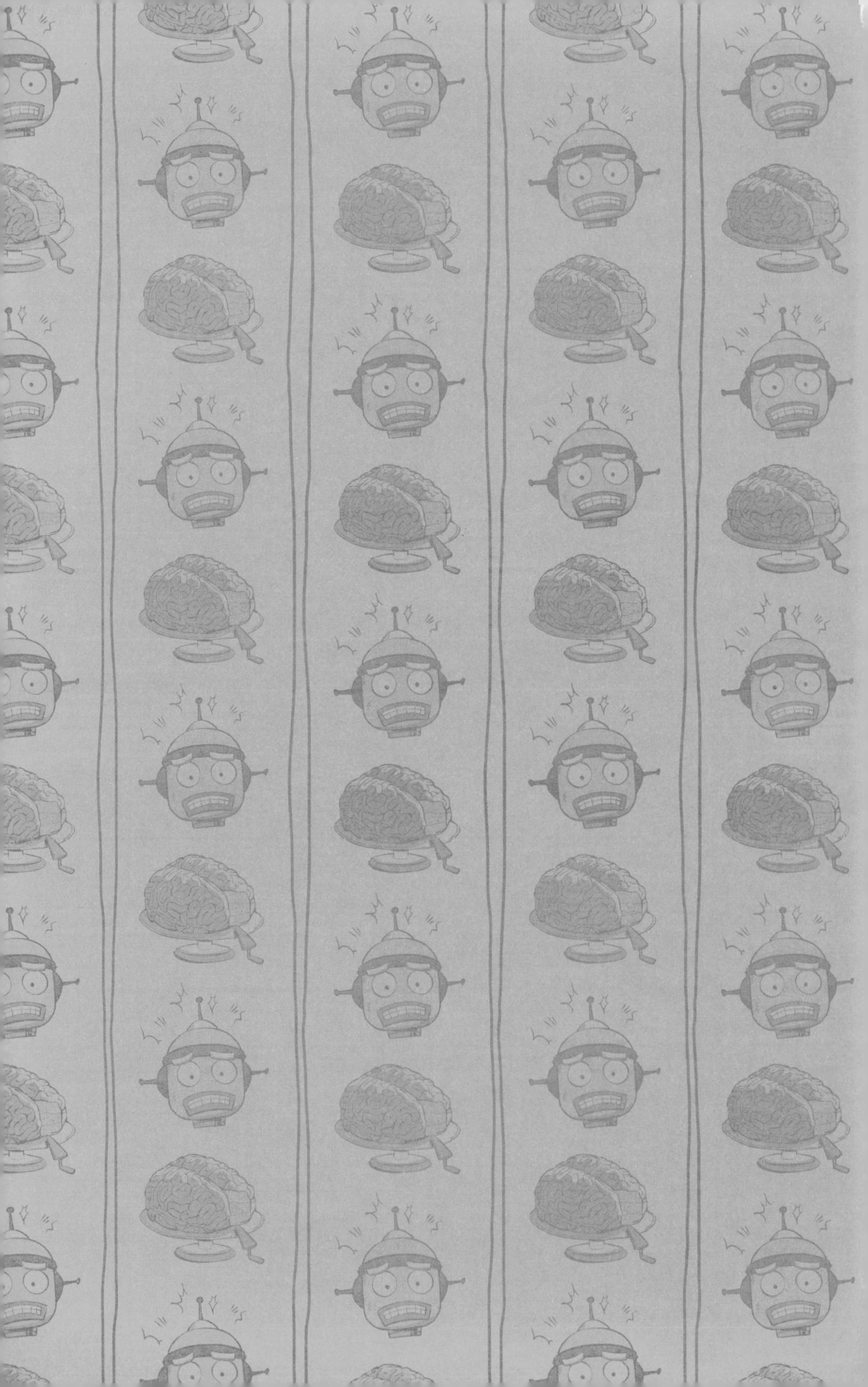